PAINTING

DECEPTION

BRIAN HEBBEL

This is a work of fiction. All of the characters, organizations, and events portrayed in the novel are either products of the author's imagination or are used fictitiously, with the exception of the named Baltimore physical locations, including Baltimore's once-famous restaurant, Haussner's Restaurant. The restaurant serves as the backdrop of the novel and basis of the events that unfold with the main character, Lily Clarke.

Haussner's Restaurant was established in 1926 and closed in 1999. It was considered Baltimore's best restaurant for many years. The history of the restaurant and the more than 600 pieces of primarily Nineteenth Century European artwork that filled it were factual. The author patronized the restaurant as a child. He never met or knew the owners. Fictitious names of the owners are used in the novel to insure no harm or damage are caused to the owners long standing reputation and memory.

Acknowledgements

The book cover was designed by David Snowden. The front cover is a photograph taken with a cellphone by the author on the Northern Central Railroad trail in Baltimore County, Maryland. Take note, the front cover is upside down. The back cover is right-side up.

A special thanks to Jordy Alperstein, Gabrielle Durham, Jane Porter and Fat Cat Studios for providing editing support for this novel. I am very thankful for their help, input, and the time they dedicated to this project. There were many others who provided honest critiques of the draft versions. Each of you spurred me on to complete the novel.

Also a warm-hearted thanks to the following reviewers:

Marcia Scherr: "The story is imaginative and really kept me intrigued. Once I started the book, it was very hard to put it down. I was amazed by the details and character development."

Ella Curtis: "The plot had many twists and turns…. My heart swelled, my eyes filled with tears as I read late into the night to see where the story would take me next."

Marilyn Toveg: "The book was riveting. I especially enjoyed the humor and it kept me in suspense."

Myra Katz: "Your book just grabbed me and I couldn't put it down. … I cried …. Again, thank you for allowing me to read this wonderful book."

Pam Collins, Mimi Miller (rest her soul), Robin & Pat Smith, Linda Rosati, Scott Scherr, Diane Seltzer, Nancy Sall, and Carol Paxson.

Finally, a very special thank you to my youngest child and only daughter, Ashley. She is the kindest person I know, has a pure heart, and is beautiful inside and out. She has spent days reviewing my books prior to their releases to eliminate errors. She always puts her best foot forward to support our family. I could not ask for a better daughter.

My wife Janet, deserves a lot of credit for helping me finish Painting Deception. She has had to listen to the book pitches to family, friends, and a lot of strangers. She was supportive for more than two years as I wrote a little at a time, in the wee hours of the morning, nights, and weekends.

May this book serve as a small piece of my lasting legacy to my family and future generations whom I will never know. It was written to urge them to continue pursuing creativity and learning throughout their lifetimes. Live your life to the fullest!

In Memory of:

My father, Earl Hebbel. He always supported his family and quietly showed it through acts of kindness and giving throughout his life. He was always proud of his family's accomplishments. He was the quiet rock of the family. He died of Alzheimer's disease in 2013, just shy of his 90th birthday.

My sister-in-law, Carolyn Caldwell Hebbel. She lived with grace and died in 2015 of AML leukemia. She was a beautiful person inside and out. She introduced the spoken word of "love" to our family when she married my brother. I always knew she was a strong woman, but didn't realize how strong until she faced her final struggle.

CHAPTER 1

The old saying goes that everyone has a story. Unfortunately today, October 2, 2016, Lily Elizabeth Clarke's story was coming to a quick end. It was a sunny day at the Sacred Heart Cemetery in Dundalk, Maryland, as cars began pulling up shortly after noon for her 1:00 p.m. funeral. Old rusted smoke stacks from a bankrupt steel mill could be seen in the background of the cemetery in this gritty part of Baltimore. Neighborhoods with seventy-year-old brick weathered rowhouses surrounded the neatly manicured cemetery.

The funeral was taking place exactly as Lily had arranged it. No details were left out of the planning. While she was alive, she made sure that her funeral, burial arrangements, and reading of her Last Will and Testament were organized and would be executed exactly to her wishes. No one knew what would take place over the next twenty-four hours and weeks to follow except Lily, and she was deceased. Not even her lawyer and confidant, Jake Snyder, knew all of the hidden details that Lily had intentionally failed to disclose to him; some of which had remained bottled and silenced for a lifetime. He had been Lily's lawyer for more than twenty years, and over the next two days, he would implement her final plan exactly as she had instructed.

Jake knew her for almost his whole life and thought he knew everything about her, but he didn't know the dark secrets about her past or the ones she intended to reveal in stages following her death. The health crisis that led to Lily's death was nothing compared to the mental struggle she faced as a result of the long forgotten secrets resurfacing during the final months of her life. Lily's struggle whether to reveal her secrets while she was alive and how to reveal them after her death would change lives and define her legacy.

Lily didn't want to have a formal viewing at a funeral home. She wanted her funeral to be short and sweet at the gravesite, so that everyone could get on with their lives.

Lily's three daughters didn't remain close to her after they graduated from college and settled in the state of their college alma maters. Lily was unsure why her children didn't stay close to her. She wasn't sure if it was her sometimes overbearing husband or the fact that her children wanted to get out of the dirty blue-collar town Baltimore was in the 1970s. Maybe they were a little rebellious, stubborn, and adventurous, all rolled into one. In truth, Lily often wondered if the secrets she harbored created impenetrable barriers in her relationship with her daughters. However, it seemed the longer they were away from Baltimore, the further they grew apart from Lily, and she didn't have the strength or courage to correct the situation.

Her three children didn't have the strength or courage to correct it either. They had their own problems and issues that Lily couldn't correct once they became adults and left her nest. As she grew older, not needed and then elderly, she learned to accept the emotional and physical distance while silently hoping their relationship would one day get better. Her secrets and experiences with her dysfunctional children shaped the course of events that took place at the end of her eighty-six-year-old life, and a short period of time after her death. When she was alive, she prayed that God and her late husband Frank wouldn't chastise her too harshly in heaven for her final earthly judgments.

CHAPTER 2

The first car that pulled up at the cemetery was Lily's oldest daughter Mary, who was sixty-three years old. She was always punctual to the minute. She was also always dressed impeccably, trying her best to look striking on a shoestring budget. As she made her grand appearance exiting the Uber cab, she threw her pudgy neck back to adjust her lively pixie cut hair. She put her double chin up and pulled back her shoulders, like a famous movie star. Her makeup and nails were always splendidly prepared, and her mother's funeral was no different.

Mary's recently acquired jewelry, obtained under not the best set of circumstances, included two pair of one carat diamond earrings that sparkled in each ear, three gold bangles dangling on one arm, and two diamond tennis bracelets on the other. Her thick gold necklace and diamond pendant finished off her jewelry and created an elegant appearance that was out of place for a funeral.

She was not the perfect daughter, but on this day Lily would have appreciated her flying in from California at her own expense. However, she wasn't the only living person knowledgeable about her recent jewelry heist. She strutted fearlessly to Lily's cemetery plot and nodded in confidence to the other attendees along the way to her front row seat at the burial site.

Mary's husband and two children did not attend the funeral. The "dirty East Coast" and its "white trash" inhabitants created too much of a culture clash. Mary stopped coming to visit Lily in her later years because she was too busy; maybe because they didn't always necessarily see eye to eye; or maybe because her mother always seemed unapproachable to discuss her feelings; or because she didn't have the money to spend on the flight, even though she acted like she was independently wealthy. In later years, she and her husband adapted to the "lesser things in life" as they reached the conclusion that lower paying jobs were better than get-rich quick schemes that always seemed to fail, leaving them more broke than when they started. For some reason, she always perceived she was better than

Lily and her husband, Frank. Little did she know that Lily was significantly richer than her in many ways. Mary's last encounter with Lily proved this to be true and she would learn the truth regarding their last encounter shortly after Lily's burial.

The next car to arrive at the funeral was Lily's second oldest daughter, Sharon. Everyone was surprised she came on time, because punctuality was never a concern of hers. Her reckless lifestyle hadn't changed much since 1973, the year she went off to college. Her alcohol and drug abuse spiraled out of control in the late 1970s, and never got any better throughout her sixty-one years. As she grew older and rarely came back to Baltimore, it got to a point that her impulsive personality and addictions were no longer Lily's problem. Lily went through the pain of losing her many years ago. Sharon's troubled life had been spent on the run, living in one apartment or motel, and then the next. Sharon's troubled past, along with Lily's own gloomy one, made Lily feel like a total failure. However, she understood Sharon more than her other two daughters. Lily's secret past often left her with a sense of helplessness and unfelt grief. Its origin always obscurely resting below in her conscious state of being, never outwardly resurfacing, but always impacting her sense of self and the impenetrable wall she placed between her husband, family and close friends.

Lily would have been surprised that Sharon actually showed up at her funeral, considering the events that took place the last time they were together. As she stepped out of the taxi, the attendees could quickly see that Sharon had a few missing teeth, an anorexic physique, uncombed hair, and shabby clothes. She appeared nervous as a mouse trapped in a corner by a cat. Her dowdy appearance hadn't changed much through the years. All of the attendees were hoping she came to the funeral for the right reasons. When Lily was living, she wished she had the strength to help her. Now that she was deceased, she could only hope that she made the right decision regarding her legacy.

Sharon made her thirty-yard walk towards Mary and did not stop to talk to anyone along the way. She appeared to be on a misguided mission as she clumsily rocketed toward the gravesite. Mary turned her head and saw that Sharon had actually made it to the funeral, and her face quickly grimaced with disdain toward her sister. Her eyes locked on Sharon like an eagle focusing on its prey. Sharon's misplaced energy was evident by her fast pace and nervous walk. Mary didn't know what to expect. Was she going to bring up old pains or was she going to try to move on now that their mother was dead?

As soon as Sharon got within five feet of her sister, she blurted out venomously, "Are you still sleeping with my ex-husband?"

"You've been divorced from him for over thirty years now and you'd probably still be married to him if your drinking and drugs didn't get in the way," Mary answered condescendingly. "Can't you simply get over it and move on? Or have you moved on to some other addictive and destructive habits?", she said pouring salt into the unhealed wound.

"I would have if you hadn't stolen my baby girl, too," Sharon replied as she began to sway apprehensively back and forth like a large lyre pendulum of a grandfather clock.

As people gathered around at the cemetery, they were shocked by what they saw and heard. But this was how Lily's children acted every time they were together. After Mary married Sharon's ex-husband, Lily's children were rarely together. Now that Lily was deceased, there was nothing to keep her children from arguing or waging war with each other. Lily had always been the driving influence to force her daughters to act civilly to each other when they were together.

The next two cars to arrive at the cemetery included the health care aides who took care of Lily in the final stages of her life. Lily was indebted to one of them. One was caring, kind, and considerate regarding her physical well-being. The second aide wasn't too kind or caring when it came to her belongings. She wasn't as honest as she should have been given Lily's situation. Sharon was surprised she came to the funeral considering the circumstances surrounding her short stint providing care to Lily. Guilt plays strange tricks on one's mind, and it was no exception for this aide. However, in the end, Lily deceived them all.

A few more cars pulled up carrying a dozen or so extended family and friends. As a result of living until the age of eighty-six, most of her friends were deceased, or had moved away, or didn't have the physical or mental capacity to make it to her funeral. Lily had lived a very full life with her husband, and only had one regret that created a major impact on her entire life, as it does with women in similar situations. She would have been fine with her funeral turn out, regardless of the number of attendees. Lily and her husband led quite simple lives, and this is the way they both wanted it to be.

Her longtime friend, confidant, and lawyer, Jake, had known Lily for more than fifty years. The sixty-year old Jake even knew Lily's mother and father. Through the health crisis Lily faced, Jake also helped Lily to deceive everyone, even though he didn't know he was doing it. He prepared her Last Will and Testament and the medical directives, including the "Do Not Resuscitate" instructions. Even as her funeral was taking place, no one but Jake had been allowed into Lily's house. That was a part of her plan. Jake had complete control of most activities taking place before her death, arranging the funeral, and most importantly, scheduling the meeting with the representatives who would hear her Last Will and Testament.

In accordance with Lily's instructions, Jake notified her family upon her death and scheduled the funeral on a date that all of her children could attend. He planned the funeral so that all of the intended parties could hear Lily's Last Will and Testament read out loud the day after the funeral. He also made sure it was documented that Lily was fully competent to sign her final will. The most important part of the will was making sure that beyond any reasonable doubt, she was competent to make the decisions. Lily felt sympathetic toward Jake in her final few months of living, knowing what his responsibilities would be after she died.

Jake was never totally sure that Lily was fully honest with him prior to her death. He had a keen suspicion about her seemingly calculated behaviors, but couldn't put his finger on the driving force. Now that Lily was dead, he thought he might uncover a few hidden secrets over the next day or two. Lily tried her best to keep her deceptive actions hidden from everyone when she was alive, just like she kept her dark secrets hidden from everyone, including her husband. Jake simply hoped that her final plots, whatever they were, worked out as she had intended.

The last car to arrive was Denise, Lily's toughest daughter. Denise kept her distance from Lily and her husband and was always secretive. Lily wasn't sure until recently whether or not she was even married. She had always kept Lily in the dark about what was taking place in her life. Everyone said she had Lily's personality. However, when Denise visited the last time, Lily found out the truth about her youngest daughter.

Denise walked slowly toward the crowd. She had on a pair of blue jeans, a neatly pressed plaid shirt, and a biker's key chain for decoration hanging from her back pocket. Her hair was cut tight on the sides and long on the top; bangs covered her forehead. She had a big snake ring on her right hand and a ring on her left hand, but no other jewelry was visible. Her two sisters didn't recognize her at first. She looked out of place for a funeral, but didn't appear to care what anyone thought as she strutted to the burial site, arms swinging back and forth like a French Guillotine.

Lily's three daughters were finally together, something she would not have expected while alive. The three women were quite a contrast. Denise was dressed and looked like a man, Mary's personality and jewelry sparkled in the afternoon sun like a queen, and Sharon looked wrung out like an old gypsy, wearing very wrinkled, old, and dirty clothing.

Denise broke the silence between them. "I didn't know Mom was going to die this quickly."

Mary and Sharon looked somewhat distraught by Denise's words.

"Mom never indicated that the end would be this soon. I'm in a state of shock," conveyed Sharon as she continued to sway back and forth like a grandfather clock.

Mary began to cry. Denise gave her a huge hug and they all began to sob.

Jake wasn't sure if they were crying for Lily or because they were thinking about their own mortality. Whatever it was, he was happy that they were attending Lily's funeral, and over the next twenty-four hours, hoped they would have warm and lasting thoughts of their mother. Jake also hoped that the decisions Lily made regarding her legacy were prudent and practical. Looking at the three children together, he began to realize that they were unaware of the cause of their mother's death.

After a few minutes of crying and sobbing, they moved to the front row of chairs adjacent to their mother's casket. From the looks on their faces, Jake guessed they were wondering how they had ended up at their mother's funeral so soon after their last visits. Nonetheless, it was too late for second guessing.

CHAPTER 3

The priest from Lily's church started the service, and the youngest daughter would end it with Lily's eulogy. She would have been proud that Denise was going to give it. Jake wished Lily could have heard it.

After the priest finished, Denise stood up and turned to the attendees.

She proudly spoke in a strong, robust voice, "I'm Denny, Lily's youngest child." A woman for most of her life, she had recently and privately made the transition to a man.

The people attending the funeral looked at each other, confused. Mary and Sharon finally looked at each other and nodded their heads. Most of the people hadn't seen Lily's children in years. They knew the person speaking could have been a male or a female, but it wasn't until the person spoke that they were one hundred percent sure of the speaker's gender. Denny waited a few seconds so that the attendees could fully comprehend what he had said to be sure they were listening to the eulogy. It was not his intent to be the center of attention at his mother's funeral. He then began reading from a handwritten piece of paper.

"We are all devastated by my mother's death from Alzheimer's disease. Mom was a great mother. She always did special things for us. She loved teaching us how to cook and clean, even though none of us actually liked the cleaning part. She taught us the value of finding a bargain. She loved to take us along Eastern Avenue, which was one of the Baltimore's major shopping districts in the 1960s and 70s.

"Mom was a classy lady, even with her Baltimore accent. She used words like 'Hon' and would say the word 'zinc' instead of 'sink'. I can still hear her yelling out the window saying 'How you doin Hon', or 'you want a glass of worter on this hot day'. She never forgot her strong Baltimore roots and that's one reason she never moved away from Patterson Park.

"Growing up in our house, we never used curse words, never had arguments in the house, didn't mind hard work and never understood people who complained. Mom had strong values."

Denny hesitated for a few seconds. "She always protected us and made sure we were safe. She never let us walk alone in Patterson Park because she said bad things could happen to girls walking alone. Yet she walked it every day because she said that she wouldn't let one bad event that happened to her in Patterson Park define her life. She never told us what it was, but she did her best to protect us."

Mary and Sharon were sitting as far away from each other as possible. Mary flaunted her jewelry in Sharon's direction as Denny spoke. Sharon took Mary's bait and began peering uneasily at the jewelry and squirming on her chair like a fish dangling on a hook.

"Growing up, many of my friends told me our family was like the Cleavers in "Leave It to Beaver". They always used the word "stoic" when they described Mom. I guess it fit her quite well.

"Mom made a great oyster stuffing for Thanksgiving and on Christmas we had her special spaghetti and crabs, not turkey. The inside of our house was decorated impeccably for the holidays and lots of gifts were always found under the tree. She always opened her home to family and friends and hosted many anniversaries, birthdays, weddings, and baby showers.

"I'd like to tell you a few of my favorite funny stories of Mom. When Mary first received her driver's license and only had a learner's permit, if she saw a boy while she was driving, she would make Mom lie down on the car's floorboard so the boys would think she was driving alone. Mom always went along with it," Denny continued.

"Through the years, she was busy driving us from one activity to another, and we would often eat at McDonald's. As a result of one of these frequent trips, she felt something scrambling around her feet. After a few days, she realized she had a mouse living in her car surviving on McDonald's food scraps. It took a few more trips in the car and a mouse trap to take care of the problem."

Sharon squirmed to the edge of her chair to move as far away from Mary as possible. Mary's flaunting had its desired effect as Sharon slipped off the seat and clumsily fell onto the ground. Denny waited a few seconds for Sharon to compose herself and place herself returned to her seat.

"Mom was a great actor. She could have received an Academy Award for how she could get Dad to bend to what she wanted. If she was mad at him, she would immediately turn around and give us a beautiful wink and then a big smile. Dad never caught on. She could act upset in the store to get the price she wanted and walk outside like nothing happened. Dad used to call her Harriet Houdini because she could escape any predicament she got herself into."

Denny continued, "Mom had high expectations of herself and her children, and expected others to live up to them. She expected you to be supportive of each other, dress well, and act in a respectful manner. I think we missed some of those lessons."

Mary and Sharon began to laugh.

"As I got older, I realized she had an amazing memory despite her bout with Alzheimer's disease. She didn't forget much, remembering all of the details about her Baltimore family, as well as our extended family and friends. If you wanted to know what happened on this or that occasion, Mom rarely forgot the details. And even if she did forget, she was able to look them up because she kept a log.

"She was always exceptionally dressed and fashionable and had beautiful and expensive jewelry. She never missed an opportunity to be on a dance floor. Mom always said dancing allowed her mind and body to feel totally free.

"It wasn't only her outer beauty that was to be admired, it was also the beautiful person she was inside. Even a few weeks ago, she continued to give me words of encouragement, though I could see that the Alzheimer's disease was taking its toll.

"The two most important aspects of Mom's life that will make me miss her more than I would ever have imagined were her commitment to quietly supporting us, even when we didn't always support her, and the dignity and strength she showed in her fast and final struggle with Alzheimer's. We were all shocked by her quick death. We love you, Mom."

To end the service, a young Catholic priest read the 23rd Psalm from the Bible. The final words were "Go in Peace." His words were very ominous considering what Jake would soon express to the attendees.

After the priest finished the service, the funeral home attendant stood up and said, "I have an announcement. A luncheon will take place at Sabatino's Italian Restaurant in Little Italy immediately after the service. Before we leave, there is also an announcement to be made by Lily Elizabeth Clarke's lawyer, Jake Snyder."

Jake stood up and peered over the attendees. Without a written paper in his hand, he broadcast in a calm, yet loud voice, "I know this isn't the best place to make this announcement, but I wanted to make it right after the funeral so that Lily's children have the next twenty-four hours to contemplate the decision she had made regarding her Last Will and Testament. At her request, she instructed me, immediately upon her death, to change the locks on the doors of her rowhome. I placed a written notice on her front door directing any questions to me."

Lily's three children had not yet approached her rowhome because the funeral had taken place with such short notice.

Jake then announced, "At Mrs. Clarke's request, I invite her children Sharon, Denise, I'm sorry, I mean Denny, and Mary to my office tomorrow at 10:00 a.m. and I will read your mother's Last Will and Testament. In addition, it is requested that Ms. Jackson also attend the reading of Lily Clarke's Last Will and Testament. At Mrs. Clarke's request, no one is allowed in her house to distribute any of her personal belongings. Some of the belongings in the house and the items contained within it will be disbursed tomorrow in accordance with Mrs. Clarke's instructions detailed in her Last Will and Testament. My office is located at South Bond Street, Room 300. I hope this meeting time doesn't inconvenience any of you. Thank you."

With that, the funeral was over. It had been pretty routine until Jake spoke up. His words were a big surprise to Lily's three children. In an instant they found out that the Last Will and Testament would be read tomorrow, that they couldn't get into Lily's home after the funeral to divide up her belongings and assets, and that someone else, in addition to them, would be attending the Last Will and Testament reading.

Up to this point, Jake thought he had all of Lily's bases covered with this announcement, but there were surprises that Lily put in place prior to her death, that no one, including Jake, knew about.

As the funeral ended, Lily's children slowly moved away from the burial site, and they continued to appear to be in a state of shock. The other person who appeared to be in a state of shock was Ms. Jackson. When Jake made the announcement, only he noticed that her face turned blood red. No one else at the funeral knew Ms. Jackson including Lily's children. They would be surprised the next day to find out who she really was.

CHAPTER 4

It was a typical warm summer afternoon in Baltimore in 1952. As Lily looked out of the second floor front window of her rowhouse, she could see her husband Frank on their front porch nervously tapping his feet and smoking a cigarette. Dressed in a suit and tie as the afternoon sun hit his face and sweat eased over his brow, Frank watched the cars move up and down the street outside their South Ellwood Avenue home.

"Come on Lily. Get a movin, hon," yelled Frank in his Baltimore accent. "It's Friday and the restaurant is gonna be crowded."

Frank continued to tap his feet and puff on his cigarette, exhibiting his nervous energy.

Lily could hear the loud engine of a car that was quickly moving down the street. It sped up as it got closer to their rowhouse.

"Hey Frank," yelled the driver out of the car window as he reached Frank's location.

"You're goin' too slow Buck," Frank hollered back as the driver pushed the accelerator to the floor.

"Yee-ah," the driver screamed as he raced past.

Frank remained seated on his marble porch steps, shaking his head and smiling as Buck raced another block and hit the brake as he approached an intersection.

Frank and Lily's neighbors were also sitting on their front steps to get some relief from the heat and humidity on this typical Baltimore summer afternoon. Frank and Lily felt pretty lucky because they had recently purchased their rowhouse on Ellwood Avenue and it was situated directly across the street from Patterson Park in East Baltimore.

The park's fifty-five acre landscape served as the site where American troops stood ready to defend Baltimore from a British land attack during the War of 1812. It was the also the first gift of land donated to a city in the United States for the purpose of public recreation. The park often provided Frank and Lily a nice breeze they had quickly come to enjoy on hot, summer nights when the only way to stay cool was to relax in the basement or have a fan in your window. To get a break from the summer heat, neighbors would also sometimes sleep in the park.

"Tell your friend Buck to slow it down, hon. He goin' to wake my babies tonight if he keeps it up. And I need to keep my winders open tonight, hon," voiced a lady four rowhouses away.

"Will do," Frank conveyed in a polite but nervous voice as he continued to anxiously tap his feet.

"I hope the car blows up," shouted another man from the other end of the street who was wearing a sweaty tank top and had a few beers sitting next to him on his marble steps. "If he comes by again, I'm gonna throw my empties at his car," hollered the man.

The remaining neighbors stared and shook their heads at each other and whispered. Frank and Lily were new to this block and the neighbors had barely gotten to know them. Frank didn't really care about what his new neighbors thought, but Lily did. Therefore, Frank kept his mouth shut, knowing what Lily would have wanted him to do.

Now that the neighbors were in tune to Frank's nervousness, he decided not to call out Lily's name again. He knew it would only make her mad and make him more nervous than he already was at this early point on their special night.

Special nights out on the town were very uncommon in the 1950s on this gritty east side of Baltimore. Many of the residents were blue collar workers or held office jobs at the manufacturing plants that surrounded the area. Whether it was the Bethlehem Steel Mill, the General Motors automobile manufacturing plant, Crown, Cork and Seal Bottling Company, the various beer makers, or McCormick Spice, most of the men and some of the woman in the area worked hard and rarely took off for a vacation or a had a night out on the town.

Many of the workers were thinking about moving into the country, which at this point in time was only about two or three miles beyond the city limits. However, Frank and Lily had no intentions on moving. Frank could walk to work, they could quickly and easily take a bus downtown, and they could even sleep in Patterson Park if a summer night got too hot. They had everything they needed in their new home on Ellwood Avenue, and most importantly they had each other.

There had been some recent talk about Baltimore getting a professional baseball and football team. If that happened, Frank and Lily hoped the stadiums wouldn't be too far from their rowhouse. A lot of the men in the neighborhoods spent their evening after dinner in the local bars, while the women worked together to run the households. Going to the local movie theater or shopping on Eastern Avenue or downtown were ways to enjoy a free day. There was also excitement in 1952 about the much-anticipated completion of a bridge spanning the Chesapeake Bay. It was scheduled to be completed in late 1952 and once finished, would become the world's longest continuous over water steel structure. Lily had never been on the eastern side of the Chesapeake Bay. She, like most residents, would often spend a long weekend at a local river beach on the western side.

But tonight, Frank and Lily were celebrating their one year anniversary. They had been married at the Martin Luther Lutheran Church the year before, just three blocks away from their rowhouse. They had the wedding reception at Frank's parent's rowhouse, five blocks from the church. It was a typical wedding reception for Baltimore newlyweds. Frank and Lily had only dated for four months before they were married and Frank was seven years older.

Frank was twenty-nine years old. This was his second marriage. He had been married before World War II started when he was seventeen. He had immediately joined the Navy at the breakout of World War II, and one year later had received a "Dear John" letter from his wife requesting a divorce. She had fallen in love with another man while he was overseas.

After a few years of being single, the day he met Lily, he told her that she was the woman of his dreams, so this night was going to be a special night for them to celebrate their love and talk about their future together. It was also special to Frank because he had received the "Dear John" letter from his first wife on their one year anniversary. Tonight was the night to break the anniversary curse, and Frank wanted it to be special.

Although she was twenty-two years old, Lily was wise beyond her years. As she continued to get ready for their special night, she remembered what an extraordinary woman had told her a few years back about what to look for in a man and she thought that Frank had all three of these things; good looks, a nice, friendly personality, and the means to take care of her.

Twenty minutes after Frank had yelled up to Lily to finish getting ready, Lily finally made it down the steps. As she looked through their front window, she could see Frank, but he couldn't see her. Their newly installed window screen blocked outsiders from looking into their house, but they could see out. A country scene painted on their window screen appeared to be the newest and freshest painted window screen in the neighborhood. Lily was sure that it would not even come close to the painted scenes they were going to see at Haussner's Restaurant later in the evening. As she peered out at Frank, he definitely appeared more nervous than usual.

Without further delay, Lily hurried toward the front door, sprung it open and looked at Frank with a big smile, and spinning around in her beautiful, white summer dress. "How do I look?" she asked Frank, her dress flowing up her leg.

"Oh my God," Frank burst out loudly as he stood up and turned around on the marble step to look at Lily standing slightly inside of the rowhome doorway. All of the neighbors within the block heard Frank's voice and turned their heads with nosy anticipation.

"What's wrong Frank?" Lily murmured in a soft low voice and with a disappointed expression. "You don't like the dress."

"No, not at all. Precisely the exact opposite," reiterated Frank. "I've never seen such a beautiful, green-eyed creature in all of my years on this earth. You are one beautiful creature Lily."

"Creature, huh?" Lily asserted, as her expression immediately changed from disappointment to delight.

"Is the top cut too low Frank?" Lily whispered as she looked down at the crevice of her bust that was quite exposed. "I'm not sure what my mother would say if she saw this dress. I've never worn a dress cut this low."

"Well, all I can say is that I think the dress and you look like an angel. And you're my angel tonight," affirmed Frank as he grabbed Lily's hand and pulled her out the door. "Let's go celebrate."

Lily pulled her hand back barely long enough to grab her pocketbook and lock the door while Frank continued to gently pull on her arm.

At this point in the very early evening on a Friday night, many of the men and woman in the neighborhood had finished their dinners and were sitting on their front porch steps to cool off. All of the men in the immediate area turned their heads and began to stare at Lily as they began to walk down the street.

The women looked at Lily with a different set of eyes. Although she considered herself shy, for some unknown reason, on this night, Lily felt very confident as she walked parading in her dress, her high heels striking the pavement and making a clicking sound with each step, causing more heads to turn their way. In addition, her beautiful dark brown hair that was curled at the neck line, her new stylish clothes, shoes, and pocketbook were all perfectly matched. As she walked, Lily wondered why everyone along the way continued to stare at them.

"Is it my makeup and the self-confident strut of my body?" she thought. In actuality Lily wasn't sure, but was enjoying the moment.

"Tonight is going to be a night to remember," avowed Lily in a spirited chuckle as her head bobbed up and down like a Hollywood movie star.

As they continued to move down the sidewalk, their pace began to pick up as they remained excited about the dinner that was ahead of them. Frank still appeared nervous as he puffed away on another cigarette, and Lily appeared to be floating slightly above the ground as she walked with her dress being tossed about by her walk and the summer breeze.

"I hope there is no line at Haussner's Restaurant this evening, Frank," Lily said as her heels continued to click in a rhythmic beat on the sidewalk.

"There probably will be a long line. If there is, we'll have a drink in the Haussner's bar," asserted Frank with an exuberant grin on his face.

"I've never been in that bar. I did peek in it once," Lily admitted as her face blushed with an innocent, yet sensual expression that was directed at Frank.

"Well, I'm sure none of the paintings hanging in the bar match your beauty," professed Frank.

"I don't think I can sit in that bar," contended Lily as her face remained pinkish in color. "It's a stag bar and I'll be too embarrassed to sit around all of those paintings of nude women."

"Lily, you're married, you're old enough, and you're with me. Besides, I'd like to take a good look at the paintings," Frank teased.

Lily gave him a sharp poke in the ribs with her right elbow.

The restaurant they were dining at was Baltimore's top rated, and one of the top-rated in the United States, Haussner's Restaurant. It had the three qualities a diner would look for; a pleasing environment, impeccable service, and delicious food. It wasn't only a restaurant, it was also a museum filled with original artwork by European master painters and an assemblage of other decorative European artwork. The owners, Tomas and Anna Becker, opened the restaurant in 1926 and expanded the quantity of original masterpieces that filled the restaurant through the decades.

Haussner's Restaurant's expansive menu included more than five hundred unique selections, including frog legs and turtle steaks. The individuals who prepared the menu selections at Haussner's Restaurant were not cooks; they were master chefs. If you peeked into the small windows of the stainless steel swinging doors leading into the busy kitchen, the glare of the shiny stainless steel stoves, pots, and pans would almost blind your eyes. The cleanliness of the kitchen that prepared over fourteen hundred meals for patrons each day would bring into question any woman's housekeeping skills. But the menu was not the only unique thing about Haussner's Restaurant.

Waitresses were always dressed in white uniforms. Menu selections were not carried on trays by waitresses, but were rolled to the table by the waitresses on stainless steel carts. The delivery of the prepared food by the waitresses was organized like an assembly line. Waitresses always knew where they were supposed to be and performed their duties meticulously and professionally as the owners demanded. Waitresses could be seen working there over many decades and they knew the menu backwards and forwards.

The most unique treasure at Haussner's Restaurant was the original artwork that hung on every square inch of wall space and the sculptures and unique items that sat on pedestals that dotted the restaurant along with a second floor museum containing additional 19th-century artwork. Frank and Lily were lucky because the restaurant was located only a few blocks from their home.

Haussner's owners began collecting artwork in the 1930s and filled the restaurant with over six-hundred original paintings, with a majority of paintings being from the late 1800s. Mr. and Mrs. Becker not only had a keen eye for selecting paintings that would look superb in their restaurant, they also understood the paintings' value now and potential value in the future. Although the "master painters" were unknown to most of the diners, they were often highly regarded by the experienced museum curators. Some of the paintings that hung in the restaurant were purchased from the estates of J.P. Morgan and Cornelius Vanderbilt. Most of the paintings were purchased in Europe from painters that were highly regarded.

If you decided to have a drink in Haussner's Restaurant's bar, it was an adults only bar and was filled with 19th century paintings of nude women. The unique atmosphere of art coupled with the menu selections and the expert chefs made a meal at Haussner' Restaurant an extraordinary experience. That's why Frank and Lily and thousands of other patrons from across the United States considered a dinner at Haussner's Restaurant a very special event.

There were two rather unique art pieces in Haussner's Restaurant. One was the world's largest painting, depicting a battle scene from World War I. The original painting was four hundred and two feet long and forty-five feet tall. The second and most outrageous item in the restaurant was the world's largest ball of twine that was four feet in diameter and weighed eight hundred and twenty-five pounds. The twine, if stretched out, would measure three hundred and thirty-seven miles in length. The twine came from laundry material that was used to secure bundles of laundered table napkins over a three decade period.

When they turned the corner on Ellwood Avenue onto busy Eastern Avenue, they barely noticed the stares they received and the occasional honk of a car horn. As they approached the restaurant and rounded the corner to enter the front door of the restaurant, more than fifty people were waiting in line to enter it.

"Well you know what this means? It looks like we may be headed into the stag bar," proclaimed Frank with excitement.

CHAPTER 5

Lily immediately began to feel embarrassed at the thought having a drink in a bar covered in paintings of nude woman. Her anxiety level increased and she began taking deep breaths as she neared the restaurant.

Frank looked down at her cleavage that became more exposed with each of her deep breaths.

"Be careful with those tonight, hon. I don't want you to lose one of them or else you may end up in a painting hanging in the stag bar."

Lily gave him a friendly smack on the butt.

"We can put our name in at the front desk and relax in the bar before the meal," voiced Frank in eager anticipation of Lily's reaction.

"I bet those paintings of naked women won't relax you Frank," Lily murmured as she snuggled Frank as they neared the front door.

Frank gave his name to the hostess. She told him the wait would be forty-five minutes. Lily could see the hundreds of original paintings that decorated the formal dining room; however, before she could focus on any one of them, Frank grabbed her hand and began to gently pull her toward the direction of the bar. There was a large sign directly above the door that stated in big letters, "STAG BAR ONLY." Lily had never been in a stag bar before, but that would soon change and begin the course of events that would shape the end of her life.

Frank knew that the "STAG BAR ONLY" was a sign for decoration purposes only, but Lily wasn't exactly sure what the words actually meant. Before she could contemplate their meaning, Frank pulled her into the bar. As soon as they stepped inside, Lily's eyes looked up in amazement at the quantity and beauty of the artwork. She had never seen such beautiful original painted artwork, much less paintings of nude women. Each painting was more beautiful than the next. However, before she could fully enjoy them, she and Frank quickly found a corner spot in the small bar immediately inside the door that was tucked away so that no one entering or leaving the restaurant could see them. Lily didn't want anyone to see her in the stag bar, so she quickly scooted into the booth and began to admire the dozens of paintings that covered every nook and cranny of the bar.

Frank was enjoying the paintings for other reasons, and Lily now felt happy that she had agreed to have a drink in the bar as they each enjoyed eyeballing the paintings.

"Where are the nude paintings of men? I want to see some of them," whispered Lily into Frank's ear.

"What will it be?" asked the bartender who quickly appeared at their table.

"Tell the bartender what you want, Lily," insisted Frank with a grin.

Lily blushed with embarrassment. She was speechless.

"She'll have a dry martini and I'll have a Natty Boh beer in a can, no glass," Frank ordered.

Lily continued to admire the paintings. Most were rather large, but some were small. In all, there were sixty 19th century paintings scattered around the bar. One painting larger than the rest hung directly behind the bar. Frank lifted his arm to point at it. Lily slapped his arm down not wanting to make any motion that would draw attention to them.

Lily was awestruck. She sat still not knowing what to do or say. She thought anything she said about the paintings could be thought of as inappropriate if overheard by others in the bar.

The bartender sat the drinks down in front of them asking, "What's the special occasion?"

"Our one year anniversary," Frank disclosed exuberantly.

"Would you like a glass of water too? It's a hot one outside. One of these days some restaurant is probably going to start charging for water," swore the waiter, trying to make Lily feel at ease after noticing her discomfort.

"That'll be the day. The day someone charges people for water is the day a movie star, like say, Ronald Reagan will become President," vowed Frank as they all began to laugh.

Although they were both uncomfortable drinking in the stag bar, Frank was a little more comfortable and worldly than Lily, considering he was seven years older. They slowly sipped on their drinks. Over the next several minutes, few words were said, as they both enjoyed the moment.

As they continued to stare at the paintings, a man dressed in a suit and tie strutted into the bar, peering at the patrons. As soon as he saw the looks on Frank and Lily's faces, he approached their table.

"Enjoying the paintings?" he asked. He was impeccably dressed and presented himself as cultured and refined. His perfectly combed gray hair and neatly trimmed mustache made him appear intellectual and highly educated. His suit showed no signs of wear or use.

"We sure are," Frank answered nervously.

"My newest painting is the one right over there," indicated the man. "It's a painting by Fried Paul. I have a few of his paintings. He's a gifted artist and his paintings' value will appreciate greatly in the future," he contended in a thick German accent.

"Are you the owner?" broached Frank.

Mr. Becker turned his head and then looked to the right and to the left, as if looking for someone else; and then looked right at Lily as he addressed Frank's question. His arrogance shone like a bright morning sun.

"I am," he disclosed.

Mr. Becker began to look at Lily in a way a person would look at a painting.

"How did you find such a beautiful woman?" he asked Frank in a complimentary manner as he began to exhibit his extraverted charisma.

Frank was nervous about talking to such a famous restaurant owner.

"I got lucky I guess," Frank continued nervously and bumbled, "I, I think Lily is prettier than all of paintings in the bar."

Lily hit Frank on the arm and began to blush.

"I agree," declared Mr. Becker, continuing to focus his attention on Lily. He then switched focus to the dozens of original nude paintings that surrounded the bar. As his eyes moved from painting to painting, he turned his head back to Lily looking at her up and down. This continued for what was a long and uncomfortable time for both Frank and Lily. Frank and Lily didn't know what he was doing or know what to say. Their nervousness began to subside with each additional sip of their drinks.

"I started buying these paintings in the 1930s," articulated Mr. Becker as he continued his shifting attention. "I got hooked buying them and my hobby got somewhat out of control. But my restaurant continues to be successful and it has afforded my wife and me the opportunity to buy these paintings. I'm a lucky man. I was lucky because I started buying these paintings when all those terrible things started happening in Germany and throughout Europe. I bought and continue to buy because they are still relatively inexpensive and not that old. Europe's misfortune over the past twenty-five years has made it easier for me to buy and save this beautiful art. I'm truly happy that the paintings in my restaurant have created an atmosphere that the patrons appreciate as much as I do. They are all my children and I know each one intimately. That's why I look at the painting and stare back at you Lily. I'm looking to see if any of the women resemble you in terms of your beauty."

Lily blushed a little more and quickly downed the rest of the dry martini after hearing Mr. Becker's last statement.

Mr. Becker glanced to the bartender and he quickly got busy behind the bar. Within a minute, Lily had another dry martini and Frank had another beer.

"How much do the paintings cost?" inquired Frank.

Mr. Becker chuckled as he took notice of a seven-foot tall painting of a nude woman, "Quite frankly, it all depends. See that painting over there? That is the Greek goddess Aurora. The artist was James Bertrand. It is one of my biggest paintings, but it is not my most expensive one. I acquired this painting only three years ago. I bought it for a great price considering how depressed art prices are in Europe right now. Isn't she a beauty? She looks as if she could come right out of the painting."

Lily wasn't sure if he was referring to the beauty of the painting or the beauty of the woman, but the beautiful life size painting of a nude angelic woman was something that was hard even for Lily to take her eyes off of.

Mr. Becker pointed to a painting that was hanging not too far from where Frank and Lily were seated that was no larger than two feet by two feet.

"That is my favorite painting in the bar," revealed an enthusiastic Mr. Becker. The artist was Charles Chaplin and the painting is actually called ECSTASY."

The painting depicted a young woman, nude from the chest up, flushed in the face from what one would assume was her first erotic and pleasurable sexual experience.

"For some reason, when I look at that painting, I think of youth and the freedom you have when you are coming to the age of maturity. I think the woman in the painting exhibits the pleasure of our youth and how I felt when I was her age. When I stare at the painting, the woman makes me feel young again. I think he did a good job naming the painting. Wouldn't you say so?" Mr. Becker professed. "I didn't pay a lot of money for it, but it is worth every penny I paid because of how it makes me feel. Every painting I buy makes me feel something inside. If not, I won't even consider buying it. I have other paintings in the dining room that make me feel, I wouldn't say old, but make me realize that time continues to tick away. But you two lovers wouldn't know that because you are so young."

"Are you sure that painting is not titled 'Painting Deception'?" Frank inquired with a grin on his face. "Are we sure she is as relaxed and satisfied as she appears?"

"What are you talking about Frank? She looks flushed and satisfied to me," claimed Lily in a tone that made Frank know she wanted him to be quiet and not say anything out of place or inappropriate.

Mr. Becker continued to talk about other paintings, naming and describing each one in detail including the artist, how it was acquired, and how the painting made him feel. He continued to give Lily more attention than Frank, but her low-cut dress and her thirty-four double D's were having an effect on the length and intimacy of their conversation.

"These are not all of my prized paintings. I don't even show them all in the restaurant. Would you like to see some more of them?" he asked.

They all stood up to begin a personal tour of the artwork and sculptures that decorated the restaurant. Little did Frank and Lily know that their evening with Mr. Becker would become more memorable than they ever expected.

CHAPTER 6

Frank and Lily were pleased to be getting this special attention from the owner of Haussner's Restaurant. They headed past the restaurant's front door, where the line of people appeared to have shortened significantly since Frank and Lily had entered the bar. As they walked, Lily began to neatly sip on her second drink, ensuring that it would not spill on the restaurant floor. Frank clumsily carried his can of beer and a lit cigarette with him as they slowly strolled through the restaurant.

As they moved past the restaurant's entry way, a pleasant and cultured-looking woman with straight gray hair appearing to be around the age of Mr. Becker, stood in the front area of the restaurant behind a pastry counter.

"Welcome to Haussner's Restaurant," voiced the neatly dressed woman to Frank and Lily as she stood in a straight and proud stance, like she had been a fixture of this front counter for many years.

"Here is my beautiful painting and exquisite sculpture all rolled into one," declared Mr. Becker as he looked at the woman. "This is my wife Anna."

"Get back to work honey," asserted Mrs. Becker in a witty and charming voice, with a strong German accent bleeding through her words.

Everyone began to snicker and Lily struggled to balance the liquid in her martini glass.

"See that painting above Mrs. Becker's head," noted Mr. Becker. "That painting is called 'The Venetian Flower Vendor.' It's the first painting we ever bought. The artist was Eugene de Blaas. We like to keep it above the front desk to remind us of how far we've come," Mr. Becker acknowledged.

With that, the tour inside the restaurant began.

As they moved through the dining area of the restaurant, Lily began to feel a little tipsy as the second dry martini began to take effect. Frank felt no effects from his two beers. As they slowly strolled, Mr. Becker began to tell Frank and Lily the history of the restaurant in a proud and enthusiastic tone.

"We bought five row homes in 1936 that allowed us to expand the restaurant. After that, we continued to add more and more paintings. As of today, we've accumulated over 600 paintings." As he began to talk about the paintings, his eyes opened wide with excitement discussing their acquisitions and achievements.

Mr. Becker gave them intricate details about every painting and every artist. The masterpieces in the dining room included rural and country scenes, childhood scenes, religious scenes, and cavalier scenes. There were even pictures of Paris street scenes that were scattered throughout the restaurant.

The significant artists that filled the walls he mentioned during the tour included Josef Israels, Giullaume Seiggnac, L'eon Jean Basile Perrault, and Elizabeth Jane Gardner Bouguereau. The restaurant tour had gone on for ten minutes, and they had only gotten through the detail of ten paintings, and still had hundreds to go.

Lily's high heels were beginning to hurt her feet from standing for such a long time, and with two martinis in her belly, she began to slightly sway from side to side. She could feel it, but no one else could see what she was feeling.

The patrons in the restaurant were staring at the three of them, and in particular, Mr. Becker, as they slowly wandered through the restaurant. He was a celebrity in Baltimore.

"See those French street paintings that are scattered around the dining room? I bought dozens of them from my good friend Edouard-Leon Cortes. You can buy them in the gift shop for less than five hundred dollars a pair, along with other paintings. The others are priced accordingly, of course," said Mr. Becker. "The painter Edouard is coming to visit Anna and me in six months."

Shortly after he had finished talking about the tenth painting, the front desk called Frank's last name. Mr. Becker told Frank and Lily to "stay put" and quickly raced to the front door of the restaurant. He quickly scurried back with two menus in his hand.

"I'm going to give you the best seat in the house," revealed Mr. Becker.

He escorted Frank and Lily to an empty table in the middle of the restaurant that allowed them to view the great expanse of paintings throughout most of the restaurant. Mr. Becker, gentleman that he was, pulled out Lily's chair. "Enjoy the view this evening and I hope you enjoy the paintings as much as I do. I'll come back later to make sure you're making the right selections, and to see if you have any questions about the dinner or the paintings," conveyed Mr. Becker, before he raced to the back of the restaurant and through the kitchen's stainless steel doors.

Frank and Lily remained amazed and speechless with the attention they were being given. It would be a night to remember.

Within minutes of sitting down at the table, the bartender from the bar moved across the restaurant and delivered another round of drinks to their table.

"Compliments of Mr. Becker. Enjoy," claimed the bartender as he hastily turned and headed back to the bar.

Frank and Lily giggled at each other, thankful of their choice for celebrating their anniversary.

CHAPTER 7

As Frank and Lily painstakingly peered through the extensive menu, Lily became bewildered trying to determine which section she should look at first. Frank had the identical problem.

"What page are you on?" questioned Frank with a puzzled look. "How many items are on this menu?"

Frank began to count the menu selections one-by-one. When he was nearly finished, he expressed in frustration, "I lost count somewhere over five hundred items. Can you believe there are that many items on it? I wonder what happens if the price changes on one item?"

They both laughed and continued contemplating their selections on the menu. Between Lily finishing the first two dry martinis and beginning to enjoy the third one, she didn't care what she was going to order from the menu. Frank and Lily were having the time of their lives looking at each other, admiring the paintings, and sipping on their drinks. Their waitress came by their table numerous times asking them if they would like to order, but they had no idea how to make a selection because of the quantity of items on the menu.

After another ten minutes passed, Mr. Becker came back to their table.

"Have you made your selection?" he inquired with spirited anticipation of Frank and Lily selecting unique items from it.

"What would you suggest?" asked Frank.

"I would suggest the Whale Steak Swiss Style," suggested Mr. Becker in straightforward manner. "I think you would especially like it Frank. And for you Lily, I recommend you try our signature dish, Hasenpfeffers German Style Spaetzles. You can't get either of these two dishes anywhere but Hassuners."

"What are Hasenpfeffers German Style Spaetzles?" questioned Lily.

"It's a farm-raised tender rabbit with a munificent portion of German noodles in a fully bodied brown sauce. It's more than delicious. I have a lot of patrons that come here and order it regularly," Mr. Becker stated with pride.

"I bet no one else serves it," said Frank, a little bit of jocular skepticism in his voice.

"I like you two a bunch. Since you are so skeptical Frank, I'll have to bring you a double order of the Hasenpfeffer," declared Mr. Becker as they all began to laugh. "Trust me, once you try it, you'll want it every time you come here. I can't put the order in until you say the name of the dish, Lily."

Lily began to try to say the dish name, "Hasenplepper, Howsinfedder, Howsintheworld. How am I going to be able to eat this dish if I can't say it?" uttered Lily in a sincere, yet humorous tone, as she gave up trying.

"I'll put the order in anyway. You'll love it," insisted Mr. Becker as he continued laughing out loud. "That is the funniest thing I've heard all week my dear."

Mr. Becker raised his hand and within seconds, a waitress was attending the table. With the drinks impacting her senses, Lily had totally disregarded what had been ordered for her. Mr. Becker stayed at their table and passed on his recommendations to the waitress before hurrying back toward the kitchen.

Prior to the dinner arriving, Lily and Frank downed their third drink. By this time, Lily was doing a good job of not showing anyone how drunk she had actually become. Shortly after her fourth drink arrived, the appetizer and their dinner were not far behind.

The waitress wheeled the Hasenpfeffers German Style Spaetzles and Whale Steak Swiss Style to the table on her stainless steel cart.

Lily gazed at the fully cooked rabbit sitting on her plate. Frank noticed Lily gazing at it.

"It looks like you're about to eat the Easter Bunny," Frank joked as the amusing sight caused his eyes to tear up.

Lily joined in with laughter, but kept it restrained since Mr. Becker had been so generous and courteous to them.

Frank and Lily sat daring each other to taste their meal first. Frank decided to try his dish first. As soon as he took one bite of it, he grinned with delight. Lily gradually and reluctantly followed suit, gently placing a piece of the rabbit in her mouth. She, too, smiled after taking pleasure in its taste.

As they ate their meal, they continued to be in awe of the paintings and sculptures that surrounded their table.

Lily couldn't take her eyes off of a painting on the wall by Adolf Schreyer titled "FLEEING WALLACHIAN HORSES." The visual imagery of a dozen wild horses busting through a wooden fence captivated her imagination with the strength and power of the untamed animals.

The large painting "A ROMAN MATRON" by John William Godward stared at her throughout the dinner. It featured a Roman woman in a red dress who looked and appeared to be a real person with a cynical expression.

There was a small painting by Martin Rico y Ortega close to their table, that appeared to have a smudge of spaghetti sauce on the bottom corner of the painting, demonstrating how close the paintings were to the tables.

By far Lily's favorite painting was by Paul Charles Chocarne-Moreau titled "I TOLD YOU SO." It was a funny depiction of a young boy with a live lobster hanging onto his index finger on a busy, city street. An older boy is seen holding a basket full of live lobsters on his lap and shaking his finger at the young boy. Lily was not sure if it represented mischief or the greed of someone getting their hands caught where they shouldn't be. In any case, it was a funny spectacle to see the boy screaming with a lobster dangling from his finger.

CHAPTER 8

Frank and Lily continued to study the paintings over the next thirty minutes and gained a strong appreciation for what Mr. and Mrs. Becker had accomplished at their restaurant. They enjoyed each other's conversation and their surroundings as their bellies were stuffed to capacity. Frank was now on his fourth beer. The three dry martinis Lily had downed left her feeling like the angels that appeared in some of the paintings; floating above the ground. But the meal and a continuous supply of water absorbed some of the alcohol.

Frank announced to Lily with a grin on his face, "My mother and father told me that these paintings are for sale. Mr. Becker said it earlier himself. My father said the week before he died that if we ever have enough money, we should think about buying some. He said they're not that expensive and they'd be a great investment for the future. You know he was a pretty smart guy."

"Your dad was smart Frank, but where would we get the money?"

"Well I brought some of the money my father left me. When we leave here tonight, I'm going to honor his wish if we can afford it," Frank revealed as he became somewhat emotional as he thought about his father.

Lily realized that the money Frank had in his pocket was from his father's estate and it was his money, not hers. Consequently, she had no problem with what Frank was contemplating.

"It's your money Frank. Do with it as you wish. I know your father would be happy with any decision you make. He always said you had great intuition. I trust you honey," Lily professed as she reached for, and squeezed Frank's hand.

Lily grinned at Frank and slowly tugged on her dress revealing more of her best and biggest assets. She looked at Frank and said with a grin, "Will these two assets help?"

"They sure have helped me," Frank quickly countered as they lifted their glasses and said in unison "Toast to the heir presumptive," which was the title of a rather large Adrien Moreau painting that was hanging near them.

After the toast, they began their quest to convince Mr. Becker to unload a few of his treasured paintings. They were both happy the alcohol had kicked in because they were way out of their league trying to purchase paintings from an art expert like Mr. Becker. Nonetheless, Mr. Becker had left a slight crack in the door that two East Baltimore working class newlyweds were hoping to enter.

Lily's alcohol consumption was having a much greater impact on her state of mind than Frank's. As each minute passed, Lily's words began to jumble together and sound slurred, but nothing was going to get in her or Frank's way of their mission. Their one year anniversary was already a memorable occasion, regardless of the outcome of events over the next hour.

Before they knew it, their waitress was heading their way again, her white uniform showing stains from the long night of serving food. She was holding two plates filled with Haussner's famous strawberry pie.

"This dessert is compliments of Mr. Becker," touted the waitress. "He also wants you to see him before you leave."

Frank and Lily took her words as an omen. They continued to remain confident that they could potentially afford one or more of Mr. Becker's paintings. Lily admired the paintings in the dining room and Frank was drawn to the paintings in the stag bar.

As Lily ate the strawberry pie, she proposed to Frank "Okay, I'll let you buy any painting you want if you first buy me the 'I TOLD YOU SO' painting."

Frank shook his head in agreement as he devoured his dessert.

As they finished eating their slices of strawberry pie, they pondered the best strategy to convince Mr. Becker to sell a painting to them.

Lily began to get a little nervous about what to say. She asked Frank, "What should we say? How should we act? Should we act smart? Should we act stupid? Should I act sexy? Should we be aggressive?"

With each separate thought, Frank merely shrugged his shoulders. He didn't know what to do either. All of these thoughts were running through both of their jumbled minds.

It was getting late and many of the restaurant's patrons had left or were exiting the restaurant. The waitress brought the bill to their table and much to Lily's surprise, Frank pulled out a wad of one hundred dollar bills. He quickly gave a one hundred dollar bill to the waitress because he did not want Mr. Becker to pay the bill on their anniversary. The complimentary drinks and dessert were already a very generous gesture from Mr. Becker. The waitress quickly brought back their change and they waited at the table for Mr. Becker in accordance with his request.

CHAPTER 9

Lily continued to contemplate how to approach Mr. Becker when he came back to their table. Frank kissed her on the cheek and nervously tapped his left foot on the floor.

After another tug at her dress to expose her assets, Lily said, "Good things happen to good people and we've been good people, haven't we love."

Frank looked at her with a shifty grin and proclaimed, "If you are not getting what you want, you are doing something wrong. If we don't get these paintings, we are doing something wrong hon."

Lily replied, "It might help a little if you get rid of your East Baltimore slur. In my case, I think the alcohol makes me sound like I'm in East, East Baltimore. I'm not sure I could say woter (water) if I tried. Here goes. Weter, worter, woter, woter, worter."

Mr. Becker was standing right in front of them as Lily finished trying to say "water" without an East Baltimore slur.

"Do you need some water dear?" he asked with a contagious smile on his face.

"No thank you," answered Lily. "We were simply having fun with those good old Baltimore accents."

Mr. Becker countered in his thick German accent, "Oh. I've been trying to get one now for fifteen years and you two are trying to get rid of yours. We had a great night tonight. The customers were fun and the staff is happy. We must have had good tippers," proclaimed Mr. Becker.

"How many other paintings do you have that aren't visible to the patrons?" inquired Lily.

"Well, we have the paintings regularly cleaned. You'd be surprised what cigarette smoke and spaghetti sauce can do to a painting."

"Do you have any paintings that you don't put out because you don't like them," Lily further inquired.

"Well let's go into the bar, have a drink, and I'll show you the paintings I'm not that fond of."

Before Frank and Lily knew it, they were seated in the stag bar again. Only one other patron remained. They sat on high bar stools this time, right at the front counter. Mr. Becker went behind the bar and quickly made Lily another dry martini and poured Frank another draft beer. He also poured himself a shot of scotch on the rocks and immediately started sipping away at it.

"To be honest," he whispered, "now that we have acquired so many paintings, I'd like to see some of them placed in good hands. There are still a lot of great buys in Europe and we'd like to buy some larger more expensive paintings for the restaurant. Right now we have too many small paintings."

"Which paintings would you like to pass onto us?" Frank asked in a low voice.

Hearing Frank's misstep, Lily jumped in before Mr. Becker could say one word, "Which nude painting does your wife want you to sell or remove?" Lily questioned with a quick smile.

Mr. Becker was either getting a little tired or a bit tipsy because he slowly leaned over the bar and said, "I think she'd like to get rid of the bar altogether and make room for more dining room patrons. I wouldn't budge on that demand. However, I'm thinking about selling a few of them only to appease her. Are you interested in any of the paintings in the bar?"

Frank was confused and couldn't tell if the offer was real.

"Well, I think we may be interested if the price is right," said Lily as she leaned over on the bar unintentionally exposing a large portion of her breasts as she sipped on her martini. Even though she didn't know it, Mr. Becker was taken aback by what Lily said and what he saw, and didn't know what to say or do next.

"I think these paintings would look great in our bedroom, don't you, Frank," Lily prompted with an air of reckless and sexy drunken confidence. They were words she would never say if she was sober, but they were effective nonetheless. She even made Frank blush.

Mr. Becker was somewhat perplexed as to what to say next.

To break the awkwardness, Mr. Becker quickly blurted out, "Which one would you like to buy from me?"

"Well, I don't think you'd consider selling the painting 'ECSTASY' would you? I like the feeling the painting gives me as much as you do, Mr. Becker," expressed Lily, as her unconscious amorous state of mind kicked in full gear.

Frank shook his head in agreement not knowing what to say or how to control Lily's borderline lurid speech and antics.

"Call me Tomas," insisted Mr. Becker, thoroughly enjoying Lily's effulgent state.

Lily was now drunker than she had ever been in her life. She felt free and unrestrained, and the words were now coming uninterrupted from her mouth.

Mr. Becker was now also beginning to calm down from the busy night. As Frank peered out into the dining area, only two tables remained and they were on the verge of leaving.

"I don't think I could sell her. Even Anna likes that painting. I love every painting in the restaurant, but some more than others, just like the patrons who frequent the restaurant," professed Mr. Becker in a cordial tone.

"Tomas, would you consider selling 'AFTER THE BATH'. I love the detail in the painting and the woman's reflection on the water. The painting makes me want to relax. I feel a sense of calm when I look at it," Lily conveyed in a slow and comforting tone as the alcohol left her uninhibited.

"Well, which 'AFTER THE BATH' painting would you like to buy? I have the 'AFTER THE BATH' by William Adolphe Bouguereau and 'AFTER THE BATH' by Jean-Le'on Ge'rome. Both of them are exquisite works," replied Mr. Becker as he poured another shot of scotch on the rocks into his glass.

As Lily looked at both paintings, she eyed and appreciated the details of the masterpieces. Like the painting by Jean-Le'on Ge'rome, "AFTER THE BATH" by William Adolphe Bouguereau was a stunning picture of a woman leaning on a tree and putting on her sandals after she had taken a bath in a nearby stream. Her light white sheet of clothing only covered her leg, and her upper body remained unclothed. Her innocence and sensuality jumped off of the canvas.

"How much would it cost to own both of these together?" asserted Lily. "It would make our lives that much richer having these hanging in our bedroom, wouldn't it, Frank," Lily stated with a drunken sexy smile as she began rubbing Frank's upper thigh.

Mr. Becker stared across the room as he was performing calculations in his head.

Lily then quickly blurted out, "You know, I love the 'I TOLD YOU SO' painting too. I think that painting would be a great lesson for our children when we have them, wouldn't it, Frank?", Lily advocated as she peered into Frank's eyes with her breasts still dangling over the bar.

Frank remained speechless. He wasn't sure if it was the alcohol, his confidence in Lily, or his inability to know what to say that formed the basis for his silence. Regardless, his silence remained golden for Lily as Mr. Becker contemplated his next move.

Lily's only advantage was to continually tug at her dress to use her best assets to complete the sale. But at this point in the evening, and after a very long day, Mr. Becker was too tired to enjoy the view. He was strictly business when he thought about selling his prized paintings he and Mrs. Becker had worked so hard to acquire.

Lily's mind shifted and conjured the goal of acquiring more than one painting before the evening ended.

"You know, I especially like the painting over there," Frank disclosed, pointing to a large painting of a very pale pregnant woman sitting on the edge of an ocean beach seconds before waves crash onto her.

However, at this point in the evening, upon viewing the painting, Lily suddenly lifted her slumped body up from the bar counter.

"Excuse me please. I have to run to the bathroom," she announced as she headed hastily to the bathroom. The painting of a pregnant woman on the edge of a turbulent sea had immediately made her sick to her stomach.

Mr. Becker turned his attention to Frank to continue negotiating.

"The 'LA VAGUE' painter was Ojjeh Bouguereau. 'LA VAGUE', depicts the changes the wave will bring to her, similar to how the birth of a child changes a woman's life."

"I think you have to sell us that one with the other two since it's our one year anniversary," suggested Frank in a persistently polite tone.

Mr. Becker poured himself another shot of scotch on the rocks.

After ten minutes passed, Lily came out of the bathroom ready to have one last shot at the negotiations.

Frank began to do more listening than talking as Mr. Becker talked garrulously about other paintings that hung around the bar. Before they knew it, another hour had gone by. As Mr. Becker talked on, Frank did his best to keep him on task, continually mentioning the four paintings he and Lily wanted to buy.

CHAPTER 10

The bar was now empty except for the three of them. Mrs. Becker had not been seen in the past hour. Mr. Becker assumed she was on the second floor counting the day's receipts or asleep, knowing she was not feeling well. In any case, Mr. Becker was on his own to make the decision. Frank realized this and pressed Mr. Becker a little harder. Lily, on the other hand, struggled to stay awake and focused on their mission.

"You know you'll make our one year anniversary special if you sell us these four paintings. We won't tell anyone, I promise. If you do, we will both be in your debt forever," swore Lily as her body gently swayed from side-to-side.

Even Frank and Mr. Becker began feeling the alcohol's side effects.

"Well, what would be a good dollar figure for us to pay for these paintings, Tomas?" asked Lily, her eyes beginning to feel heavier with each passing moment.

"Well, since it is your anniversary, I would say thirty thousand dollars. For you Lily, I'll give you the woman's discount, but you both have to agree to one thing," disclosed Mr. Becker. "I'll sell you the four paintings if you agree to be a nude model for one of my artists who may be coming to the states from Europe sometime in the next year or two." Mr. Becker stipulated it as though it was a normal matter of business. Modeling nude was a customary event in Europe.

Frank sprung to attention, with a concerned look on his face. Lily thought he was going to immediately jump over the bar and punch Mr. Becker in the face.

Instead, he drunkenly blurted, "That's a great idea. Where will you hang her portrait in the bar?"

Before Lily knew it, she was completely out of the conversation as Frank and Mr. Becker contemplated where the nude painting of Lily would hang in perpetuity. She didn't want anything to do with it, but was too drunk to explain why it was a bad idea.

She immediately downed the dry martini sitting on the bar untouched in one swift gulp, as if she had found an oasis in the middle of a desert. That martini was the knockout punch for Lily.

As Frank and Mr. Becker continued the discussion, Lily got up from the bar stool and stumbled to the booth that they were sitting in earlier in the evening. She stood up on the booth seat, struck a sexy pose, tugged on her dress to expose her cleavage and yelled to the men, "Would I look good here?"

Lily then clumsily crawled her way like a baby across bench seats to the next table, stood up and struck another drunken pose and shrieked again, "Would I look good here?"

Mr. Becker and Frank remained speechless and allowed her to carry out her frantic temper tantrum.

"Hold on, hon," Frank asserted as Lily crawled to the next table. "I thought this was what you wanted."

"To pose nude and hang in Mr. Becker's bar? Is that what we agreed to?" Lily yelled in a panic as tears ran down her face, smearing her eyeshadow.

"Now, now dear," Mr. Becker responded in a reassuring voice. "If you don't want it hung in the restaurant, we won't do that. I didn't mean to upset you. I know this artist, Edwardo-Leon Cortes. I think he can do a great job painting you. I think you will be a great investment for Anna and me."

With that stated, and as drunk as she was, Lily began to feel better about the terms and conditions of the purchase. However, her tears made Mr. Becker and Frank feel terrible. Mr. Becker was a true gentleman, and their experience with him had been wonderful and unforgettable up to this point in the evening.

As Lily settled down, Mr. Becker poured himself another scotch on the rocks.

"How are you going to pay me tonight?" Mr. Becker stated, hoping to put an end to the discussion.

"I have some cash tonight," Frank said in a tone indicating that he did not have that much money.

Mr. Becker continued to gaze at Frank and Lily as dollar figures ran through his head. He had almost always been on the buying side of a sale.

Frank and Lily had no idea of the value of the paintings. Mr. Becker knew the value of the paintings, but also wanted to appease his wife Anna by selling a few of the paintings in the stag bar. Selling one, two, or three of the paintings would not hurt Anna's feelings at all.

"I'll make you a deal," he proclaimed.

Frank and Lily sat up straighter as the evening was about to reach its climax.

"If you agree to model for my friend Edwardo-Leon Cortes when he comes to town, I'll agree not to hang the painting in the restaurant and I'll sell you the four other paintings for twelve thousand dollars. I'll call this a package deal."

Mr. Becker knew his numbers, knew his strengths, and was getting what he wanted, including Lily as a nude model.

Frank, on the other hand, quickly decided his next move because Lily was in no shape to help him make a decision. Before Lily knew it, Frank was pulling out his compressed wad of one hundred dollar bills, agreeing to the sale price. Mr. Becker had seen piles of paper currency at his restaurant each day, but was surprised that Frank had such a wad of one hundred dollar bills scrunched up in his pants pocket.

"I think we can manage twelve thousand dollars," admitted Frank. He slowly placed the one hundred dollar bills in piles of ten on top of the bar. When he was finished, he counted out the remaining seven one hundred dollar bills and sloppily shoved them back into his pocket.

"It looks like we have enough money to come back for dinner tomorrow night," Frank touted with a renewed confidence as he and Mr. Becker laughed.

Once Mr. Becker counted the money a second time by Mr. Becker, the deal was done. Mr. Becker came out from behind the bar, and they all hugged each other. Lily could barely stand at this point. In her intoxicated state, she was totally oblivious of the final terms of the sale.

"I love you Frank, I love you Tomas," Lily slurred over and over again. She had already forgotten that her nude modeling career had commenced with the agreement.

Lily got out her tenth "I love you," when Frank and Mr. Becker began to pull the paintings off of the wall. Mr. Becker told Frank and Lily that he would call a taxi so that they wouldn't have to carry the paintings back to their home.

After he made the call, Mr. Becker began wrapping them in clean dining room table cloths.

"These table cloths should do the trick. I only ask that you bring them back to me in the next day or two."

The walls were barren where the paintings had been removed. Frank was trying to determine how to carry all four paintings to the front door without dropping them. Lily made one more trip to the ladies room and when she returned, the empty spaces on the walls were being covered with additional nude paintings.

"This is one of our new acquisitions I was hoping to hang," indicated Mr. Becker. "The painting is titled 'LOVE CAPTURED' and was painted by Rudolf Rossler. It's a depiction of a woman in love. The detail, size, and colors are a great match for the bar; that is if we don't turn the bar into additional dining space. I think Anna may like this painting more than the three paintings you bought."

As soon as he finished the sentence, there was the honking of a taxi cab outside. They hugged each other and Frank carried the paintings outside and placed them in the trunk of the cab. Frank and Lily quickly sloshed into the back seat. No sooner than the taxi cab driver hit the accelerator, Lily passed out on Frank's shoulder.

Their one year anniversary would truly be one of the best nights of their marriage, one they would never forget, and hopefully one that would make them wealthy in the years to come.

CHAPTER 11

It was 11:10 p.m. when the taxi cab pulled up in front of their rowhome. The neighborhood was quiet with the exception of the fans spinning in the second floor windows. The sudden braking of the taxi cab aroused the neighbors from their sleep.

"Come on, Lily. Wake up," Frank insisted as he gently shook her. "You didn't fall asleep that fast did you?"

"Where are we Frank?" mumbled Lily, acting if she had been in a deep sleep, even though the taxi cab ride lasted about two minutes.

"Come on, Lily. We're home," whispered Frank hoping not to awaken their neighbors.

Frank instructed the taxi cab driver to wait at the curb while he took the paintings into the house. Lily sat slumped over waiting for Frank's return. Frank didn't want to leave the paintings in the cab in case the driver mistakenly drove off with them. Frank knew the cab driver wouldn't drive off with a drunken woman in the back seat.

Frank quickly paid the taxi cab driver and attended to Lily.

"Come on Lily," Frank pleaded in a low voice.

She did not move. Like Lily, Frank had very minimal control over his body movements. However, he had to help Lily into the house and into bed. Frank reached into the taxi and gently pulled Lily out, picked her up, and then closed the door of the taxi. When the taxi door closed, he could hear a baby begin to cry from a house a few doors away. Frank stumbled through the doorway with Lily in his arms. He slowly moved up the stairs, tripping on two occasions, and plopped her into their bed. That was the best he could do in his condition. Her one hundred and ten pound body remained almost totally limp; she could no longer move or wake.

He slowly removed her dress and placed her head on a pillow. "She looks like a beautiful angel lying on the bed," Frank thought. However, Frank hoped that she would not awaken because of the hasenpfeffer and strawberry pie mixed with the dry martinis that lay in her belly. This was not the way Frank expected their anniversary to end, but it was still an incredible evening.

Now that Lily was sleeping like a log, Frank was excited to place their new acquisitions on the walls of their bedroom. The mere thought of the future value of the paintings, coupled with the fact that there were nude women hanging on his bedroom walls made Frank proud of his new possessions.

Within a few minutes, Lily began to snore.

Frank sat on the edge of the bed for a few minutes staring at the walls and wondering which painting should be hung on which wall. He laughed and hollered in triumph of the acquisition. As soon as he quieted, he again heard a baby crying a few doors away.

Frank knew that he had to remain quiet or his neighbors would hear him wrestling around with his new acquisitions. As he continued to stare at the wall and paintings, he realized that he fulfilled his father's bequest. Frank grinned and looked toward the sky, hoping somehow that his father would be proud of his selections. He then began to second guess his picks, wondering if anyone else in Baltimore would have picked out the same paintings under similar circumstances.

His drunken mind was telling him to lay his head down on the pillow next to Lily, but his conscious mind knew the paintings had to be on the wall when she awoke.

"I'm going to hang them tonight, Dad," Frank avowed.

He staggered in a zig-zag manner down to the basement workbench to find the tools he needed to hang the paintings. As he made his way, he had to duck down to ensure his head would not hit the floor joists on the floor above. The workbench was Frank's first handcrafted piece of furniture he had ever built. Much like the beautiful paintings that now sat in the bedroom, Frank's workbench was painstakingly built over hours of thought and labor. It was eight feet in length and reached to the ceiling. He single-handedly built the frame, the drawers, and the shelving that rose above the counter top. He stained the whole workbench a honey oak color and sealed the stained wood with three coats of lacquer. It shone to perfection and had hardly been used since he completed it. It looked like a handmade piece of furniture that the Pennsylvania Dutch cabinet makers would have been somewhat proud of, or at least that's what Frank thought.

He reached into the second highest drawer on the left hand side of the bench and quickly grabbed a can of small nails, and then reached into the bottom drawer and selected one of the six hammers that lay in the bottom. Frank knew his workbench like the back of his hand and was happy his hard work was finally paying off with this small project.

It was easier for Frank to force his way up the stairs than it was stumbling down the stairs. The painting "I TOLD YOU SO" with the boy being bitten by a lobster was not going to hang in the bedroom, so Frank picked it up and moved it into the hallway. As he peered at each painting, he thought that the "LA VAGUE" painting would look best at the head of their bed and that the two "AFTER THE BATH" paintings would go on the left side of the bed.

Frank picked up his hammer. His hands shaking from drunkenness. He clumsily tapped the nails into the wall. Once the nails were in, he wryly examined his fingers to make sure he had not whacked them in the process.

The "AFTER THE BATH" painting by William Adolphe Bouguereau was the first painting Frank decided to hang. As he peered at the woman, she appeared almost real. As he picked up the painting, it had a calming effect on him that allowed him to hang it on the exposed nail with ease.

Once the first painting was on the wall, Frank quickly moved to the next one. As he began to bend his back over to pick it up, he stumbled forward and dropped the painting onto the hardwood floor.

"Oh, shit," Frank yelled as he hit the floor after the painting.

Realizing that he had almost ruined the painting before it was even up on the wall, he found that the only damage was a chip in the bottom of the frame. As he again rocked his body forward toward the painting's final resting place on the wall, Frank felt like the walls were moving back and forth. He quickly lunged his body and the painting forward, placing both of his fists on the wall to steady him. He slowly moved the painting up and down the wall, releasing his hands in hopes that it was successfully latched onto the wall.

In an instant, painting number two was successfully hung. The next and final painting was going to be a challenge. However, Frank was determined to hang it before Lily opened her eyes. Not only was it the largest painting, it was also going to be hung right above the headboard under which Lily was in a deep sleep. He envisioned a positive, passionate, and romantic morning when she awoke to see their newly decorated bedroom.

Frank bravely positioned himself at the head of the bed, with Lily's head and body directly below his. He attempted to discreetly hammer the nails into the wall. He was able to steady himself by leaning on the headboard, but his legs began to shake. He bent down slightly to grab the painting and used Lily's back to support his right knee.

She still did not move an inch.

As he turned to hang the painting, his legs continued to shake again. Once it was hung, he walked on the bed away from the painting in a hurry to ensure he wouldn't knock it off of the wall. He turned and studied it realizing it was hung in the perfect spot.

"I think this is a good omen to have a sexy pregnant woman watching over our bedroom" he thought.

Frank moved his eyes from painting to painting, until his brain finally registered that his mission was accomplished and it was time to join his wife in a deep sleep. He decided to call it quits and joined his motionless wife. The bedroom lights remained lit, exposing a partial view of one of the paintings from the street for any neighbor to see.

CHAPTER 12

Frank felt movement next to him as he looked at Lily and the alarm clock that sat on an end table. It was 9:05 a.m. and the sun was beginning to shine into their bedroom window and it began to move across the southern sky. The cool breeze of the night was gone as the day began to heat up. Lily got up from the bed with her eyes closed and moved into the bathroom, sat on the toilet, and hung her head between her legs.

"I'm feeling rotten," Lily mumbled to Frank. "What time did we get home last night?"

"Huh, a little after 11:00 p.m.," Frank replied, still half asleep and in a morning stupor.

"I can't believe I ate Bugs Bunny last night and liked it. I can't remember what I had for dessert or anything else after that," Lily admitted with a little more vigor in her voice as she slowly began to awaken.

"We both had their famous strawberry pie and topped it off with another drink in the stag bar," Frank. said quietly.

"Did I have another drink? I don't remember."

"You sure did you lush. You had another martini."

"We had a great time, didn't we honey?" expressed Lily looking for validation.

"The best second one year anniversary I've ever had. I didn't know you couldn't hold your liquor," professed Frank who was somewhat puzzled by her lack of memory of the evening. "You seemed in almost total control until the very end."

Lily eased herself off of the toilet, washed her hands, and slowly walked into the bedroom holding her head down with her eyes shut to ease her hangover headache. As soon as she reached the bed, she lifted her head up and saw the "LA VAGUE" painting hanging on the wall behind her head. The large painting of the nude pregnant woman swiftly and painfully stirred Lily's soul with raw emotion.

She began to yell, "What is this Frank, huh?"

She continued to yell uncontrollably so that the neighbors could hear her piercing screams. Her face turned blood red.

"Frank, what did you do?" she screamed in a panicked and frantic high pitched shrill.

"What did we do Lily?" Frank backpedaled, not knowing how to react.

"Francis," she burst out using his official name; which she would only use when she was extremely mad. "We did not, I repeat not, both agree to buy that painting?" she countered in sharp and downright scary tone.

"There wasn't one painting honey, there were four altogether. There are the other two," Frank revealed slowly and sheepishly pointing to the two "AFTER THE BATH" paintings that hung on other walls.

Lily screamed louder as she quickly assessed the other two paintings. She continued to yell and hopped up on the bed and began jumping on it in frustration.

"How could you? Are you stupid? You dumbass! How could you do this on our anniversary?" she chided in a loud, livid, and panicked tone. "I'm furious and you should be too," she vented with her arms wheeling about.

As Lily continued to scream at Frank, neighbors gathered in the street to catch a glimpse of Lily jumping up and down on the bed in her bra and panties. Frank didn't notice the crowd gathering below as Lily continued to yell and call Frank a lot of names he had never heard before.

"You're going to be sleeping in the next bedroom tonight Francis Clarke," Lily squealed.

With that, a voice from outside yelled "Can I sleep with you?" followed by the loud laughter of thirty or so young men. Hearing the fracas, some of the older neighborhood men and a few of the women ventured into the street to see what was taking place in Frank and Lily's bedroom.

"Lily get down off of that bed. Stop acting foolish. The neighbors can see you," Frank demanded as she continued to jump on the bed with the nervous energy of a two year old and the frustration of a woman whose husband had been wrongfully duped.

"Acting foolish. You've got to be kidding me. Who did I marry one year ago, a fool or a sucker?" she cried with her anger and outrage continuing to build like a volcano before its eruption.

"If you are foolish enough to buy these paintings, I'm foolish enough to continue jumping on my bed. You already have three naked women in the room, why not have another one?" she vented in a menacing voice.

Before Frank could react, Lily bent down and slipped off her panties and pulled off her bra and began jumping on the bed with all of her naked assets clearly exposed to the street crowd below. The neighbors were now vying to get the best view of the action from an angle in the middle of the street.

She continued as hoots and hollers echoed from the street below. Cars from both directions were forced to stop, as the crowd created a roadblock.

Frank tried to grab her, but she kept moving and hopping from side to side of the bed, giving the horde of people more entertainment than they would experience at a circus.

After what seemed like a prolonged period of time chasing Lily around the bed Frank could hear the uncontrolled hooting and hollering of the boys and young men getting louder by the second.

Frank was unable to pull her off of the bed without hurting her.

After a few minutes of shuffling around the bed, he quickly resolved his dilemma by hastily pulling down the two window shades, completely covering the window. However, the damage was done. As soon as he closed the shades, he was treated to a round of boos that sounded as loud as a crowd at a professional wrestling event. No sooner did the boos begin, the cars stopped honking as the crowd began to disburse from the street.

"I don't care what you do with those paintings Frank Clarke, but get rid of them right now if you ever want to have sex with me again," Lily threatened. "We'll talk when these paintings are off of my bedroom walls. This is my bedroom now. It's not yours and I want these paintings gone right this instant," she insisted as her voice started to rise again.

"Can I close the windows first?" Frank said in a low voice. "The neighbors may be able to hear us."

"I don't care if the damn neighbors can hear us. Get these naked and pregnant women off of my wall now," Lily demanded and screamed in frustration.

"Okay, okay," Frank conceded as he first removed the painting that hung above the headboard. Lily fumed unrelentingly and watched as Frank continued following her orders and took the two "AFTER THE BATH" paintings off the wall.

Frank proceeded to move the paintings immediately outside of the bedroom. He came back and walked over to the window and closed the first window sash. He quickly moved to the second window, closed it and squatted down with his arms crossed and back leaning against a wall. Frank felt demoralized after berated by his wife while the whole neighborhood watched.

The room became eerily silent as Frank and Lily sat motionless.

As time passed, Lily began to reflect on her morning outburst and started to feel guilty about the way she had treated Frank. Through the years, she learned how to quickly shut down and bury her raw emotions whenever her past pain resurfaced in her mind. Today was no different. As she focused on Frank, she thought he looked innocent and cute as he leaned against the wall. Lily's thoughts and attitude began to quickly change as she accepted her culpability in the night's events. As she stared Frank down, an amorous look began to appear on her face.

"What is the other painting we purchased Frank? I hope you were fair and bought at least one painting of a well-endowed naked man," Lily contested as her voice became sexually suggestive.

She turned her bent leg slightly and began to rub both legs together as she slowly caressed her thigh with her hand. Lily erotically commanded, "You better get in this bed right now if you know what's good you, you bad, bad boy."

Frank confusedly grinned at Lily and slowly made his way to the edge of the bed as he collected his thoughts. No other words were spoken for the next two hours as Frank followed each of Lily's unspoken commands. Lily remained in control of Frank for the next two hours and got what she wanted to alleviate her pent up frustrations. As they enjoyed each other, Frank smiled realizing that the paintings were worth this moment they were spending together. The morning rendezvous brought Lily sexual pleasure she had not yet experienced in their first year of marriage. The prior evening's and morning's events would be an experience they would never forget.

CHAPTER 13

Frank looked at the clock as it revealed it was 2:06 p.m. as he sat up in their bed.

"What happened to me last night?" Lily asked.

Frank explained the events of the evening at Haussner's and what had happened when they arrived home. She was finally calm and was able to talk normally.

"Frank, the money you spent last night was your father's money. I know he would have been happy you spent his inheritance on the Haussner's paintings. However, I can't have these paintings hanging in my house. I don't care what you do with them. You can give them back to Mr. Becker or you can do something else with them. I don't want to see or discuss them ever again. Do you hear me? Never, ever again," Lily said emphatically.

Frank nodded his head, acknowledging Lily's wishes.

Lily's frustration began to build again, "I can't have them. After what happened a few hours ago, the neighbors are going to think we are absolutely crazy. Just please get rid of them. I don't care what you do with them or where you put them. Just get them out of my sight," she said.

There was a brief period of silence.

"Where's the fourth painting we bought? That's one I haven't seen yet. Is it another risqué' painting Frank?" Lily skeptically probed.

"I think you'll like this one," Frank touted to Lily trying to keep the discussion amicable. "I'll go get it."

Frank left the room, grabbed the painting, and walked back toward the bedroom.

"Close your eyes," he directed.

"I'm nervous Frank. Three's a charm, not four."

Frank sat the painting on the edge of the bed.

"Open your eyes."

Lily opened her eyes slowly. She took one look at the painting and began to laugh.

"I loved that painting when we were in the restaurant. I can't believe you bought that painting for me Frank. What is the name of the painting?" she said.

"I TOLD YOU SO," Frank declared.

"I TOLD YOU SO," Lily acknowledged to Frank as if pontificating the meaning of the painting. "Well, I guess I told you so today Frank, didn't I?" reminded Lily in a lecturing manner.

"You sure did," replied Frank submissively. "I think I made up for it over the past two hours. I hope you're not going to make me hide this picture too," Frank requested in a nervous voice.

"Well," Lily stated as she peered at Frank with her eyes squinted as if examining Frank's soul. "Regarding those other three paintings, I'm still the judge, jury, and executioner," Lily maintained.

"Okay, okay," Frank said, knowing that he was going to have to accept that only the painting "I TOLD YOU SO" would ever be seen by anyone.

"Frank, if we have children, I think the 'I TOLD YOU SO' painting will deliver a good daily dose of medicine to them. It will be a reminder for them to listen to what we tell them," Lily stated with conviction.

Frank remained silent, proud and content that he was going to be able to hang one of his newly acquired trophies in their home.

"Let's go down and decide where we are going to hang it," Lily proposed with enthusiasm.

Frank carried the painting down the second floor steps with Lily trailing right behind him and proceeded to hang the painting on a wall immediately next to the front entranceway.

"Hopefully in the future our children will ponder this painting every time they walk in our door Frank. It is the perfect location. Now let's get rid of those other paintings," Lily insisted relentlessly.

"Do we have to?" Frank appealed with a dejected tone and his head lowered to the floor, relinquishing any further hope of persuading Lily to change her mind.

"You know the deal we made," maintained Lily as she sternly reminded Frank.

"I think it was a one-sided negotiation. You'll be eating these words when we get old."

"We're never going to grow old."

"What's the alternative, hon?"

"That is the smartest thing you've said all day," Lily touted.

A quick-witted Frank replied, "At least I remember what I did last night and this morning, and I wasn't jumping up and down on the bed naked so all the neighbors could see me."

"I hope they enjoyed the view. It'll give them something to talk about for a long time. I've never done anything like that before and I won't ever do it again," promised Lily.

"I don't know. I kind of liked watching you jumpin' on the bed."

Lily moved toward Frank quickly in an effort to wrestle and tickle him. Frank, upon seeing Lily's intentions, turned and started running away from Lily. She chased after him around their rowhome.

CHAPTER 14

Frank moved each painting one by one into the basement, ducking his head slightly so it would not hit the basement rafters. Lily remained upstairs.

Frank studied the basement. "Where could I place these paintings so that I won't have to worry about them for a long time?" he carefully thought as his eyes scoured every inch of the basement.

As he contemplated the paintings final resting spot, his thoughts kept wandering back to his beautiful new workbench. With it in mind, Frank's plan and final resting place for the paintings was resolved.

Frank's idea and strategy was to place the three paintings in a hidden compartment behind his recently finished workbench. He spent so much time building the workbench, it was going to be mentally challenging for him to rip some of it apart so soon after he had completed it. Frank's plan included unsecuring it from the basement wall and constructing a new compartment directly behind it to conceal the three paintings. He needed to build this compartment and make it look like new again.

Frank started the work immediately.

"What are ya doing down there?" Lily questioned.

"I'm adhering to your wishes, dear. I'm working on hiding the paintings."

"Well if you're going to do that, I'm going to go back to bed. I still don't feel that great," Lily maintained.

"No more jumping on the bed while you're up there," Frank shouted back.

Frank could hear Lily's footsteps above as she headed back to the bedroom. He began to take action on his proposed design. Frank removed anything that could fall from the workbench. It took half an hour to unbolt and unscrew his new beautiful workbench from the basement wall where it was anchored.

With this plan in mind, he didn't need to make significant changes to the workbench, but he did need to make it look brand new.

Frank also realized that he would need to do some research to determine the proper temperature and humidity necessary to preserve the paintings for years to come. A dehumidifier and heater were on his list to purchase at some point in the near future.

When the job was officially finished, with the exception of the final staining and lacquering, Frank sat back and admired his handiwork. His workbench was again his masterpiece. The paintings were now safely sealed for years to come. He wasn't sure when he'd ever see them again, but was happy nonetheless with his investment.

At the end of this crazy course of events, Frank realized that his father and Lily were both right. He categorically couldn't hang three of the paintings in his home, but he could use his father's inheritance to take a risk on a potentially excellent investment. Frank began to hope that years from now, the paintings would be a legacy that Lily will be proud of. He also hoped that the painting "I TOLD YOU SO" would remind his future children to listen to their parents' advice.

CHAPTER 15

The next evening, Frank grabbed the Haussner's Restaurant's tablecloths from his rowhouse and made the short trek to the restaurant to return them. As he walked into the front door of the restaurant, it was crowded with patrons waiting for tables. Making his way past the line, he saw Mrs. Becker standing proudly behind the front counter.

As he approached Mrs. Becker she blurted, "I am so glad you came back. I was looking for you all day yesterday."

"I'm sorry. I should have brought the table clothes back yesterday."

"No, no. I wasn't worried about that. I'm just upset with the deal my husband made with you. Is your wife okay?" probed Mrs. Becker.

"She's fine," replied Frank.

"Good. I'm so sorry Mr. Becker sale's price included your wife modeling nude. He still thinks he's in Europe. I was so embarrassed for you and your wife when he told me this morning what he did. You got a great price for the paintings. I hope you all learned a valuable lesson," chided Mrs. Becker.

"To be honest, I haven't told her yet. She had too many martinis that evening and doesn't remember the full extent of the deal. I was too afraid to tell her," Frank said as he handed Mrs. Becker the table cloths.

"You got a good deal and I'm happy we got rid of three of those bar paintings. I lectured my husband that from now on he must confide in me on any future sales. He may be the face of our restaurant, but I'm the brains," insisted Mrs. Becker in her thick German accent.

Frank listened and shook his head acknowledging his luck.

"Thanks for saving my marriage, Mrs. Becker. I'm not sure what my wife would have said when I told her about the modeling. I think I was in denial," admitted Frank.

"You better get out of here before Mr. Becker sees you. He might demand the return of the paintings. He's a stubborn German you know," insisted Mrs. Becker.

"You're a lucky young man. Enjoy those paintings."

"Thank you. Thank you Mrs. Becker," Frank mumbled in excitement as he shook Mrs. Becker's hand and honored her request, turned and exited the restaurant quickly so he would not be accosted by Mr. Becker.

As Frank headed back to his house, his mission was accomplished. He had completed the art sale of his lifetime, and was elated knowing his wife's nude modeling career had officially ended before it had begun.

CHAPTER 16

Lily nervously smoked her cigarette as she made her way past the admissions desk and was slowly escorted to her hospital room for the delivery of her first child.

"Don't forget your suitcase," the admissions clerk yelled to Lily as she began to walk down the hall. "Best of luck to you," she uttered, scaring Lily.

Amniotic fluid continued to drip down Lily's leg as she walked down the hall. She was petrified knowing that none of her family members would be allowed into her hospital room until after the delivery. She was totally unprepared and in complete denial this event was even taking place. It was the middle of September and Lily had a small suitcase in hand as she waddled gingerly down the long hospital hall. Her anticipated hospital stay was going to be one long week if she had a normal delivery, which she had hoped for.

The nurse attending to Lily met her as she walked her down the hospital hall. She was not all that friendly and very few words were spoken as they entered her hospital room. The hospital was busy with a lot of women having babies in the aftermath of World War II.

"Lie down on the bed and get comfortable. Put on this hospital gown. I'll be back in a little bit," the nurse said.

The room was semi-private, and as luck would have it, no other expectant mother was in the adjoining hospital bed. There was no television in the room and the walls were barren. She was hoping to watch some of the fairly new television shows like "The Ed Sullivan Show" or the "CBS Television News". Instead, Lily quickly determined that she'd be reading a lot of magazines and newspapers and also hoping her stay would be much shorter than one week.

Lily had a window in her room, but it looked out onto a parking lot. She unpacked her suitcase. She was happy to be at the hospital to deliver the baby, but she was not happy with the pain she was now beginning to experience.

The same unfriendly nurse returned and stayed in the room, waiting for Lily to have a cycle of contractions.

After two contractions came and went, the nurse concluded, "Your contractions are coming fairly steady. The next time you feel a contraction, breathe in deep, which will push the baby further down the birth canal. After you push your air out of your lungs, relax. If you keep doing that, it will help to push the baby out quicker. So let's start to get ready now," she directed in a non-personal manner.

"To prepare us for the baby's delivery, I have a couple questions for you before we start," indicated the nurse. "Did you smoke while you were pregnant?"

"Doesn't everybody? Expecting made me nervous," admitted Lily as she pulled another cigarette out of her pocketbook and began the process of lighting it as the nurse continued asking questions.

"Did you drink during the past nine months?"

"Doesn't everybody?" Lily responded to the nurse in the same impersonal tone the nurse had been directing towards her. "It helped to relax me at night. I would only drink when I could get away with it."

"How about medications? Did you take any medications since you've been expecting?" probed the nurse, acting as if Lily was inhuman.

"I took black beauties for most of the expecting period because I didn't want to gain too much weight. I didn't want anyone to think I was getting fat during the nine months," contended Lily as she became perplexed by the nurse's questions.

"Well you did a good job at that. Other than that little belly sticking out, you don't look like you're pregnant to me. You must have fooled a lot of people," countered the nurse.

As another contraction came and went, Lily countered to the nurse, "Well, I think that's the nicest thing I'll hear from you all day."

Once the contraction ended, the nurse gave Lily a snooty grin and proceeded to help her take off her gown

"Let's start to get ready for your exciting day," the nurse insisted with a smile seeing that Lily had a terrified look on her face.

"When did you find out you were pregnant?" questioned the nurse with sincere curiosity.

"I sent a urine sample into a lab a while back. When they injected the rabbit with my urine, it died very quickly. That's when I knew I was expecting. I think I was as shocked as the rabbit," Lily divulged as she stared with a blank look on her face, puffing on another cigarette.

"My first baby was the toughest," advised the nurse as if it would make Lily feel better. It didn't.

"The first thing I'm going to do is shave your pubic hair," revealed the nurse as she indiscriminately poured cold water and dabbed shaving cream around Lily's pubic area.

"Do you know if it's a boy or girl?"

"No I don't. I wasn't interested in finding out," Lily disclosed as another contraction began.

"What are you going to name it?"

"I haven't decided yet. Why is it so cold in here?" Lily responded, trying to avoid her questions as the pain grew stronger.

Although the contraction was painful, the nurse proceeded to ask one more question in a joking manner.

"Well if you don't know the answer to these two questions, do you know who the father is?" she probed as Lily's pain worsened.

"Shut up, bitch," Lily swore as she began to grunt and then scream uncontrollably, dropping her cigarette, as the pain level significantly increased from the previous contraction. At this point, Lily didn't care what she said to the nurse and the nurse didn't care either. The nurse had heard it all over her career and continued to smile and grin at Lily as she screeched through the contraction.

After the contraction ended, the nurse ordered in a curt manner, "Put the gown back on, lie down, and wait for the doctor. How strong are your contractions in terms of pain?" probed the nurse.

"On a one-to-ten scale, they're a nine," responded Lily.

Lily had never had felt pain like this before.

"Is this normal?" Lily appealed, indicating that she was totally unprepared for what to expect next.

Once the nurse realized Lily was totally unprepared, she rolled her eyes and started to walk out the door saying "You have a long way to go, honey. The doctor will be here in a couple of minutes."

That's when Lily realized she was in big trouble and was heading directly into rough and uncharted water.

The doctor walked in shortly thereafter. He was an on-call doctor and that was fine by Lily.

"Hi, I'm Dr. Scherr. Lie down and let's take a look."

The doctor proceeded to examine Lily.

"Well, your baby is quite far along, but you also have a long way to go unless you help it along."

Since this was her first baby, Lily didn't know what that meant or what to say. She simply replied "Okay Doc."

Dr. Scherr responded, "I'll be back in a little while," as he exited Lily's hospital room.

Lily sat for another hour as the contractions began to occur on a more regular basis. The nurses came in from time to time to check on her. The pain brought about by each contraction remained excruciating.

"Relax and take a deep breath," the nurse would repeat each time she came into Lily's room. Lily did her best to abide by the nurse's instructions as the contractions continued to grow stronger.

Lily felt dreadfully lonely being in the hospital room by herself. When the nurses did come in her room, they were strictly business. As the contractions became more frequent, her mind raced, thinking that maybe this was her payback for getting pregnant in the first place. After all, this baby was unplanned and didn't come at a very good time in her life.

After being in the hospital room for six hours, the doctor and nurse came into her room and gave her a further examination.

"I think you're almost ready to deliver," confirmed the doctor.

The pain was so great at this point that Lily only heard half of what the doctor said.

"I don't care what you do. Can't you please give me something to make this pain go away or put me out of my damn misery?" Lily implored to the doctor.

"Okay, let's take you in. Are you all set?" countered Dr. Scherr.

"No, not at all," confessed Lily as her sweaty face began to turn blood red as another contraction developed.

As the nurse prepared Lily for the delivery, little did she, the other hospital staff, or Lily know the shocking event that would take place during the delivery of Lily's first born child.

CHAPTER 17

The doctor left the room, and the nurse proceeded to put Lily onto a mobile hospital bed and began to wheel her down to the delivery room. Immediately upon entering, Lily was placed on an operating room table, her feet were placed in stirrups, and sterile bedding was placed around her whole body. Sterile metal tools and instruments surrounded her. Dr. Scherr was already waiting.

"I don't think I can take this pain. Will you give me something to help, damn it?" Lily demanded in a condescending tone. Her pain was now so bad that she didn't care what she said to anybody. Her mind was beginning to race, wanting to make the pregnancy end and return her body back to its pre-pregnancy state.

"Well," Dr. Scherr uttered.

Lily knew that the doctor was going to give her a rather detailed explanation of what her choices were for the delivery. As another strong contraction began to surge, the doctor explained to Lily her choices.

"I think your best option is the twilight sleep" he recommended in a calm manner with confidence in his voice. "This procedure has been around for a long time and involves giving you two intravenous drugs that are mixed together. We'll give you small doses of these drugs. One drug will be morphine to provide you relief from pain. The other drug is scopolamine, which will put you in a twilight sleep. During the twilight sleep, you'll be able to respond to our instructions. The twilight sleep will give you amnesia so that you won't remember the pain you're going to endure during the delivery process. Other than this, some women don't take medications so that they'll be totally alert during the delivery. It's your choice."

As the contraction reached its peak, Lily was in excruciating pain and completely bewildered by her situation. She didn't want to endure the pain anymore.

"Will you please give me the drugs and put me out of my misery? Let's get on with it," asserted Lily as she grimaced through the contraction.

As the contraction subsided, the nurse quickly pulled over to Lily the two bottled solutions that were hanging from a hospital pole and immediately began to stick Lily's arm with the intravenous concoction that she so desperately needed.

"Please begin administering the drug," the doctor instructed.

The two drugs began to drip down the tubes and would eventually reach Lily's arms.

The nurse began talking to Lily slowly.

"In two minutes, you will feel no pain and in fifteen minutes your baby should be here. But watch what you say when you're in the twilight sleep. The drug is also known as a truth serum. You'd be surprised what we hear coming out of the mouths of mothers during the delivery process. We often hear their best- kept secrets. It's the best part of the job, besides the babies."

The nurse continued to talk as Lily slipped into her twilight sleep.

CHAPTER 18

"Let me know when she is fully engaged in the twilight sleep," requested Dr. Scherr.

"She's a feisty one. You know how those feisty women are," aired the nurse with a worried expression. "The heavier women are much calmer in the twilight sleep. The skinny ones seem to have a lot more energy in it."

As the twilight sleep began to kick in, Lily's hands began to move wildly at her sides and each leg began to move back and forth banging together at the knees. Two nurses began to hold her legs to ensure her feet remained in the stirrups. Her head began to move from side to side.

"Here comes another contraction," announced one of the attendants as she pressed on Lily's stomach.

Lily began to scream and move hysterically and managed to move her legs away from the stirrups; her arms moved up and down and side to side and her head was blood red and sweaty as she pushed, yelled, and screamed.

As each contraction subsided, she would calm down slightly, but only briefly until the next contraction began its progression.

As the contractions continued, Lily's wild and crazed screams increased in intensity. The doctor, nurses, and attendants looked at each other knowing her behavior was uncharacteristic compared to the hundreds of other deliveries they had each performed. All of the hospital staff began to realize that this delivery was going to be far from ordinary.

As the next contraction came, Lily's yells and screams began to take the form of coherent language and her whole body began to shake as she screamed. The scopolamine truth serum had now taken full control of Lily's mind. As soon as scopolamine took its full effect, Lily's mind placed her immediately back to an event that had occurred nine months earlier. She began to recall the cold winter's night in January as her body continued to shake and shiver with deep felt anguish on the delivery table.

In her mind, she was placed right back to the January night when she was returning home from a friend's house who lived on the opposite side of Patterson Park. She had made this half mile walk across the park dozens of times each year over her lifetime. It was only 6:00 p.m., on this dark moonless winter evening.

"No, no," Lily yelled. "No, no," she screamed in a terrified voice as the hospital staff continued to hold down her arms and legs.

"Please don't, please don't. I'm only a girl. No, No, please no," she cried out again in a horrified voice as she began to recall, as if it was happening again, the torment of her body being pulled into the bushes.

The collegial mood in the delivery room quickly grew silent. Dr. Scherr continued to perform his work as any doctor would, through Lily's horrified screams. He glanced up at his medical team with an alarmed look in his eyes.

Lily's bizarre movements and screams became nonstop, even after the contractions subsided. Her arms and legs began to flail as she tried to escape the barbaric demon that completely filled her mind.

"I'm only a girl," she screamed. "I'm a good girl," she repeated as she began to sob. "Please don't. I'm still a virgin. Please no," she continued to cry as she thrashed her arms and legs on the delivery table and recalled being violently dragged belly first into the bushes.

"Please don't. Oh, God. Please don't rape me. I'm a good girl. I'm a good girl. Please don't," she pleaded and begged to her imaginary attacker.

"The baby's head is crowning very well," Dr. Scherr disclosed in a quiet tone. Let's deliver this baby."

Lily's mind was still at the Patterson Park Lake as the baby moved further down the birth canal and its head became more effaced.

"What are you doing? Please, please stop it. Please let go of my legs."

In her mind, the attendants were her attacker.

"You're hurting me," she shrieked in a combination of a howl and a cry.

"Give us one big push Lily," Dr. Scherr demanded.

With that push the baby's head popped out. As the baby's head popped out, Lily began a long period of silence. In her cloudy and darkened mind, her attacker was in the middle of his heartless act and she was totally defenseless. She could see his brown-skinned hand holding the knife he held close to her throat making her a hostage to his vicious cruelty. She knew it was better to remain quiet and live rather than scream, fight, and die.

Exactly in the way the twilight sleep would make her delivery memoryless, the only actual memory she had of the rapist was the glimpse she had of his tanned hands and the black knit hat he wore on that cold January evening. He could have been Greek, Italian, Jewish, African American or any other dark skinned ethnic group that populated the Baltimore neighborhoods around Patterson Park.

She stared in the air, as she continued to recall his body thrusting into hers.

She briefly speculated again about his ethnicity or nationality.

"One more big push and your baby will be here," repeated Dr. Scherr.

Lily followed the doctor's instructions and gave the final push. With that, Lily's first girl was born, the product of her encounter with a rapist in 1948. She was only seventeen years of age when the rape occurred and had barely turned eighteen years old one month ago. She would not meet her future husband Frank for another three years.

She had been too afraid to tell her parents about the rape until it was too late for her to have an abortion. Luckily, she was able to hide her pregnancy from her classmates and stayed at her father's brother and sister-in-law's house outside of Baltimore in the summer months. No one knew about the pregnancy except them.

Lily felt lifeless as she lay motionless in her twilight sleep on the delivery table. She felt dead, like she had nine months before. Her baby, now delivered, would never be seen by her again.

September 11, 1948, was an event that she was hoping the twilight sleep would take from her memory forever.

Lily began to awake from her twilight sleep in the delivery room. She could hear noise around her, but had a towel drooped over her head to cover her eyes.

"It's okay. It's all over. You're safe now," Lily heard a nurse reassuring her.

"What's wrong? Is the baby okay? Am I okay?" Lily probed in an alarmed voice.

"You're fine dear. Everything went according to plan. Your baby daughter is fine too. You simply rest your bones and we'll have you back to your room in no time."

With that said, Lily relaxed as the hospital staff continued their clean-up tasks. She could hear the attendants moving about the operating room. The delivery room was eerily quiet, unlike the discussions that were taking place as she was being prepped for the delivery. Lily wasn't sure what took place during the delivery of the baby, but she was hoping that the dreams in her mind during the delivery were not outwardly expressed to the operating room staff. But as the silence continued longer, Lily's fear was that the twilight sleep truth serum's characteristics gave away the secret that only a few of her immediate family knew.

Although the towel was still draped over Lily's head, she felt a woman lean on the operating table. Unbeknownst to her, she was leaning in next to Lily's ear to whisper to her.

"I understand that you want to give this baby up for adoption," she whispered. "Is this true?"

Lily's head remained under the towel draped on her head.

"What do you want to name the baby?" the woman asked.

"I'm not ready to name the baby. Name her Baby Doe for now," suggested Lily.

Within minutes Lily was cleaned up, the towel was removed from her face, and she was whisked down the hall to her new hospital room. Lily kept her eyes closed until she entered her new room. The room she entered was different than the room she had previously been in. She was still in the maternity ward, but on the opposite end of a long hallway, away from most of the other expectant and new mothers.

The nurse helped Lily off of the mobile hospital bed, and helped ease her onto the permanent bed where she anticipated spending the next week in recovery. The room was cold and barren of any objects. Within minutes, another nurse brought Lily her suitcase from the room she had previously expected to be in for the duration of her stay. Although the new room was a semi-private room, the bed next to Lily's was empty, which was fine by her. Within minutes she was in a deep sleep.

CHAPTER 19

Hours later, Lily was awoken by the sound of a woman crying in the bed next to her. As she looked at the faint light on the clock, she could see that it was 1:30 a.m. in the morning. A drape was pulled between Lily and the crying woman, giving each one some privacy. Every few minutes, Lily could hear her gasping for breath between the whimpers and the sniffles.

"Are you okay?" Lily asked in a concerned voice.

"Not really," countered the woman.

"Is your baby okay?" Lily probed again, not knowing what she might say.

Before she could get out the word "okay" the woman on the other side of the curtain began again to cry, sniffle, and whimper.

"I'm sorry. I'm very sorry. I should've known better," Lily said intuitively knowing the woman must have lost her baby and that anything she would say wouldn't make her feel better.

There was silence for a long period of time.

"When did you come into the room?" Lily inquired in a quiet voice.

"About two hours ago. I didn't even know you were there because you were so quiet. What's your name?" asked the woman.

"Lily."

"My name's Ella. What happened to your baby?"

Lily didn't know how to respond to the question. Her mind was racing for an answer. She hesitated for a long period of time and then confided "I'm sorry, but I actually don't want to talk about it now."

"Well, you eventually will," contended the woman. "This is the end of the hallway where they put all the misfortunates like me and you. They put us together because they don't want to put us in a room with a woman who's happy with her new baby. Misery loves company you know. I've been here five times. My husband and I have tried to conceive for years, and for some reason we've never been successful," she disclosed in a whisper. "They say it has to do with some kind of build-up on my ovaries. They told me this was my last try. I'd be real happy with one beautiful child, just one. Is that too much to ask from the Lord? Just one Lord is all I asking for," vowed Ella.

There was a long period of silence in the room again.

"Where you from?" Ella expressed inquisitively.

Before Lily could answer, the woman spoke again.

Ella continued, "I'm a west side girl. I live right on the other side of Greenmount Cemetery. Do you know John Wilkes Booth is buried there? I still can't believe that he shot President Lincoln, who freed our people."

Lily sat quiet for a second trying to think again how to respond to Ella. With a childlike giggle Lily inquired, "Whose people are you referring to?"

Ella began to pick up Lily's silly tone.

"Well, I guess you ain't one of my people after all, but I think I'll like you anyway," Ella proclaimed as her mood began to sound a little better. "I can't believe I have to share a room with a white woman. I think I'm gonna call security and change rooms," she insisted in a teasing way as she began to cackle.

"Now you know everything about me. I'm from the west side, I'm black and I've had five miscarriages. Now can you please tell me everything about you?"

Lily didn't know what to say. "Well, I'm from the 200 East block of Linwood Avenue. How old do you think I am?" Lily countered in an attempt to change the conversation.

"Well, judging by the fact that you was pregnant, hope you're married which would make you at least eighteen, so I say you're twenty. Am I right?" Ella replied trying to get additional information out of Lily.

"How old are you?" Lily countered trying to get her to change the subject.

"I'm thirty-eight years old, and I think this might've been my last chance to have children. That's one more piece of information I gave you. Now you have to give me one."

Feeling backed into a corner, Lily didn't know what to say. "I'm white," she disclosed in a jovial tone. "And that's number two. I don't want to be here. That's number three and I'm eighteen years old. That's number four. You might feel better now, but I don't. I can't wait to get out of this place," Lily professed.

"Come on now, baby. We're gonna be here together in solitary confinement for a couple days. We might as well make the best of it. The past four times I was here, I never had a white woman in my room. I'm hoping it'll make the experience enjoyable because we think the white women always have more fun. That's what we black folk see on T.V.," Ella declared as she began to chuckle.

"You're a real hoot," Lily proclaimed to Ella. "It sounds to me like black folk have more fun," Lily contended with childish giggle.

Ella and Lily continued to talk throughout the night. They talked about their families, dreams, and religion. As the night wore on, Lily realized that they had more in common than their differences. Ella dispensed wisdom, knowledge, and insight over the next few hours. As Lily talked and listened to Ella, they continued to laugh and cry about their successes, failures, and difficulties. Lily realized that Ella was a strong and independent woman, who was a resourceful survivor of life's challenges. She would have made a good mother, but for some reason it wasn't meant to be.

Sometime during the night, Ella decided to give Lily some worldly advice regarding finding and keeping a man.

"Baby, you never told me yet if you're married, but if you are or ain't, I'm gonna give you my rules for finding and keeping a man. They were taught to me by women in my neighborhood when I was your age. It's called the Rule of Three," Ella expressed as she began to talk in a lower tone so she would not be overheard by anyone.

"The Rule of Three means that a woman gotta have two of three things if she wants to attract a man and keep him. First, she's gotta take care of him by running the house, including doin' the cookin' and cleanin'. Second, she's gotta be good looking. And third you gotta give him good sex. If you're taking care of him and you ain't too pretty, you better be givin' him some good hard sex, or you ain't gonna keep him too long. If you're taking care of him and you look like a goddess, you don't have to have sex with him if you don't want to. And if you look like a goddess and give him good sex, you don't have to take care of him. He'll cook, he'll clean all night long and do anything you tell him to do."

"But I've never had sex with a boyfriend. How do I know if I'm givin' him good sex?" Lily broached in an innocent and uncertain tone.

"I guess you're not married after all, are you?" contended Ella.

Lily remained silent.

"You'll know. I promise. You'll know if you're givin' him good sex," Ella continued. "And if you're a man and you want to attract and keep your woman, you have to take care of her by earning a good livin', be nice, or be good looking. That's it for the man. If he has two of those three things, you'll be happy for the rest of your life, baby. He doesn't even have to give a woman good sex to keep her. Please make sure the man you decide to marry has two of these three things. If he doesn't, you better quickly walk away, baby, or you're not gonna be too happy," confided Ella.

They continued to chat until it was almost sunrise and then both closed their eyes for some well-deserved sleep.

CHAPTER 20

By 8:00 a.m. they could hear movement and muffled voices down the hallway. A nurse walked in and pulled Lily's curtain back so that they could finally see each other.

"Nurse," proclaimed Ella in a loud kidding voice, "I'm shocked that you would stick me in the room at the end of the hall with a white woman. I'm going to call my congressman," she vented with a laugh as the nurse looked at her with a blank, cold stare, not knowing how to react to Ella's comment.

Lily kept quiet as long as she could until she could no longer hold back her laugh. The nurse could see that they were enjoying each other's company and cracked a grin.

"Let's get up and take your first pee. Who wants to be first?" she questioned.

"Well since I delivered my baby first and had to wait for the longest time, I should be first. And besides, I don't think I can hold it much longer," Lily admitted as she immediately got up and waddled to the bathroom.

"You go child. Babies first," Ella replied referring to Lily's youthful age.

The nurse exited the hospital room to attend to other patients.

Lily did her business and exited the bathroom. Ella went in right behind her and closed the door.

No sooner had Ella entered the bathroom and closed the bathroom door, then a different older nurse quickly appeared at Lily's bedside.

"Do you want to see your baby? She's beautiful," disclosed the nurse not knowing that someone was in the bathroom. The nurse was hoping Lily would want to see her new baby.

Lily immediately began shaking her head back and forth to indicate a strong "no."

The nurse blurted, "If not then, I'll go get the papers for you to sign so that we can work with the city's adoption agency to find your baby a good home."

"I can't. I can't." Lily responded and started to cry frantically as she began to realize the decision she was about to make.

Forgetting that Ella was in the bathroom next to her bed, Lily divulged, "Do you know I was brutally raped? Do you know I don't know who the father of the baby is, other than the fact that he is a rapist?"

The nurse remained silent and after an uncomfortable period of time, countered, "I'll go and have the papers drawn up."

The nurse began to leave the room, but before she could, Lily blurted out a question.

"Is the baby light-skinned or dark skinned? I never got a good look at the person who raped me."

"It's hard to tell with any baby, white, black or other when they are a newborn. But she has black, curly hair and it appears her skin could become darker when she gets a little older. However, you never know with a baby until they are a year or so old. I'll see you in a little bit."

As soon as the nurse was gone, the toilet flushed. Lily had totally forgotten that Ella was in the bathroom. Lily had provided a lot of detailed answers to questions to the nurse that she was trying to avoid giving Ella. Ella hadn't known much about Lily up to this point, but now all of Lily's shameful and hidden secrets were out. She was afraid the overall conversation she had with the nurse did not paint her in a good light.

The bathroom door opened and Ella slowly walked back to her bed, her eyes turned away from Lily. As Ella moved past Lily's bed, she slowly pulled the curtains between their two beds so that they could not see each other. Lily was mortified.

"How could I have hurt such a wonderful woman who was already in so much pain?" Lily thought.

There was silence between Lily and Ella for a long time. Lily was trying to determine what she could do or say to her to apologize or make it right between the two of them. She wasn't sure what she was thinking, but knew her words tore right through Ella's soul.

"How could this woman have suffered year after year trying to conceive a baby and Lily got pregnant when the fateful opportunity presented itself? It truly doesn't seem fair," Lily thought. During the period of silence, Lily began to pray.

Her prayers continued in her head over and over again until she was able to clearly see a righteous path forward.

Tears began to flow unabated down Lily's cheeks as she sat in silence knowing what to do to make her life peaceful and balanced and Ella's complete. Slowly Lily got out of her hospital bed and pulled the curtain back that separated their two beds. Ella's head was turned away.

"Ella. I want you to know that this room at the end of the hallway, it's like a dungeon. It's the place where both of our lives became whole again. I want you to have my baby," Lily professed as tears began to flow down her cheeks.

"I mean it with all my heart. I want you to raise and love my baby. She wouldn't stand a chance with me as her mother. I still have not moved beyond being raped. This baby was meant to be with you, not me. That's why God brought us both together to this dark and dubious place. Out of this dark place, the light of your life and mine will shine brightly again."

Ella sat quietly for a few seconds as her mind absorbed what Lily had said. As she slowly turned her head, tears were streaming down her face. Ella got up from her hospital bed, and they met hugging each other and crying hysterically for a long period of time.

"I'm gonna honor you somehow with this baby, so that I'll always remember your kind generosity Lily Ellen Ewing. I'm not sure what that will be, but every day when I look at that baby, I'll think of you," Ella vowed as she continued to cry.

From that minute on, Lily totally blocked out the thoughts of being a mother to the baby she bore. Ella was now the baby's mother, not Lily.

As the next few days passed and the adoption paperwork was not yet formally completed, the few times the nurses would come into the room, Lily asked the nurses to give the baby to Ella and not her. Ella took to being a mother instantly. Lily, on the other hand, kept the curtain closed or left the room, separating her from the baby. She didn't feel connected and wanted to remain emotionally uninvolved with the baby. She knew she was doing the right thing. It was not always easy during that week stay for Lily to bury her feelings about giving away her baby.

Lily had barely turned eighteen, and any push or interference she received from her mother, father or hospital staff was quickly brushed aside, particularly after she confided to the hospital staff that her rapist had dark brown skin. The baby's features supported her admission. Eventually the hospital staff and social workers reluctantly abided by her decision and the adoption process began to take shape.

Lily's mother and father had been in total denial throughout the pregnancy. She was also in denial of what was going to happen after the baby was born. She questioned herself as to whether Ella was merely a convenient solution to her problem and genuinely wanted her to have the baby. But whatever the case, it was a positive solution for the both of them.

The hospital staff went into quick action as soon as they were on board with her decision. Even though Lily was white and was giving up her baby for adoption to an African-American woman, there were enough circumstances and biological traits the baby had to generate support from the hospital staff. They knew that Lily was ill-equipped to take this baby home, much less try to raise it.

By the time their stay in the hospital was over, Ella was going home with the baby and Lily was going home alone. That's the way Lily wanted it to be. She was happy to go home alone to try to remove any memory of the rapist and the pregnancy that followed. She was happy to resume the normal life she had prior to the event in Patterson Park in January of 1948.

CHAPTER 21

With Frank's death five years earlier, Lily's life in 2016 had become routine. Each day consisted of coffee and a review of the morning newspaper, a three-mile walk in the park followed by lunch, "The Price Is Right" television show, and hopefully dinner with a few of her friends. Like Frank, many of her friends had died or were in poor health, so her list of friends grew smaller and smaller. Evenings brought shows such as Jeopardy, Fox News, and CNN. She often passed the time by doing genealogy research on her computer until bedtime.

As the week after Memorial Day passed, Lily developed a persistent combination of coughing, dizziness, cold sweats, headaches, and joint pain. It seemed to grow worse with each passing day.

She decided to stop walking around the park so that she could regain her strength. On the tenth day of the persistent symptoms, she decided to drive to the local Urgent Care Center a few blocks from her home.

A doctor with an Indian accent came into the room where Lily was waiting on a small, medical exam table.

"Hi. I'm Dr. Patel. So you're not feeling well today? Tell me why you're not feeling well." inquired the doctor.

Lily appeared pale.

"For the past week now, I've had a persistent cough that seems to be getting worse. I have constant chills throughout my body and cold sweats," she weakly confided.

"Let's take your temperature."

The doctor proceeded to put a thermometer into Lily's mouth and waited for it to record her temperature.

"103.5 degrees. That's pretty high. I want you to take a deep breath and I'm going to listen to your lungs."

Lily pulled in her stomach and sucked air down her passageway. She did everything she could not to cough.

"Your lungs sound very congested. I need to take an x-ray of your lungs and do a blood test. Someone will be in shortly."

The doctor left the room. Lily waited for additional staff to arrive. Within minutes the attendant arrived and drew blood to determine if Lily had pneumonia or an infection. Lily was then whisked down the hall where an x-ray of her lungs was performed.

Much later, Dr. Patel opened the door and studied Lily's x-ray report.

"We won't have your bloodwork back until the morning. It looks like you have pneumonia. I'm going to prescribe amoxicillin. You also need to drink plenty of fluids and get some rest until you're feeling better. I'll call you about the blood test results when we receive them."

"Thanks," said Lily.

Lily struggled to get into her car to drive to the local pharmacy. When she arrived home, she was exhausted. She laid down on the sofa.

The next morning the telephone rang and Lily slowly got up from the sofa to answer it. She had slept there the whole night and into the next morning. Lily looked at the clock as she moved to the telephone. It was now one o'clock in the afternoon.

"Mrs. Clarke," voiced the person on the other end of the phone. "This is Dr. Patel. Your bloodwork looks questionable regarding your red and white blood cell counts. I'd like to have you retested once the pneumonia symptoms clear up."

"Thanks, Dr. Patel. I'll be happy to come in as soon as I'm feeling better. I'll hopefully feel better in a few weeks."

As a few weeks passed, the weather in Baltimore grew warmer and Lily's health improved slightly because of the amoxicillin. However, most of her symptoms persisted. She went back to the Urgent Care Center to have her blood redrawn. Lily had some apprehension because of the doctor's concern.

At 6:43 p.m. the next day, her telephone rang.

"This is Dr. Patel, Mrs. Clarke. Your blood test revealed that your white blood cell and red blood cell counts are still low. I would like you to make an appointment downtown at the University of Maryland Medical Center. The doctor's name I want you to see is Jeffery Baum. He's a great doctor and they have a great facility for blood disorders," confirmed the doctor. "There's no need to be concerned until after you meet with him."

"Thanks for all your help and concern, Dr. Patel. It is very much appreciated," Lily replied after which she quickly hung up the phone and contemplated what this meant.

CHAPTER 22

As soon as the offices opened at the University of Maryland Cancer Center, Lily called to schedule an appointment.

"The next appointment we have is in six weeks," advised the woman on the phone.

"If I have to wait six weeks to get an appointment in my condition, I'll probably be dead. I'm eighty-six years old," Lily asserted with desperation in her voice.

"Hold on ma'am and let me see what I can do. We have an opening today at 3:00 p.m. if you'd like to come in," indicated the receptionist.

"That'll be absolutely fine. Thank you," replied Lily.

Lily didn't know what to expect since she was going to a hospital. As a result, she showered and packed a small bag in case she was going to be admitted. She tidied up the loose ends in her house too. By 1:30 p.m., she was exhausted, but made her way to the University of Maryland Cancer Center.

"Please sign in," instructed the receptionist.

"Thank you for fitting me into your schedule today," replied Lily.

"Please take a seat and we'll call you back in a few minutes," noted the receptionist as she typed on a computer.

A half hour later, Lily was called back from the waiting room.

Dr. Jeffrey Baum walked into the patient room with Lily's medical record in his hand and a pleasant smile on his face.

"I see you recently had pneumonia and your white blood cell and red blood cell counts were quite a bit low."

After reviewing Lily's vital signs and checking her breathing, the doctor was ready to talk to Lily about the next steps.

"I have some concerns about you continually feeling tired and weak, and your mild fever and cold sweats. I'm also concerned that you've lost a few pounds since your last visit to your doctor. And you don't have a lot of meat on your bones in the first place," advised the doctor. "Your lymph nodes also seem to be slightly swollen."

"You're in relatively good health for an eighty-six year old woman, but we need to draw some blood and take a look at your red and white blood cells and platelet counts. If they appear abnormal, we're going to take a further look at some of the individual cells to make sure they're not cancerous. Once we've done this check, we'll have a better idea of what's going on. Do you have any questions?"

"When do I need to come back and see you?"

"I'd like you to come back next week after the testing is completed. Do you have a family member you can bring with you? You may want to have another set of ears here on the next visit," recommended Dr. Baum.

"I have three daughters, but they all live out of town. I'll bring my friend Jake Snyder with me. He's my lawyer and a personal friend. By the way, he doesn't practice in the area of medical malpractice," teased Lily as they both begin to laugh.

"I'll see you next week," said Dr. Baum. "In the meantime, call me if you have any questions."

CHAPTER 23

Jake pulled up in his car to the front door of the hospital for Lily's follow-up appointment. Jake dropped her off and pulled his car into the parking garage. Lily remained weak and tired and didn't want to use her limited strength to walk the two blocks from the parking garage to the hospital. Upon Jake's arrival, they headed up the elevator to the eighth floor in anticipation of her medical results. Once they made it to the front desk, they were immediately sent into Dr. Baum's office. Neither Jake nor Lily viewed that as a good sign.

Dr. Baum's office was filled with medical degrees and medical certificates. Pictures of his family on various vacations stretched across a credenza behind his desk. It was a small room and only included three chairs.

"Hi Lily," Dr. Baum stated in a serious voice. "And this must be the friend you mentioned, the medical malpractice lawyer I presume," Dr. Baum joked.

"I stopped suing doctors because you guys were too smart. Only kidding," Jake stated.

Dr. Baum opened Lily's medical file.

"The results from your previous blood tests produced similar results to our testing. Your blood tests revealed that you have a problem with your white blood cells. Some of them are cancerous and are a form of cancer we refer to as leukemia. The type of leukemia you have is referred to as AML, which stands for acute myeloid leukemia (AML), and is formed inside your bone marrow. Instead of normal white blood cells being produced, immature cells are being produced that are cancerous. These cancer cells grow very quickly, and replace the healthy blood cells. Unfortunately, your body may stop producing healthy white blood cells altogether. Patients with your form of leukemia, have difficulty fighting infections. Do you have any questions so far?"

Lily and Jake shook their heads and remained silent.

"There are some risk factors that can cause the disease, but generally we don't know what causes it. That's the bad news. The good news is that we do have some limited ways to treat it depending upon the exact type you have and how far it has progressed. Do you have any questions?"

"Does my age affect how you will treat me?" Lily inquired in a dejected voice.

"Because of your age, your treatment options are limited if the disease is in its advanced stages, you have one of the more aggressive forms of leukemia. Unfortunately, AML in older patients tends to be more resistant to treatment. If we administer chemotherapy, research has shown that there's a good chance it may kill you and a better chance it won't extend your life, if you are in the advanced stages. A bone marrow transplant, another form of treatment, can only be performed on people under the age of seventy years. Most adults over seventy years of age in the advanced stages of this disease survive three to eight months, with or without treatment."

Lily remained quiet and solemn. She appeared to be aging by the minute upon hearing this dreadful news.

"But let's talk about what we have to do next. To get a better handle on the progression of your leukemia, I'd like to do a procedure called a bone marrow aspiration and bone marrow biopsy. These are very routine procedures that are performed at the same time. We will have you lay down on the table, and we're going to put a needle into your hipbone and we'll remove a little bone marrow, blood, and a small piece of bone. A lab technician will review the samples taken to determine what percentage of your white blood cells are cancerous. They'll also look to see if you have any chromosome abnormalities, which will help us determine if we can administer chemotherapy. After we receive the lab results, we'll have a better idea of how far the cancer has progressed and how you'll react to the chemotherapy treatment."

Lily looked at Jake as her thoughts raced about what the doctor had just disclosed. Lily let out a big sigh.

"Thank you, Dr. Baum. That's not what I wanted to hear," Lily indicated as her mind moved a million miles a second.

"I think it would be best if you scheduled an appointment to have the procedure done as soon as possible. As soon as we find out exactly what form of AML you have and how far it has progressed, we can hopefully begin some form of treatment," advised Dr. Baum.

"Will I be under anesthesia when you do the procedure?" Lily asked.

"Normally when we do the procedure, the patient is awake. All you'll feel is a slight stinging sensation. The procedure sounds more difficult than the pain that it inflicts on the patient. You'll do absolutely fine."

"Okay, let's get on with it," pronounced Lily

Lily and Jake got up, scheduled an appointment with the receptionist, and made their way toward the exit.

"This doesn't sound good, Jake. I'm a little concerned that my days on this earth may be numbered. I don't want to tell my children yet. They've never been concerned about me, and I don't want them to fake it and be concerned now. Let me give it a little bit of time to soak in and think."

"I agree with you. You need some time to soak it all in and think about what you might need to do to tidy up your affairs," Jake acknowledged in a concerned voice.

"I haven't had any boyfriends since Frank died. So I wouldn't say I needed to tidy up any affairs," Lily joked. "But I don't want anyone to know yet. Promise me you won't call my daughters."

"I think you should give that some real consideration. If I was your child, I would want to know," Jake responded.

"They hadn't known what's going on in my life for years, so why do they need to know now? I'll think about it, but I'm pretty sure I won't change my mind."

"You wait here and I'll go get the car," replied Jake.

As they headed home, Lily's fate remained uncertain.

CHAPTER 24

The day after Lily's bone marrow aspiration and bone marrow biopsy, she rested anxiously waiting for the lab results. She began to think about what would happen if the test determined she only had a limited time to live. She thought about her Last Will and Testament. She thought about each of her daughters, who she had not been close with over the last forty plus years.

Lily had completed her will and twenty years prior to Frank's death and much had since changed. In reality, she didn't feel comfortable leaving her assets to her daughters because they still exhibited dysfunctional behaviors when she saw or spoke to them. She felt guilty about feeling that way toward her own flesh and blood; however, Lily knew she had to start going through her financial paperwork in the event that her test results revealed terminal news.

As she rested in her home, she moseyed into the bedroom office that had been primarily used by Frank and remained virtually unchanged since his death. Framed pictures of Lily and Frank hung on the wall, memorializing the few vacations they took over their lifetime together. Other awards Frank received over his career dotted the desk and a few spaces on the wall. A John Wayne movie poster filled another space along with a framed picture of President Kennedy and President Reagan. For all practical purposes, it was still Frank's office.

Frank was also the bookkeeper for the family. He spent a lot of time in the office, maintaining the bank checkbooks and keeping meticulous track of their assets.

Frank and Lily never discussed their finances. She remained in the dark about them, and that worked totally fine throughout their lives. However, his heart attack and sudden death five years ago had changed all of that. Once Frank died, Lily didn't maintain the bookkeeping duties or manage the paperwork in the same meticulous manner as Frank. She never balanced the checkbook, but merely kept an eye on it electronically on the bank's website. Bills and other paperwork were thrown into an unorganized pile.

Frank's office still remained somewhat of a mystery to Lily, even five years after his death.

Lily sat down at the cluttered desk covered with paperwork that had continued to pile up through the years since Frank's passing. She had never mastered the art of organizing Frank's workspace.

She opened the largest drawer on the desk, revealing many files that Frank had labeled and neatly organized. As she moved her eyes from file to file, she reached down and found a file labeled "Financial Information-Assets." She opened it and began examining the monthly handwritten entries. As she peered through the file documentation, she surveyed his outstanding bookkeeping skills. Frank wasn't proficient on a computer and considered it a badge of courage to never use one.

Lily peered at Frank's last journal entries. It was dated "January 2011," the month before he died. Her eyes scanned the page.

At the top, it stated "house - $225,000." As her eyes moved lower on the paper, an entry noted "Checking - $5,735.00" and "Mutual funds - $187,435.23."

Lily's eyes continued moving further down the page. As she reached the bottom of the page, a journal entry stated "Haussner Paintings 1999 estimate from auction - $3,700,000."

She couldn't move beyond that line. Her mind was wedged on the meaning of Frank's handwritten note. Lily wasn't exactly sure what it meant.

Finally, after a few minutes mulling over and studying Frank's notes, Lily's head began to rise up as her eyes slowly peered above the top edge of the paper.

Until this moment, Lily had totally forgotten about the paintings they had purchased in 1952. Lily wasn't even sure if three of the four paintings still remained in her possession.

"Frank, how could you?" Lily burst out. "Why didn't you ever talk to me about those damn paintings? I've been looking at the 'I TOLD YOU SO' painting for over sixty years Frank, and you never mentioned it may be worth a lot of money," Lily scolded out loud to her late husband.

She continued staring at Frank's notes trying to determine why he logged the value to be worth over three million seven hundred thousand dollars.

"Was it possible for those paintings we purchased in 1952 on a whim be worth that much money today?" she thought.

Lily began combing through more of Frank's old records. One by one, she went through each of the remaining files in the desk drawer. As she flipped file by file and paper by paper, the last file in the back of the bottom drawer appeared to be what she was looking for.

Inside was a Sotheby's auction catalog titled "The Haussner's Restaurant Collection, November 2, 1999, sale 7372." She quickly flipped through the one hundred and eighty-nine-page catalog, which contained a partial collection of the six hundred paintings that had hung in the restaurant, which closed in 1998. Based on Frank's notes that were scribbled throughout the catalog, it appeared that he had a strong interest in the 1999 Sotheby's sale.

After assessing the basic contents from the catalog, Lily slowly turned each page of it, attempting to ascertain the meaning of Frank's notes on each page and trying to visualize the paintings.

It appeared to her that Frank had systematically recorded the auction sale price of every painting in the catalog. Much to her surprise, Frank recorded wide ranging selling prices, from under one hundred thousand dollars to over one million dollars.

She found a piece of paper Frank had placed in the catalog listing the names of four master painters, the sale prices of their painting at the auction, and the page numbers in the catalog where they could be found. Frank noted the paintings' sales value at three million seven hundred thousand dollars. In a column next to it, Frank had listed the titles of other paintings by those same artists.

Lily noticed that one of the master painters name was the same artist who painted "I TOLD YOU SO", which was still hanging on a wall in her house.

Lily began attempting to recall information regarding the other three paintings they purchased and soon realized with a high degree of certainty that the names of the master paintings noted by Frank were the same artists of the paintings they had purchased in 1952.

As Lily continued to finger through Frank's records, she became more and more convinced that the painter's names on the paper were the same paintings they had purchased long ago.

Lily couldn't understand why Frank had never mentioned the value of the paintings to her through the years. Lily thought that maybe Frank was afraid to move them from their hiding spot, or just didn't want to bring up the bad memories surrounding their purchase.

She wondered if they were still hidden somewhere in the basement.

She logged onto her computer and started looking online at the sale prices of all of the Haussner paintings sold during the 1999 Sotheby's auction. As she studied the website links, Lily quickly discovered that they had sold for more than forty-two million dollars. She was flabbergasted as she clicked on three additional websites to verify the information.

In her excitement, she quickly got up, made her way down to the first floor, and began to kiss the "I TOLD YOU SO" painting.

"I told you so, I told you so," Lily yelled out loud as she talked to the painting. "That's what you'd be saying to me right now, wouldn't you Frank," she thought. "And I would deserve it based on what I know now," Lily added.

At Frank's insistence, one painting remained on their living room wall in the same spot where it was placed in 1952. Frank had it professionally cleaned and treated through the years to ensure it retained its value, much to Lily's constant consternation.

Lily stared at the painting, shaking her head at what Frank may have pulled off.

Lily grabbed a flashlight from the kitchen and carefully maneuvered into the basement, looking around for the most obvious spot where Frank could have hidden the paintings. Her eyes quickly focused on his workbench.

Frank's workbench remained virtually untouched since the day he had died. The wood molding Frank had added to hide the paintings remained attached to it, exactly as it was constructed by him in 1952.

Lily studied and peered at the workbench until she noticed a small gap between the workbench and the basement wall. Frank had done a pretty good job securing the workbench to the wall, but it appeared he had left small gaps on each side.

Lily turned on the flashlight and bent down to peer into a gap on the right-hand side of the workbench. She could see two wooden crates, tightly sealed and secured. As she moved to the left side of the workbench, she peered into the other small hole. Inside she could see another wooden crate tightly sealed.

"You did it Frank," Lily yelled. "You were right all along, you son of a gun. And you kept it a secret from me all of these years. Why didn't you tell me," Lily proclaimed as she looked to the sky thinking of Frank. "Wait till I come up to heaven and see you. We're going to have a good laugh together," Lily said as she sat and leaned back on the workbench chair with a huge smile on her face.

The mystery of the nude paintings they had purchased was no longer a mystery. As she stood by the workbench, she thought about what she should do next.

"What would Frank do?" she thought.

Her final conclusion was that her health was more important than the paintings, and it was better not to worry about the paintings until after she received the results of her lab test.

Lily realized that she was now a multi-millionaire.

CHAPTER 25

Lily and Jake found themselves once again in Dr. Baum's office. Lily had no plan to mention her recent discovery to Jake or anyone else for that matter. Dr. Baum came into the office with another doctor by his side. They said their hellos, and right away, Lily knew by the look on their faces that the results were not good.

Dr. Baum leaned back in his chair and began to talk calmly and slowly.

"The test results gave us a clear picture of what's going on inside your body. As I suspected, our examination discovered you have too many immature white cells in your blood. You also don't have enough red blood cells or platelets. The immature white blood cells are the cancer cells and everyone refers to them as blasts. Blasts are not normally found in a healthy patient's blood."

Dr. Baum stopped and did a quick study of Lily's medical record. He peered down at the file as he spoke.

"Unfortunately, your results are disconcerting and problematic in terms of the number of blasts. A normal range is one to five percent for leukemia patients. If the percentage is over twenty, you would be diagnosed with acute myeloid leukemia, otherwise known as AML. In your case Lily, about thirty percent of the white blood cells are cancerous cells. That's a very high percentage."

Jake looked down as he patted Lily on the hand to comfort her.

Dr. Baum finally looked up with a grim look on face.

"We also did another test to determine if you have any defective chromosomes. Studies have proven that older AML patients have a greater risk of having defective chromosomes. You have two abnormal chromosomes, which makes it difficult for you to receive treatment. You have an advanced case of AML. Unfortunately, your defective chromosomes do not give you much long-term hope of survival. Elderly patients like you generally only live six months or less," disclosed Dr. Baum.

"Oh my, oh my," declared Lily. "That is not good news. That's not what I was expecting to hear." Lily looked up to the sky. "Start getting ready for me Frank, here I come," she pronounced in a quivering voice.

In an effort to provide Lily with a little bit of hope, Dr. Baum backtracked and said, "There is a small chance that you could still live an additional three months if you have chemotherapy. However, there is also a good chance, because of your age, the chemotherapy will kill you."

"This isn't what I was expecting," conceded Lily as her face grew grim and she began to sob.

Jake put his arm around her and gave her a small hug, but nothing he could say could make Lily feel any better. The room remained silent for a few minutes.

Lily looked Dr. Baum in the eyes and implored, "Is there anything that can be done?"

"No, I'm sorry Lily. Unfortunately, there isn't. If you were younger, you might have been able to enroll in a National Institutes of Health study. Unfortunately, palliative care is all we can offer."

"Dr. Baum, I've been recently having headaches, and my joints seem to hurt quite a bit. I'm not sure if it's just old age or the leukemia. Is there any medication you can prescribe in case the pain gets worse over the next few months?" Lily insisted.

"There are a lot of choices in pain management for leukemia patients. I'll write you a few prescriptions for a ninety-day supply of pills and you can use them when you need them."

Dr. Baum proceeded to pull out a pad from his desk and began writing numerous prescriptions for Lily.

"I'm going to prescribe some medicine in the event that you have moderate to severe pain. This way, you won't have to come back and see me unless it's absolutely necessary. If the joint pain and headaches aren't severe, only take an over-the-counter drug like Advil or Aleve. If you can't bear the pain or your headaches won't go away, the pain relievers I'm going to prescribe should help to manage it."

Dr. Baum began to hand Lily a pile of scratchily written prescriptions.

"I'm going to prescribe a ninety-day supply of codeine, morphine, and oxycodone. Take the morphine only if you are in extreme pain. You absolutely need to ensure you don't take them unnecessarily and read the labels carefully prior to taking them. Call me if you any have questions about taking them."

"Don't people become addicts from taking medications like these?" contended Lily.

"You're absolutely right, Lily," confirmed Dr. Baum. "That's why you have to be very careful taking these. But they will certainly help you with any headaches, joint pains, and any other effects from your leukemia."

"If I have any additional questions, can I call you, Dr. Baum?"

"Of course Lily. You can call me anytime. I'm just sorry I can't do more."

Lily and Jake left the office in a state of shock. Once they reached Lily's house, Lily settled in for the rest of the day. Although she was tired, she knew she had a lot of issues to resolve before her death.

"Jake, let me think about my estate and how I want to settle my affairs over the next few days. If you could come back at some point to help me tidy up my existing will, it would be appreciated. I'm not sure how I'm going to divide up my estate among my daughters. You've known my daughters for a long time Jake. Truth be told, I'm not sure if I should leave them anything. I'll have a plan in place before I visit the angels, you can be sure of that," asserted Lily.

"You always have a plan Lily, don't you? Throughout your life, you've always seemed to plot away to make the right decisions, and I don't think you'll change that, even over the next few months."

"One more thing Jake before you leave. Promise me that you will not tell anyone about my illness. I don't want my daughters to panic. I need some time to think about the best way to handle my situation. Promise?" Lily insisted.

"I promise. My lips are sealed and you have my word," Jake assured Lily.

From here on out, every minute of Lily's remaining life was precious. She had to determine how to best utilize the limited time she had left to put her final affairs in order. Little did she know that the next few weeks and months were going to be the most challenging of her entire life.

CHAPTER 26

As Lily got out of bed and moved about the next morning, her pragmatic side began to stir. She had to decide how to settle her estate, including the four paintings, three of which no one but her knew existed. Lily decided to keep that information hidden from everyone, at least for the foreseeable future.

Lily sat in her kitchen contemplating what she and Frank had purchased so long ago. Although she had the information from the 1999 sale, the paintings' current value remained a mystery.

"I wonder how much the paintings are worth today," she milled over as she sipped on her coffee.

"Frank, should I divide our estate evenly among our three daughters, or should I leave everything to only one of them?" she said out loud. "Maybe we should just give it all away to some worthy cause? What do ya think Frank?"

"How could I give my life savings Frank and I worked so hard to accumulate to individuals who will probably quickly spend it all?"

Lily thought about each daughter. She knew that Mary always spent her money impulsively and recklessly before she had earned it; she recognized that Sharon probably still had a drug addiction and any money she inherited would eventually be used to buy a tainted batch of heroin that would probably kill her; and she grasped that Denise always seemed extremely ungrateful.

Lily opened her laptop and began scouring the internet to determine if any of the Haussner's paintings from the master painters whose paintings were in her house had been resold since the 1999 Sotheby's auction.

Her searches of the first three master painters did not initially reveal any internet hits of recent or comparable sales.

Her final chance was to find a comparable sale of the master painter, Ojjeh Bouguereau. Lily typed his name on her computer and immediately found multiple links confirming a resale of one of his paintings. A Ojjeh Bouguereau painting similar to the one they had purchased, sold for $1,300,000 at the Haussner's auction in 1999. As she peered at the computer screen, the art auction website indicated one resold at Sotheby's again in 2015 for $1,800,000.

Lily couldn't believe what she was seeing.

"Gosh darn it Frank, I wish you were here to see this with your own eyes," she uttered.

Lily quickly grabbed a calculator to determine the current value of all four paintings based on the increased in value of the Ojjeh Bouguereau painting. As she punched away on the calculator, she determined that over the sixteen year period, the potential value of her paintings had increased by almost forty percent.

Taking it one step further, Lily multiplied the 1999 value of her four paintings by forty percent. The calculator displayed almost five million two hundred thousand dollars.

"Ain't the beer cold," she declared.

Lily sat back in her chair, staring at the calculator, flabbergasted by the value of her paintings. She continued to peck away, adding her other assets to the total. As she peered at the calculator, it totaled just under six million dollars.

She let out a big sigh realizing the responsibility now placed on her to insure that her estate would be placed in the right hands after her death.

Lily stared at the air as she contemplated her decision. She then got up and began pacing the kitchen as she further considered if her daughters moral and ethical standards may have improved through the years. All three were now close to sixty years old.

"Do they deserve my money? If my children had changed for the better, it would be very unfair of me to not give them one more chance to prove themselves worthy of inheriting one third of my estate," Lily reasoned to herself.

Lily continued pacing around her kitchen as she contemplated the best course of action to gain a thorough understanding of their true characters.

"I need to give them one more shot at proving and redeeming themselves to me," she concluded. "How could I do this? It won't be an easy task," she pondered.

Lily felt alone as she paced with her head pointed down at the floor. She had no one else to call to discuss her dilemma other than Jake. However, Jake had already done enough for her, so she decided not to bother him any further.

"If I call my daughters to let them know that I'm gravely ill, I'd never discover their true character; they'd be coming to Baltimore solely to remove any guilt they may have about not seeing me through the years; or coming only to harass me about what I am going to leave them."

As she paced about the entire house, Lily continued ruminating the best way to engage her daughters to determine their true characters.

"They need to come and see me one-on-one for the last time," she acknowledged to herself. However, she remained stumped on how to lure them to Baltimore without tipping them off about her incurable illness or on how she should act when they arrived.

Lily knew her physical limitations would be a challenge if or when her daughters came to town.

"I'm gonna have to be defenseless and helpless in front of them, I think Frank. Don't you?" Lily debated out loud. "I know I'm gonna be physically weak from leukemia, but what can I do to convince them to let down their guard, so I can see their real personalities?"

Knowing she had to do this quickly, Lily began thinking about what would happen if she became mentally vulnerable, in addition to being physically vulnerable. "Maybe that would encourage them to let their guard down."

Lily stopped pacing and let out a big grin as she plopped onto a kitchen chair, relieved.

"Alzheimer's. That's it Frank," she pronounced out loud. "I'm gonna act like I have Alzheimer's disease. That'll throw them off Frank," she declared as she looked toward the ceiling.

Leukemia was her actual physical vulnerability, but Lily contrived that Alzheimer's disease would be her mental vulnerability if and when her daughters came to Baltimore. However, she was still as mentally strong as she had ever been.

"I'm going to fake Alzheimer's. Yes sir. If I do this, we'll see who our daughters truly are. What do you think of that idea, Frank?" Lily stated out loud still looking towards the sky. "If they think I have Alzheimer's and I'll forget everything they tell me, I may be surprised what comes out of their mouths."

Lily continued pondering her next steps.

"I can't tell my daughters I'm going to die in a few months, particularly if I want to assess their true character," she further reflected.

"Wouldn't it be great if I ended up dividing my estate among my three daughters? If I could do that, my life would be complete," she fanaticized.

Lily contemplated her next steps over the next hour, stuck in her kitchen in thought.

"Am I fooling myself about this scheme?" she pondered as she further thought about the lie she would soon be imposing upon her daughters. "Is it unethical, immoral, or deceitful?" she asked herself.

Lily began to question the manipulative plan she was conceiving, wondering if it was a characteristic she had passed on to her daughters. But her plan had to be implemented relatively quickly because she knew her health condition was going to deteriorate on a fairly fast and continuous basis.

As Lily's plan began to materialize in her mind, her next steps began to take form.

"I need to hide my financial records, including the current will so that my daughters won't see them during their visit. I also have to stop my mail so no hospital information or financial information is delivered to the house," Lily concluded.

"I need to organize and categorize my jewelry too," she said as she stewed over the details in her mind.

Through the years, her husband often bought her jewelry on special occasions. Over a lifetime of anniversaries, birthdays, or other occasions, Frank had a knack for picking out jewelry that Lily loved. Through the years, Lily had not passed any of it to her daughters.

"If any of my daughters are thieves, I'll know it if my jewelry is missing. I'm really concerned about Mary and Sharon plundering my 'free' jewelry," she worried.

"Mary needs the jewelry to feel important and rich, even though she's probably still dirt poor and probably still loaded down in debt. Sharon probably still needs it to support her drug habit," Lily thought.

However, at this point, knowing the approximate value of the paintings in her possession, Lily was unconcerned about her daughters plundering her jewelry, and actually wanted to pass it on to them anyway. She thought the jewelry would become one of her baits to determine their true character.

When it came to Sharon's drug habit, Lily knew that she needed to determine if the habit remained. Lily didn't think it would be a problem to catch her if she was still an addict.

Lily thought it was going to be easy to discover Mary and Sharon's true character. They were sixty-two and sixty years old respectively and she did not think that their personalities were going to actually change.

Lily knew that Denise was going to be a challenge. As bad as her relationship was with Mary and Sharon, Denise always made her feel like she had failed as a mother. Lily hoped this last visit would be different.

The next few weeks would represent one of the biggest challenges in Lily's life; battling leukemia, faking Alzheimer's disease, meeting her children for probably the last time, and making a decision of how to disperse from her newly discovered fortune. It was much to bear for an eighty-six year old woman nearing the end of her life.

CHAPTER 27

Lily had no time to waste. She needed to convince her daughters to visit her in the very near future and on short notice, so she could make a final determination regarding her newly discovered wealth.

She decided to call each of her daughters a few minutes apart, so they would not have discussions with each other between her telephone calls. Lily knew that Mary and Sharon wouldn't talk to each other, because of the animosity generated when Mary married Sharon's ex-husband. However, she was somewhat concerned that they may call Denise. Even with that concern, Lily felt confident her plan could be implemented, undetected by her daughters.

The first person Lily decided to call was Mary because Lily understood Mary better than her other daughters. Mary had her share of issues; however, Lily normally had decent conversations with her over the telephone, as long as they discussed new fashion trends, luxury cars, or vacation spots, including Mary's four costly vacation timeshares.

As she sat in her recliner, Lily jotted down a few notes regarding what to say to her daughters to act like an Alzheimer's patient.

Lily took a deep breath, dialed the telephone and heard it click. She quickly and nervously voiced, "Hi Mary. This is your Mother, Lily."

"Hi, Mom. What's up?" Mary answered in her normal curt tone.

"Mary, you know I'm eighty-six years old and I'm not getting any younger. I need you to come to Baltimore to help me and your father pack up and to move us to our place at the beach."

"Mom, Dad is dead and you haven't owned the beach place in fifteen years. What are you talking about?" Mary inquired.

"Could you please come back to Baltimore to help me pack? My place is such a mess. I absolutely want to scream sometimes because your father has left this place a mess. I can't find my car either. I think the neighbor's kids keep moving it. Dear, could you please come back next week and help me clean up this mess? I think one week should be enough. When you come back, I'll take you to Haussner's for dinner. Your father loves the Surf and Turf. He orders it every time we go. I think we went last month. Frank, did we go to Haussner's last month?" Lily shouted.

"Dad's dead, Mom. When was the last time you went there?" said Mary.

"Oh, let me think. I went with Sharon six weeks ago. Your Dad wasn't feeling well and couldn't go. Sharon loved their strawberry pie," Lily insisted.

"Mom, Haussner's closed in 1999, and it's 2016. Are you sure you were there last week?"

Lily remained quiet for a period of time to let Mary absorb what she was hearing. Lily decided to avoid answering her question altogether.

"Can you please come next week, dear? I need you more now than ever. I'll even pay for your flight, but I need your help," vowed Lily.

"Okay Mom. David and the kids are too busy, so I'll come by myself. I'll be there next week."

"That's great Mary. Thank you. It's very much appreciated. I'll tell Dad you're coming. Goodbye hon," Lily mumbled as she hung up the telephone and let out a huge sigh of relief.

Lily immediately transferred her thoughts to her next conquest, Sharon. She had fooled Mary, or so she thought; so she reasoned she would have no problem fooling Sharon. Sharon normally couldn't get out of her own way, much less get in the way of Lily trying to convince her to travel to Baltimore. Lily determined that once Sharon knew that she needed help getting rid of things, with a paid ticket, Sharon would come and gather what she could and sell it for drug money; that is, if she was still an addict.

She knew that it was time to call Sharon. She took a deep breath and began dialing Sharon's cell phone.

"Hi, Sharon. It's Mom. How are you? What town are you living in?" Lily questioned.

"Mom, I'm still living in Chicago," Sharon spoke without even saying a friendly hello.

"I hear a lot of cars in the background. Are you okay dear? Are you still living on the streets?"

"No Mom. I'm living in a small apartment with some friends."

"I'm at the beach now. I drove myself down to the beach place yesterday," Lily asserted in an effort to confuse Sharon.

"Mom, you haven't had your beach place in fifteen years." Sharon argued with confusion and concern in her voice.

"Well, when I look around the apartment, I know it's my beach place even though it's my furniture from Baltimore. I'm going to drive home today if I can find my car keys. I've been looking around for them. Hold on honey, I'm going to look in the freezer. I think I may have left them there," Lily insisted.

Lily purposefully dropped the telephone and mumbled some words over the course of five minutes, acting incoherent and changing subjects constantly and keeping Sharon hanging on the other end of the phone. She could hear Sharon's muffled yelling.

"Mom, Mom! Pick up the phone. Mom, Mom. Pick up the phone dammit," Sharon pleaded.

Sharon continuously yelled into the phone over the five-minute waiting period. Lily continued shuffling her feet close to the phone and talking to herself so that Sharon could hear her.

"I found my wallet in the freezer, but I don't know where my keys are. What's this stove doing on? I must've left it turned on all night. Oh my. How did my T.V. channel selector end up in the refrigerator with my underwear? I must've put my underwear in the refrigerator because I was hot in the house. Oh my, the thermostat says eighty-six degrees. I think it should be sixty-eight degrees, not eighty-six. Oh, here are my keys. They were in the trashcan. How did they get in there with all of this money?" Lily muttered.

After five minutes Lily finally picked up the telephone. "Hello, hello?" Lily said pretending that she didn't know Sharon was on the telephone.

"Sharon, Mary is coming here next week to help me tidy up my house and clean out some of my old stuff. Can you come the week after Mary and help me and your father clean up some of the stuff in the house? I'm getting old and I surely need your help for a little bit.

I'll pay for your airfare to and from my house. And it'll actually be good to see you and your husband, Dave."

"Mom, Dave is Mary's husband. I've been divorced from him for over twenty-five years," refuted Sharon.

"Oh I'm sorry, hon. I always forget who Dave is married to. If you can come to town two weeks from today, it will be a big help," insisted Lily.

"Okay, Mom. I'll see you in two weeks. Goodbye." Sharon confirmed as she quickly hung up the phone.

"That was easier than I imagined," Lily thought.

The next and final child to convince was Denise. It was going to be tough for Lily to fool Denise, who would pick up on Lily's staged mental cues quickly if she made a misstep.

Lily thought about her plan for a few minutes and then dialed Denise's cell phone.

In Dallas, Denise could hear the cell phone ringing and picked up the call without checking the number. She had on a pair of blue jeans and a flannel shirt, relaxing at a coffeehouse. The woman sitting directly across from her was leaning across the table and they appeared to be a couple based on their eye contact and closeness. The other woman appeared to be Denise's age, and was dressed fashionably in capris and a pink lightweight top.

"Denny here. This is Denny Clarke," Denise pronounced into the cell phone.

Lily listened to the voice on the other end of the telephone, thinking that the voice sounded like a man.

"Oh, I must have the wrong number. I was trying to reach my daughter, Denise," Lily countered in confusion.

Upon hearing this, Denise looked down at the number on her cell phone and held the phone away from her body and said to the woman sitting across the table in a quiet voice, "Oh shit, it's my mother."

She then returned the cell phone to her ear and continued the conversation.

"Hi, Mom. You must not have heard me correctly. It is who you thought it was," Denise proclaimed, not wanting to say her birth name in front of her companion.

"Well, let's start over. Hi Denise. It's Mom. By the way, how is Tippy? He looked so good when I saw him last."

"You know Mom, the last time you saw him was fifteen years ago right before he died. What year is it Mom?" Denise queried.

"2001, I think, hon." Frank what year is it?" Lily barked.

"Dad is dead. He died in 2010," Denise reminded.

"Are you sure?" With that conversation complete, Lily knew she had Denise right where she wanted her. However, she was still somewhat perplexed by how the conversation had started.

"Denise, Mary is coming to Baltimore next week, and Sharon the week after that. They both think that I need some help organizing this house now that I'm eighty-six years old. They were both concerned about me. I want you to come into Baltimore too. You were always great at organizing your things and I need some help with mine. I wouldn't ask you if I didn't need you. I'll even pay your airfare. I'm paying for Mary and Sharon's."

"I'd be happy to come," Denise conveyed with a more feminine sounding voice.

"Okay, dear. Please book the flight soon so I'll know you're coming. I sincerely need you, hon," Lily said with desperation in her voice. "Book your trip for three weeks from today."

"You know, I'm your dependable daughter, Mom. Gotta go. I'll see you in three weeks." With that Denise impatiently hung up, not wanting to interfere with the event taking place at the coffee shop.

Lily thought she might discover what this 'Denny' person was all about.

For now, her mission was accomplished. All three daughters would be coming to town. None of her daughters were suspicious of her true intent. Lily didn't know what to expect from their visits, and neither did her daughters.

CHAPTER 28

Unbeknownst to Jake, Lily had quickly executed a plan to bring her daughters to Baltimore, one week at a time, to help her formulate the distribution of her newly found wealth. However, unbeknownst to Lily, Jake had also put into place a plan to help her manage her sickness, not knowing that she had already cleverly arranged her daughters stay. Jake's plan began the day after Lily had arranged her daughters visits, and it all started with a knock at Lily's front door.

As soon as Lily heard it, she slowly moved to the front door and peeked out the window. Jake was standing next to a young Hispanic woman. He had a big smile on his face. Lily opened her front door and asked, "Is everything okay? Who is this?"

"Lily, I know you'll be in need of some help over the next few months, so I took it upon myself to call on a few home health companies. I went online and found the company 'Angels for the Elderly.' They have over three hundred active home health assistants working in the city and a five star rating on a few websites. I have six aides coming over today and we'll interview them together and you can pick the ones you like. I didn't want to be prejudiced against men; however, I selected all women. Knowing that you have three daughters, I didn't think that you would want a man coming in to help you," communicated Jake.

"I hate to say it, but I would prefer women. Please don't take that that the wrong way," Lily confessed. "I wouldn't want a man moving around my house. I'm more comfortable with women. I'll have enough of a problem controlling my daughters when they come to Baltimore starting next week for the next three weeks."

"What? If I would've known that, I wouldn't have invited these six women to come to your house today. Do you think it's a good idea to have these women coming if your daughters are in your house too?"

Lily hesitantly replied, "I think it's a good idea to have them here because it'll be a good transition and breaking-in period. Besides, I'm only going to get more tired and in worse shape as time goes on. And

I don't want to go to hospice. I want to spend the last days in my own home."

"Eventually, you may need hospice nurses. But for right now, you only need aides," conceded Jake.

"I think it'll be a good idea to have them both. So what's the name of the aide who's been standing next to you?" asked Lily.

"Her name is Rosa Gonzalez and she showed up at the same time that I was knocking on your door. This is the first time I talked to her and met her too. Rosa, why don't you tell Mrs. Clarke and me a little bit about yourself?"

"Mi name is Rosa Gonzalez. Yo vivo en Fells Point y he estado en los Estados Unidos durante un mes. Usted es mi primer trabajo con esta compañía. Espero aprender mucho de trabajar con usted. Nunca he estado en la cárcel en los Estados Unidos, y sólo dos veces en México por el robo de mis hijos curso."

"What did she say? I'm totally confused. Did you understand her Jake?" Lily asked with a befuddled look on her face.

"I'm a little confused too, but I think she said that she lives in Fells Point and has been in the United States for only one month. She said that this will be her first job with this company. She hopes to learn a lot from working with you. As if that wasn't bad enough Lily, she also went on to say that she has never been in jail since coming to the United States a short time ago. She was only jailed twice in Mexico for stealing money and food for her children. Ain't that special, Lily," Jake proclaimed with a smirk on his face.

"Please, please Jake. Please send her out and tell her I'm not feeling well," suggested Lily.

Jake said to her a few words in Spanish that were totally incomprehensible to the woman in her native dialect, but she could tell by the looks on both of their faces that the interview had ended.

As the aide headed out the front door Jake said, "The next interview will take place at nine o'clock, and they will continue every hour until we are finished. So rest up, because it's going to be a marathon today."

CHAPTER 29

At 9:15 a.m., there was a knock at the front door. Jake opened the door and a young white woman stood before him. Her nose was pierced with a ring in it and each ear had half inch round ear expanders. Her arms and legs are covered in tattoos, including a large tattoo of the Star Wars character R2-D2 covering the left side of her neck. The woman appeared not to have gotten much sleep the night before, probably as a result of a heavy night of partying.

"Hey, yep. Good da be here," the woman claimed to Jake as she was stepping into the house and moving toward Lily like she owned the place.

"Had a rough night last night, but I think me and you will get along perfectly fine. It doesn't look like either of us have a whole lot of energy today," the woman commented as she peered at Lily resting in her recliner.

Unbeknownst to this woman, Lily was still right at the top of her mental game and Lily could see her issues in a nanosecond. The interview had started off on a bad foot and was only heading downhill from there.

"This will be the tenth home where I've provided aide support," admitted the woman. "Most of the time, both the men and women crapped over shortly after I started. I don't know if it was me or them, but I think I've merely had a stroke of bad luck. They didn't have strokes. That's not what I meant," denied the woman as she stumbled over her words. "Anyway, if you're sick, I have a lot of experience taking care of frail people, exactly like you," acknowledged the woman in a confident manner thinking she was saying the right words to impress Lily and Jake.

"Well that's simply great, truly great," countered Lily in a low disheartened voice. "Where did you go to high school?" Lily further inquired. "I see in your application you have a high school degree."

"No one has ever asked me that question before," contended the woman with a confused look on her face. She hesitated for a few seconds as she began to sway from side to side and then alleged, "I went to that high school by the steel mill."

"Which one is that?" grilled Lily instantly knowing that the woman was lying.

Finally, the woman confessed, "You know, I needed a job very bad, so I lied on the application. I didn't think I needed a high school degree so I dropped out after 10th grade. I never went back and took the GED class because I didn't think I needed it."

The woman's tone was becoming downright rude.

"I'm not sure how a high school degree is going to help me take care of you," asserted the woman in a nasty tone.

"Well, I'm happy you've been able to find work," reassured Lily. "I'm not sure that you're a good fit being that most people you work with died shortly after you were hired. I don't want to be the eleventh fatality, therefore I think you need to find somebody else to care for," Lily advised in a straightforward and direct manner.

The woman was dumbfounded. There were a few seconds in which no words were shared as she stared at Lily, baffled and tongue-tied.

Jake finally spoke up, "Thanks for coming in for the interview. I hope you learned something today, like we did."

The woman shook her head yes looked down in dejection, and moved towards the front door.

The number second interviewee was another bust.

CHAPTER 30

At exactly 10 a.m., there was another knock at the front door. Jake opened the door and greeted the third interviewee. She quickly stated in a strong African accent "Hi, my name is Fosuaa Bello. Thank you for having me today."

Fosuaa was dressed in an African ceremonial dress and headdress.

"Well, thanks for coming today," said Jake. "Please come in and meet Mrs. Clarke."

They walked into the room where Lily remained in her recliner.

"Can you pronounce your name for us so that we say it properly?" Jake requested.

"F O S U A A, Fosh You Ahh," acknowledged the woman spelling out her name and restating it.

Jake repeated her name perfectly.

Lily, on the other hand, had a tough time pronouncing it. She tried repeating the name over and over, and after four tries, finally got it right.

"That was hard," conceded Lily. "Now the easy part. Tell us about yourself."

With that, Fosuaa began to speak, rarely stopping between sentences to take a breath.

"My country is Ghana. We are a proud people. We are a strong people and my country is a beautiful country. It is the best country in the world. Our language is Twi. My clothing is made of Kente cloth. It is the most popular cloth in Ghana. Kente cloth is used for traditional and modern Ghanaian dress. Different ethnic groups have their own individual clothes. But mine is Kente and Kente is the best," she mumbled acting as if Jake and Lily had absorbed what she had said.

"Is that so?" mentioned Lily in a sincere voice as the woman continued talking.

"We use Kente cloth in different colors and different shapes. Each cloth's shape has its own meaning," she explained as she moved her hands up and down her dress, pointing at the different shaped patterns and colors. "We take small strips of various colors and patterns and sew them together to make larger pieces of cloth. I'm currently looking for a new dress for a Knock-Knock ceremony," muttered the woman.

"What in the heck is a Knock-Knock ceremony?" inquired Jake as the woman took a quick breath.

"A Knock-Knock ceremony is a Ghanaian wedding tradition. It takes place a few months before the wedding. The groom's family visits the bride's family with the purpose of formally announcing the wedding plans. They must "knock" on the bride's parents' front door to agree to the conditions of the marriage," the woman said as she closed her fist and made a knocking motion. It is Ghanaian tradition to knock at the entrance of a house before entering it as a visitor. The groom's family brings two bottles of Schnapps, some money, and cola to the house to present to the bride's family. The drinks are used to aid in praying to our ancestral spirits and God. When these gifts are presented, a person from the groom's family formally asks the bride's family for permission to enter the house and announce their marriage intentions. If the drinks are accepted, then permission is granted for the groom's family to state their intentions. It is a beautiful and traditional ceremony. I hope one day you will get to see one. What else would you like to know about Ghana? If you hire me, I would tell you much more about my country," proclaimed the woman with her eyes wide open and a broad grin across the face.

The more the woman spoke about how great "her country" was, the more Jake got irritated.

"I'm confused," conceded Jake.

"Now, now," appealed Lily knowing that the woman had pushed Jake's crazy button.

"If your country is so great, why did you come here? Why don't you go back? There is nothing stopping you. In fact, if you want to go back, I'll give you the airfare to send you back to your 'great' country. I think I've heard enough. Thank you for your time and I want you to know that if you don't like it here, the offer is always open for me to pay for you to go back to Ghana." contested Jake.

Before Jake could finish, Fosuaa was stomping out the door in frustration and not looking back. Her experience with the fast-tongued Jake Snyder was one she wanted to forget.

"So far, we are not doing well," Lily admitted, disappointed. "That may be okay since my daughters will be here over the next three weeks."

"I'm an optimist. I think we'll hit a winner with the next interviewee," Jake assured her.

CHAPTER 31

At five minutes before 11:00 a.m., there was a knock again at the front door. Jake got up from his chair to answer. As he began to open it, the person on the other side of the door burst out in a loud voice.

"How ya doin', hon? Thanks for invitin' me to da interview. I had no problems findin' me a parkin' space. Sometimes it ain't easy findin' a parking space down here," said the woman with a strong Baltimore accent.

Jake gave the woman a quick once over. She was small and she had to look up toward the sky to see Jake as he stood in the doorway. Her four-feet-ten-inch tall stature and flat shoes, coupled with standing one step down from the doorway, made her appear even shorter.

She was a woman of simple means. Her weathered skin and lack of makeup made her look much older than the sixty years written on her application. Her black polyester slacks and white blouse were somewhat wrinkled, probably bought at a discount department store at best. Her scuffed black walking shoes were the type worn by seniors twenty years older. The sure sign of her simplicity was her gray hair, which had a few patches of brown remaining. Her "big hair" hairstyle appeared to have been recently washed, teased, set, and doused with a generous coating of hair spray. Her pocketbook was black and looked as if it had been the mainstay of her limited wardrobe for a long time.

"Welcome and come on in. So your name is Connie Smith," stated Jake as he held her application in his hand looking at it to make sure that he had the right application and the right person.

They both moved towards Lily, who was still resting in the recliner.

"Hi, it's nice to meet you, hon," Connie voiced as she reached her hand out to Lily. Lily didn't reach back, knowing that the stranger entering her home could have a cold or a contagious illness that could land her in the hospital or even kill her.

"I'm feeling a little sick today, dear, and I don't want to give you whatever I have," Lily quickly responded.

"I understand," acknowledged Connie in a calm voice. "I always want to do what is best for my patients."

"Sit down and tell us a little bit about yourself," requested Jake.

"Will do, hon," replied Connie as she sat on the sofa to the left of Lily. "I've lived in Essex since 1965. I was raised a few blocks from your house, until I was twelve years old. Then my parents moved us to Essex, which we thought was the country back then. I've lived there ever since."

Essex is a blue-collar area located a few miles outside of Baltimore City comprised of a lot the residents who had previously worked for the local steel mill or a General Motors assembly plant, both of which closed about a decade ago. In the past, a lot of Essex residents had also worked at a Lockheed Martin (formally Martin Marietta) manufacturing facility and other factories that used to be an integral part of the Baltimore area. Many of those companies and their associated jobs ceased to exist.

"My husband worked at da steel mill until 2008. He was one of the last remainin' workers. He's been drivin' a truck ever since, when he can get work. You know hon, sometimes it gets tough and some weeks are better than others. I've been doin' this kinda work for a few years now to help out. Ya know what I mean?"

Her Baltimore accent became more apparent as she became comfortable talking to Jake and Lily.

"I do any kinda work that I'm hired to do. I can warsh your clothes and put them aways in your beero. I can clean yer windas and your toilets if need be. I can do anything ya need to do to help keep your house in order. I can also do anythink you need with any personal hygiene issues you have, like helpin' ya warsh yourself."

As Connie continued to speak, Lily and Jake were nodding their heads up and down. She was convincing them she was the right aide for Lily. She was older, experienced, and from a similar culture. She also appeared to have the right personality to help Lily through this difficult point in her life.

"How do you work with other people? I need to know because my daughters will be in town the first few weeks that you are here. That is if we hire you," stipulated Lily.

"I have four sisters and I was the youngest. Bein' the youngest of five made me pretty thick skinned. I can be as tough or as sweet as you want me to be," bragged Connie.

These words were music to Lily's ears. With those words, she knew that Connie would be her first hire. As the interview continued over the next hour, Connie made Lily feel relaxed and at ease. Her application showed that she had ten years of experience working for the company. She had good references and continued to make a strong impression on Lily and Jake.

"When can you start work?" Lily asked before the interview ended.

"I'm finishin' up a job this week and I think I could probably start the week after," acknowledged Connie. "But you have to call my employer to work out final details, even though I'll be the one givin' you the go-ahead if you want to hire me."

"It was nice meeting another Baltimore girl," conveyed Lily in a warm and heartfelt manner.

"Ain't it nice you call me a girl. In Essex, they usually call me 'honey' or 'sweetie' and I don't like either of them. It was nice meetin' you and I hope to see you again," Connie expressed as she headed to the front door. "See ya," she yelled as she exited Lily's home.

"I actually liked her," confirmed Lily. "I think I'll be comfortable with her in my house. And God knows, I want to be as comfortable as I can be over the next six to eight months."

"I understand. If you want it, it's done Lily. I'll see to that," consoled Jake. "Connie's interview lasted so long that the next woman is scheduled to arrive in a few minutes. I'll look over the next application before she comes."

CHAPTER 32

A few minutes before twelve o'clock, there was a knock on the front door. Jake opened it to a tall Asian woman who appeared to be college aged. She had long, straight black hair down to her shoulder blades and was dressed in a professional manner. She had a large handbag draped over her shoulder. She reached out her hand to shake Jake's, but remained silent.

"Hi. I'm Jake Snyder. I'm going to assume you're here for the interview?" pronounced Jake.

"Yes I am," assured the woman in an unassuming, yet confident voice.

"Please come in and meet Lily," said Jake.

As the woman walked through the front entrance way and into the house, her eyes quickly turned to the painting that was hanging on the wall. She continued to stare and began to move closer to the "I TOLD YOU SO" painting that had been hanging in the same spot since 1952 until she was face-to-face with it. Her eyes scanned it, and she appeared to forget the purpose of her invitation into Lily's home.

Jake and Lily sat quietly as the woman continued to stare at the painting for two minutes that actually felt like ten minutes. As she glanced over the painting, her head nodded up and down, and a grin appeared on her face. She looked down at the name at the bottom of the painting and finally looked back at Lily. She repeated this motion several times.

On the fourth turn of her head she blurted out to Lily in a light Asian accent "Is this a real, original Chocarne-Moreau painting? I can't believe I'm looking at one in your house. This must be worth a lot of money. One was auctioned six months ago for one million two hundred thousand dollars, and yours is better," revealed the woman. "I am so happy to be here today. I am honored to meet you. Today is a blessing," she exclaimed as her eyes became misty.

"Well, I hope it's real," contended Lily. "I purchased it in 1952. It has been hanging there ever since. How do you know so much about this painting?"

"I am a student at Johns Hopkins University. I'm a third year premed student. That's what my parents wanted me to major in. But my passion is art history. I'm minoring in that. I love 19th century art," conceded the woman.

"Dear, what is your name," asked Lily. "We got sidetracked when you came in and I forgot to ask you your name."

"My name is Cupid Wong," disclosed the woman.

"Why did your parents decide to name you Cupid?"

"My family is from Hong Kong," said Cupid. "My parents became Christian when I was six and wanted to change my name to something that better conformed to the Christian religion. In my native language Cupid means 'God is Love'. Therefore, my parents thought it meant that I was a child of God. Once we came to America, we realized my name meant something totally different. But that's my name and I like it because people always remember me once they hear my name," Cupid asserted with a cute and innocent smile.

"So you're a busy woman. Why would you want to come here and work with Lily?" inquired Jake.

"To be honest, I don't need a lot of sleep. I'm hoping to find a patient that only needs someone to sit with them and watch over them at night, so that I can do my homework and study. I'm smart, honest, and kind. I think those are some of the attributes clients are looking for during their time of need."

"Oh dear," uttered Lily. "In keeping with being honest, I'm not sure you're going to be the right fit for me. My three daughters will be coming to stay with me over the next three weeks. I'm not sure how much studying you'll get done when they're here. They each have their own issues that'll definitely get in your way. After they leave, I'm afraid that my needs may get more demanding. I have AML leukemia. I'm eighty-six years old. My story is coming to a quick ending and it won't have a happy ending, if you know what I mean," confided Lily.

Cupid listened to Lily, shaking her head up and down like she did while looking at the painting.

"I think you have a great future ahead of you Cupid," Lily said, but I don't think your wants and my needs are matching up well. I admire your work ethic and attitude. You're going to be a very successful woman one day."

Knowing that the interview was over, Cupid thanked Lily and Jake for the opportunity and turned her head back to the painting.

"You should have that painting appraised," Cupid quickly blurted out. "It may be worth a thousand of times more than you paid for it. In fact, I know an Art History professor at Johns Hopkins University who could give you a good estimate of its value. Do you mind if I take a picture of it with my cell phone?" asked Cupid.

Without thinking of the consequences, both Jake and Lily nodded their heads. Cupid carefully aligned her iPhone with the painting and snapped two shots. She then looked in her cell phone and made sure the snapshot of the painting "I TOLD YOU SO" was what she expected.

"I'm going to send a text message of the painting to my Art History professor. He may be able to give you an estimate of the value of the painting right away if he is available. I'm sure he'll be happy to see it."

After she hit the send, Cupid began to rattle off the master painters that she liked from the 19th century. As she rattled off their names, Lily heard her mention Jean-Le'on Ge'rome and William Adolphe Bouguereau.

Lily began to grin from ear to ear.

Although Lily was excited, Jake was now going to find out about the value of this painting, even though he knew nothing about the three other paintings that remained hidden in Lily's basement.

Cupid's cell phone pinged. Cupid stopped talking and stared at her cell phone. Lily waited with great anticipation hoping that her recent estimated value of the painting was correct.

"I knew I was right. Here's what my professor said." Cupid read the message.

Hi, Cupid. Thank you for the text message. How did you discover that work by Paul Charles Chocarne-Moreau? What a find! I checked some recent records of sales at various auction houses around the world for paintings by Paul Charles Chocarne-Moreau. I found a sale of one that went for one million one hundred thousand dollars six months ago. The person you're with should be very happy with the potential value of this painting. Congratulations. I see I taught you well. You have a keen eye. Thanks for the text, Professor Gray.

Lily was happy to hear what Cupid's professor had to say. It confirmed what she had estimated their value to be.

"You are a godsend, Cupid. I can't believe we were so lucky to have you come today," Lily stated as she smiled.

There was a knock at the front door as Cupid finished reading the text. It was now one o'clock.

"The past hour flew by," declared Jake. Thank you for coming today."

Jake escorted Cupid to the front door. She continued looking back to get one more glimpse of the painting. As she opened the front door and walked down the front steps, the next interviewee was patiently waiting.

CHAPTER 33

As Cupid moved down the front steps, the person waiting at the bottom gently moved aside. She was a light brown skinned African-American woman appearing to be in her mid-sixties. She wore neatly pressed dark slacks and a purple business casual knit shirt with the Baltimore Ravens logo on it. She held a notebook in her left hand and a dark brown leather COACH pocketbook dangled from her right shoulder.

"Hi. It's nice to meet you," Jake said shaking her hand.

"Hi. I'm Lee. It is my pleasure. Thank you for inviting me today. I live in the two hundred block of North Rose Street. It's only about ten blocks from here," said the woman.

"Thanks for coming today. Please come in and meet Lily."

The six interviews began to take their toll on Lily.

"Nice to meet you," stated Lee enthusiastically.

"It's nice to meet you too," Lily sighed, "Jake and I hope this is the last interview of the day. I don't think I could handle one more."

"Your wish is my command," pledged Jake. "Lee, why don't we get along with the interview because I think I may have pushed Lily a little too hard today. Why don't you tell us a little bit about yourself?"

"I don't like talkin' about myself, but I'll do my best," Lee replied in a reserved and confident manner. "I was born and bred in Baltimore. I went to the Western High School for girls right about the time that it was fully integrated. I got a great education. My mother made sure of that." Lee's expression then deepened in thought. "I didn't go to college, but I had a good payin job in Baltimore City as a maintenance person in the projects around Baltimore City. I've seen it all, both the good and bad in people. Most people think it's a hard place, but it ain't that bad. I got a nice pension and can pay my bills, but my aide job helps me to get a little bit ahead, and I get paid to help others. It is a win-win for both me and my clients. I've been doin' this job part time for over twenty years now," disclosed Lee, frank and self-assured. "You think you're picky about who you select. I'm picky too. I only agree to work with people who show me respect, like I've always demanded from my two girls. Because I'm retired, I'm pretty flexible about when my clients need me. I'm here for them and I want them to know that. I'm not here to take advantage of them in their time of need. I'm a good Christian woman. I'm simply here to serve the Lord and help others."

Lily and Jake looked at each other to acknowledge that they liked what they were hearing from Lee so far.

"Tell me about your daughters," inquired Lily, leaning forward in her chair as her energy level increased from Lee's straightforward synopsis of her life.

Lee sat up a little straighter and began to grin, "I'm real proud of my daughters. One is a nurse and the other has her master's degree in the IT field. I have three beautiful older grandchildren that I love to death. I had a brother, but he's been dead a long time, but that's a story in itself for another day."

"How about you Mrs. Lily? I'd like to know a little more about you," said Lee in an effort to determine if she would take on Lily as a client.

Lily sat back in her chair and took a deep breath and a serious look came upon her face.

"I've lived right here since I was married in 1951. My children grew up right here in this house, and this is where I want to spend my remaining days."

Lee leaned forward with a concerned and compassionate expression on her face.

"My life has been good and simple and I've witnessed lots of big events in my lifetime. I was an obedient and loving wife and mother. I've made a few mistakes in my lifetime, but I've always tried to do the best with what I had. I've had a few regrets, but more happy than sad times. I try to think about the happy times these days," Lily professed, sounding melancholy and retrospective.

Lee intently listened to Lily. Their eyes zeroed in on each other throughout the discussion. Lee reached over and grabbed Lily's hand. She squeezed it gently as Lily finished her sentence. Lily could feel

Lee's sincerity and understanding of her situation. She began to think that Lee would be a good fit for the task at hand.

"Lee, if we hire you, I want you to know that over the next three weeks my daughters will be in town. They may be a little bit difficult, but each one will only be here for a week. Will that be a problem for you?" questioned Lily as she laid the ground work for what could be a mine field for any aide starting employment at Lily's home.

Lee said in a confident tone, "Mrs. Lily, since workin in the projects, I've worked with some of the nicest and craziest people you could imagine. I've been yelled at, spit at, and even got in a couple of fist fights with the residents. And my light skin didn't help me, that's for sure. I've been called cracker, whitey, and snowflake, even though I'm black like them. So whatever your daughters throw at me will merely pass over me, like snowflakes on a windy day."

Both Jake and Lily began laughing out loud. Jake was ready to seal the deal.

"Can you start with us next week?" asked Jake.

"Well, let's both think it over for one day. I don't like to make quick decisions. My mother always taught me that sometimes people make quick decisions that end up being wrong. She always told me to think about big decisions. You should think about it overnight before you decide to hire me, Mrs. Lily," contended Lee.

"I think that's excellent advice," responded Jake.

"If you have any other questions you can call me on my cell phone," insisted Lee. My three references are also noted at the bottom of the application."

"Thanks for coming Lee. I want you to know that if I was ever in the middle of the ocean on a long voyage, it sure would be comforting having someone like you by my side," Lily confided as she got a little bit choked up.

"That is about the nicest thing anyone has ever said to me," claimed Lee as she reached down to hold Lily's hand again. "God bless you Mrs. Lily. It was nice meeting you both." She stood up and walked towards the door.

Lee made her way to the front door taking a quick glance at the painting on the wall before exiting the house.

"I think we have our two aides Jake, Connie Smith and Lee. I've decided. And what was Lee's last name?" asked Lily.

"I'm not sure. I threw her application in the pile with the rest of the candidates. Does it matter?" countered Jake as he looked down at the pile of resumes.

"It doesn't. I'm just glad we're finished," maintained Lily.

As soon as those words were out of her mouth, Lily realized that her real challenge would soon begin. With her daughters coming to town and aides helping to assist her, her acting debut and final curtain call was about to begin. Not only did her daughters not know what was planned, but neither did Jake or her aides. They would all soon be in a state of confusion as to how best help Lily.

With her paintings valued at almost six million dollars, the stakes were high for her daughters on their upcoming visit. The next few weeks would determine whether they would receive all or any part of their mother's fortune.

CHAPTER 34

The day after the interviews, Lily called Lee offering her the job. Lee happily accepted. With her home health aides in place and daughters' visits scheduled, Lily had no idea what to expect, knowing her daughters' dysfunctional pasts; Lily sat in her recliner contemplating how to prepare for their visit.

"The easy task will be safeguarding my physical possessions and accounting for items that aren't adequately secured," she thought. "The hard part will be continuously acting like I have Alzheimer's disease during their visits," she contemplated further. Being sick and performing amateur drama was new territory for Lily. She had never taken acting lessons and didn't even know how a person would act if they had Alzheimer's disease.

As Lily sat in her recliner, she combed through the Internet to determine the personality characteristics and behaviors of a person with Alzheimer's disease. She clicked onto the National Institutes of Health's website and peered at the following information on her computer screen:

"As the disease progresses, people experience greater memory loss and other cognitive difficulties. Problems can include:
- wandering and getting lost
- trouble handling money and paying bills
- repeating questions
- taking longer to complete normal daily tasks
- losing things or misplacing them in odd places
- personality and behavior changes

Moderate Alzheimer's disease:

In this stage, damage occurs in areas of the brain that control language, reasoning, sensory processing, and conscious thought. Symptoms may include:
- increased memory loss and confusion
- problems recognizing family and friends
- inability to learn new things
- difficulty carrying out multi-step tasks such as getting dressed

- problems coping with new situations
- hallucinations, delusions, and paranoia
- impulsive behavior

Severe Alzheimer's disease:

People with severe Alzheimer's disease cannot communicate and are completely dependent on others for their care. Near the end, the person may be in bed most or all of the time as the body shuts down. Their symptoms often include:

- inability to communicate
- weight loss
- seizures
- skin infections
- difficulty swallowing
- groaning, moaning, or grunting
- increased sleeping
- lack of control of bowel and bladder"

As her internet search neared completion, Lily highlighted and saved the details of a person in the first and second phases of Alzheimer's disease. She knew she had to study, memorize, act, and practice her craft over the next few days prior to her daughters' arrival.

Lily lifted herself up from her recliner and made her way to Frank's office.

I need to safeguard, organize, and record my valuables, Lily thought as she made her way to her late husband's office.

Lily began combing through and collecting key financial documents, including banking, mutual fund, and tax return information, with the goal of placing them in her safe deposit box in the next day or two.

Additional information included files regarding the Sotheby's auction from 1999 and the paintings hidden in her basement and other financial information that she knew wouldn't fit into her bank's safe deposit box. She placed this information into a small metal box that had a lock and key.

I'm going to give the metal box to Jake for safe keeping, she decided.

A few days before Mary's visit, Jake came by and picked up the box.

"I'll hold onto your lock box until your girls are gone or until you want it back. By the way what's in it?" inquired Jake.

"Oh, it's only some personal items I don't want the girls to see. What's in the box is more valuable than any other possessions I own," proclaimed Lily, not wanting to lie to Jake any more than she already had, but not disclosing to him the calculated plan she had in store for her daughters.

Jake grabbed the box and headed towards the door. Lily stopped him.

"By the way Jake, I'm not sure it's a good idea for you to see me over the next few weeks while my daughters are here."

She had never informed Jake of her scheme, and she had no intention of telling him. She felt horrible deceiving him, but knew she had to in order to ensure her sneaky plot would progress effectively.

"I'm afraid if they see you, they may get suspicious of my true intentions for their visit. If they call you during their stay and raise concerns about my health, please tell them that my will was prepared a long time ago when Frank was still alive and has not changed. That should keep them quiet. So if they call you, please be short with them, so they don't realize how much of a confidant you have been to me through the years. This is the way it has to be, Jake. I'm sorry, but you know these next three weeks are very important to me, particularly in light of the fact that the 'I TOLD YOU SO' painting may be worth a quite a bit of money."

"Okay, okay. You win, as usual. But you'd better call me if you need me. You know I'll always be here to help you."

"Jake, there is one other matter I need you to take care of over the next three weeks. Could you please contact Sotheby's in New York and ask them if they are ready to auction another Haussner's painting?"

"Didn't the Haussner's paintings sell for millions of dollars at the Sotheby's auction quite a few years back?" Jake inquired.

"The auction was in 1999, and some of the Haussner's paintings were auctioned for over forty-two million dollars," Lily disclosed.

"Wow. How did you know that Lily? You never cease to amaze me."

Lily ignored Jake's question and quickly added, "After my daughters are gone, I want it auctioned as quickly as possible so that the proceeds from it are in my estate upon my death. I'd love to see how much I can get for it while I'm still alive."

"I'll do my best and contact them right away. I still can't believe that painting you've had hanging in your hallway is worth that much money," exclaimed Jake.

"Thank you Jake. I'll forever be in your debt," Lily looked at Jake with sad eyes, knowing that she was still not being fully honest with him.

"Call me if you need me," Jake said as he grabbed the metal box and bolted out the door. The information regarding Lily's three secret hidden paintings was now safely hidden with Jake, and the key to the box remained in Lily's possession.

CHAPTER 35

The next day Lily began categorizing and logging every piece of her jewelry. She created a Microsoft Word document on her laptop computer, knowing that if she placed it there, her daughters would not have access to it. It appeared as follows:

Rings: Four Gold, Eight Silver, Three Diamonds, Four Topaz, One Sapphire, Two Quartz.

Necklaces: Twelve Gold, Five Silver, Two Diamond.

Earrings: Fifteen Gold, Eight Silver, Two Diamond.

Broaches: Five Gold, Four Silver

Watches: Three Gold

Other: Frank's 1970 Rolex Watch, Frank's wedding ring

Lily placed each of the items neatly in her jewelry box.

"Based on how organized the items are, my daughters should have some indication that I've been keeping track of each piece," Lily noted.

Once the jewelry was organized, Lily closed the jewelry box and locked it. She then placed the key back in its supposedly hidden location, a dish containing a pair of her grandmother's false teeth. Lily had kept the key in the same location since 1952, and each daughter knew its location. Lily's jewelry was now ready to serve as an indicator of her daughter's moral character.

The only other prized possession in her house was the "I TOLD YOU SO" painting.

Lily wished she hadn't known the value of the painting prior to their visit. She certainly didn't want to raise any suspicion while they were in town. She thought it would be better to leave it hanging in the same place it had been since 1952.

Little did she know that her decision would be a huge mistake when her daughters came to visit.

Lily waited another day before deciding to tackle her next problem. She knew her declining health would mean her taking a larger amount of medications to help manage the side-effects of leukemia, some of which she had already started.

Lily concluded that she needed to hide her medications so her daughters wouldn't get suspicious.

To verify her concern about Sharon, Lily sat down and opened her computer and researched which of her leukemia medications might be abused by a drug addict. She quickly discovered that the drugs prescribed by Dr. Baum, are the same drugs craved by addicts. As a result, she realized she not only had to hide her medications, but she also had to track them.

Lily began to shake her head. "Sharon's going to be a tough cookie," Lily whispered to herself.

As Lily settled back into her recliner, she began to realize that she was still missing a big piece of the puzzle.

Lily returned to her computer to search the Internet and gather information from the court systems where each daughter lived.

On the California Court System civil case website, she typed in Mary's first, middle, and last name. There were a slew of cases: two foreclosure went back to 1999 and 2008. There were multiple notices of other claims, tort cases, warrants in debt, and garnishments of wages. There were cases where Mary was sued by banks, charge card companies, and individual citizens who may have been landlords, or someone never paid for services rendered. Mary had had twenty-seven civil cases filed against her in the California court system over the past years.

"Oh my," thought Lily, "I'll bet the judges know Mary on a first-name basis."

Lily continued pecking away at the computer. She began searching the California criminal system database to see if Mary had any cases against her. Mary had no serious criminal cases other than two shoplifting convictions and numerous traffic violations including driving in an uninsured car and driving a car that was not licensed or had an expired license plate. All total, Lily counted sixty official cases of Mary's in the California civil and criminal court system over the past thirty years. The information was quite shocking and alarming.

The court records exposed how Mary's life was still filled with chaos and dysfunction. Lily began to feel sorry for Mary as she sat back on her recliner thinking retrospectively about Mary's childhood. Mary was her oldest and most spoiled child. Lily began to doubt her child-rearing skills and began to look inward at what she could have done differently. Lily began to stare at "I TOLD YOU SO" as she pondered Mary's life.

Mary and her husband always made Lily feel inferior to them even though they lived well beyond their means. Lily began to think that their lifestyle had caught up with them. Now that they were in their sixties, it wasn't going to be easy for them going forward knowing Mary's court records were the tip of the iceberg of the debt that they had probably amassed over their lifetime. Lily felt disheartened by the path Mary's life had taken.

Lily searched the Internet for Sharon's court records. She theorized the majority of her review time would be looking at the state of Illinois's criminal cases rather than the civil cases. Therefore, she began her Internet inquiry reviewing the civil cases, hoping her search would only reveal a few. However, she quickly discovered she was terribly wrong. As she peered at her computer screen, it revealed a laundry list of civil cases in her official state record. The majority of them stated "Judgment in Favor of Plaintiff Entered" and appeared to be cases where Sharon hadn't paid a landlord or had received a service that she hadn't paid for. There were thirty-five civil cases in Sharon's Illinois court record.

As Lily searched for Sharon's criminal cases, she was astonished. Sharon made Mary's court issues appear minor in nature. In total, Sharon had twenty documented court cases related to driving violations. They included operating an uninsured vehicle, operating a vehicle with expired tags, operating an unlicensed motor vehicle, driving with a suspended license, driving under the influence of alcohol, driving a vehicle that was not inspected, and failure to wear a seatbelt. Her record also included numerous tickets for driving over the speed limit and reckless driving. But these were only a small part of her court history.

As Lily continued moving from offense to offense, she was shocked to see the way Sharon led her life. Her criminal cases included possession of marijuana, possession of narcotics other than marijuana, trespassing, assault second-degree, assault first-degree, burglary, reckless endangerment, and the list went on and on. There were so many cases that Lily didn't even try to add up the total. All total Sharon's criminal cases spread across five pages and thirty years. Each page had twenty to thirty cases on it.

Lily sat contemplating the information that she had just examined for both Mary and Sharon and continued to speculate and wonder how they had gotten so far off track. The serenity prayer popped into her mind as she realized that the actions they took as adults were beyond her control. They were adults and they made terrible choices.

Lily thought she had done a good job of raising them with a simple lifestyle in East Baltimore, but for some reason, their lives went awry.

As she sat motionless, Lily eventually gathered enough internal strength to perform a search of her youngest daughter's court records, checking civil and criminal court cases. Much to her pleasant surprise, there were a limited number of civil and criminal court cases for Denise. The only civil case involved a legal matter that was less than $2500. There were criminal cases that were a little bit puzzling to Lily. Three of the cases involved sexual misdemeanors and provided little detail as to what they were. The other case involved a name change. Lily was quite puzzled and remembered that when she recently called Denise to arrange for her to visit Baltimore, she answered the phone by another name.

After reviewing her three daughters' information online, Lily began to fully comprehend the challenge she had placed upon herself. As she sat thinking about how difficult the next three weeks would be, she felt alone and scared, but knew she had to find the strength to make the right decision regarding her and Frank's legacy. Frank had the foresight and the guts in 1952 to buy the paintings and she now had to have the fortitude to engage her daughters.

"Frank," Lily yelled. "I wish you were here. How did you leave me with this mess?"

Deciding which of her daughters to give some or all of her six million dollar estate to was a big decision for a woman of simple means from East Baltimore. And once she died the decision would be final. So if there was bedlam after she died, her children would have to accept her decision.

Over the next few days, Lily continued to organize, stage her house, and practice her acting. Lily surmised that if she succeeded with her ingenious plan, an Academy Award would be waiting for her at the pearly gates of heaven. On the other hand, if she made the wrong decision regarding her inheritance, Frank would be waiting for her in heaven and would have some choice words for her, even if it was in heaven.

Unfortunately for Lily, her final decision regarding her inheritance and legacy were going to be much tougher to resolve than she had ever contemplated, particularly considering that she was an eighty-six-year- old woman nearing the end of her life. Little did she know that the turn of events that would take place over the remaining few months of her life would shake her and others to their core. She would have to make decisions that involved more than just money, but how she wanted to be remembered by her loved ones. Her final test would be much harder than trying to deceive her daughters. It would become the toughest, most soul wrenching, and most meaningful decision of her long life.

CHAPTER 36

Lily moved about her house, making the finishing touches prior to Mary's visit. As Lily masterfully untidied her house, she felt confident her plan was nearly ready for execution. In the case of Mary, Lily made sure that there was no financial information that she could get her hands on. Lily had meticulously counted and categorized every piece of jewelry in her possession. She also filled her wallet with twenty dollar bills totaling three hundred dollars, and planned on making every attempt to track and safeguard it.

Lily paced about, moving items here and then there, becoming very anxious about Mary's arrival. She became concerned about her ability to take on the personality of an Alzheimer's patient and remain in character for a three-week period, even though her health was continuing to decline. Above all else, Lily was hoping to witness that her daughters' behaviors and attitudes, particularly their ability to be kind, considerate, and compassionate toward her, had transformed.

Every hour on the hour until Mary arrived, Lily would repeat the Serenity Prayer to ask God for support and guidance.

At 1:02 p.m., there was a knock at the front door. Lily took a deep breath knowing it was Mary. She quickly shifted into her new role and began blankly staring at the television. The television blared in the background. In her new character as a mother afflicted with Alzheimer's disease, activities that were normal to the average person would now be difficult for her to perform.

Lily sat motionless. After thirty seconds, there was a second rapid knocking at the door.

Lily could hear a loud voice yelling "Mom, Mom, are you home?"

Mary listened more intently and could hear the television blaring, and waited a short minute before jiggling the doorknob. Much to her surprise, but not to Lily's, the front door opened.

"Mom? Mom?" Mary called as she walked into the house. As soon as she made it through the short vestibule, she could see her mother blankly staring at the television.

Mary was dressed impeccably. She wore a light sundress with high heels to match. Her shapely black hair had been recently cut and colored, and her fingernail and toenail colors matched her dress. Her dark tan was covered in makeup to hide the leathery skin that was the byproduct of Mary's enjoyment of the California sun. Her face now looked like a shriveled raisin, even though her big green eyes were just as beautiful and youthful as when she had arrived in California more than forty years ago. Cheap costume jewelry hung from anyplace on her body where there was an opportunity. She quickly strutted across the room, with a Starbucks coffee in her hand. The smell of her strong perfume reached Lily's nose before Mary did.

Lily was already earning her Academy Award. She wore black pants, a bright blue shirt that was inside out, and had a light house robe on top of her clothes. She was not wearing a bra, had one slipper on, and the other slipper was lying on the floor. She wore no makeup and her hair appeared as if it had recently been placed in a blender. She was a perfect mess.

As Mary peered at the state of her mother, her shoulders lowered in sympathy to her mother's pathetic appearance.

"Mom, Mom," Mary repeated as she gently shook Lily's shoulder. "Mom, Mom. Are you okay? Are you alive?"

Mary continued gently shaking Lily's shoulder in an effort to urge her out of her stupor. Lily slowly blinked her eyes and looked at Mary.

"Oh, who are you?" Lily declared acting confused by Mary's appearance. "Oh, hi Sharon. What are you doing here?" Lily inquired as if puzzled by Mary's presence. "You need to go back to school right now. Your grades have been suffering lately."

"Mom, Mom, Mom. Wake up. I'm not Sharon Mom. It is not Sharon. It's Mary, Mom," Mary implored in a very concerned voice.

Lily look confused as Mary stared at her. Lily slowly raised the recliner from the tilted-back position.

"Oh, it's you, Mary. I'm sorry. Why are you here Mary? I didn't know you were coming. If I had known, I would have left the front door open."

"Mom, you did leave the front door open. In this neighborhood, I can't believe you would leave your front door open. Someone could rob or rape you. Mom, you asked me to come and see you." Mary became even more alarmed.

"Mom, you've lost weight. Are you okay?" Mary said as her concerns began to mount.

"I'm doing fine dear," vowed Lily in an effort to give Mary a little reassurance.

"I'm not sure about that, Mom. You have all of these newspapers and mail lying everywhere and you have a robe over your clothes."

Mary helped Lily slip off the robe. As she slipped it off, she realized that Lily's next layer of clothing was inside out.

"Mom, you put your shirt on inside out. What's going on?" questioned Mary.

"I must have put it on in the dark," contended Lily with her eyes facing the ground.

"Mom, I'm worried about you," Mary vented as she began to organize the loose papers scattered about the floor.

"Don't be worried about me, dear."

Lily thought it was the perfect time to throw Mary further off. After the next statement, Lily's apparent confusion and forgetfulness would no longer be Mary's primary concern.

Lily grabbed Mary's hand. Lily in her seated position looked up to Mary like a puppy waiting for a treat. She looked at Mary for five seconds in silence.

Finally, Lily calmly proclaimed, "I've been thinking a lot over the past few months. The reason I asked you to come to town is that I want to move to California with you and Dave."

As soon as those words rolled off of Lily's tongue, Mary took a big step back and plopped onto a nearby chair. Her face turned white as a ghost as she briefly sat in silence.

"Why would you want to move to California?" Mary began to nervously rock back and forth in the chair as she considered the consequences of her mother moving to California to live with her.

"You wouldn't know anyone. It's hot, dry, and overpopulated. I think I'd have to move to a larger apartment to accommodate you. Are you sure you've thought this out?"

Although Lily had no intention of moving to California, she was happy that she had put the thought on the table. Her plan was going better than she had expected.

"Well, let's think about it over the next week."

"What?" Mary burst out as her mind was still in a cloud contemplating what Lily had just revealed.

"I said, let's think about it over the next week while you're here," repeated Lily. This brought some relief to Mary knowing that she wasn't one hundred percent locked in on the idea.

"Where is your suitcase? You only brought a carry-on bag," queried Lily.

"I thought we'd do some shopping together, so I didn't bring a lot of clothes. Remember when we used to go shopping at the department stores downtown? I loved shopping with you at Hutzler's, Hoschild Kohn's, and the Hecht Company. Those stores sure have been gone a long time. Do you remember when we used to eat at the counter at Read's Drug Store and I'd order a chocolate soda?"

"Those sure were happy and simple times," recalled Lily as her mind began to reflect on their life together going back over forty plus years.

"Do you remember the only time I ever hooked school and was shopping at Hutzler's? I was on the elevator and it stopped on the second floor. When the door opened you were standing there. I got busted," Mary declared as they both began to laugh.

With that said, the conversation quickly changed from the state of Lily's mental and physical health to reminiscing about their past time together. Mary did most of the talking and Lily remained guarded knowing the goal she needed to accomplish over the next week.

"I actually enjoyed growing up here, Mom. However, once you and Dad sent me away to college and I saw how people in other cities lived, I was never going to come back to Baltimore. Do you remember, a few years before I left for college, the 1968 Martin

Luther King riots burned most of the city down. Why would I want to come back to that?"

"I understand dear. I only wish it could have been different. Once you three girls went away, I didn't know how to convince any of you to come back to Baltimore. Your father didn't like traveling and you never seemed to have the money to travel."

"What do you mean? I came as often as I could afford to. It's expensive to fly to Baltimore." Mary said defensively.

"That is all I meant," conceded Lily as she began to back pedal not wanting to further upset Mary.

Mary continued reminiscing about the past and updating Lily about her family. Lily remained listening, nodding, and not doing a lot of talking. As they moved into the kitchen, Mary was surprised by the pile of dishes in the sink and the trash overflowing from the trash can.

"Mom, it looks like you haven't cleaned your kitchen in days. That's not like you."

Mary began to organize the trash.

Lily shrugged her shoulders and remained silent.

Mary went about the business of cleaning up the trash can and then made her way to the sink. After an hour passed, Mary had cleaned up the area.

"I'm starving, Mom. What do you have to eat?" Mary asked as she was wiping off the countertop and putting the finishing touches on her kitchen clean-up activities.

"I'm not sure, dear. Please feel free to eat anything that you'd like," replied Lily as she relaxed on a kitchen chair in anticipation of Mary's next surprise.

Mary moved to the refrigerator and opened the door. As the door opened, the only substantial items that was contained in it was Lily's car keys sitting on one shelf and her pocketbook on another.

"Mom, what is going on here? Your car keys and purse are in the refrigerator," barked Mary in an alarmed tone. "I'm really confused."

"You're confused. I'm confused too," expressed Lily in an innocent unassuming voice. "I've been looking for them for three days now.

No wonder I don't have any food in the refrigerator. I couldn't find my purse or car keys."

"That makes no sense at all. Didn't you see them when you got hungry?"

"I don't know, Denise. I've been confused lately."

Mary grabbed the car keys and purse and removed them from the refrigerator.

"You have nothing in your refrigerator to eat. Tomorrow we're going to go to the store and we're going to fill it up."

"Whatever," sighed Lily.

"Have you been driving Mom?"

"Of course. No one is going to take my driver's license away. If anyone takes my license away, that will be the death of me," Lily cried as she began to realize that she may not have fully thought out the consequences of her plan.

"I'll call out for dinner. Is there a carryout place you like?" Mary inquired.

"I always liked Matthew's Pizza. Please order from there."

"I can't believe they've been around since I was a kid."

Mary looked on her cell phone and called in the delivery order. She then grabbed her pocketbook looking for cash, knowing that it didn't contain enough money to pay for the pizza. She opened her wallet and pulled out two one dollar bills. She then frantically searched each section of her purse and couldn't find any other cash.

"Mom, I don't have cash to pay for the delivery. Do you?"

"I do, Mary," admitted Lily. "Take the cash out of my wallet to pay for the pizza."

Mary began to go through Lily's pocketbook and quickly observed the location of her mother's wallet, which included cash and her three charge cards.

Within twenty minutes, the pizza was delivered and they began to enjoy their favorite pizza that Mary had not eaten since the 1970s. Lily continued to be a better listener than talker, contemplating what the week would bring.

CHAPTER 37

Mary was still on California time the next morning. That suited Lily absolutely fine because it gave her time to prepare for her next charade. It was 9:30 a.m. and Mary was just beginning to ease out of bed.

"Mom, are you up yet?" Mary yelled from an adjoining guest bedroom.

There was no response from Lily. Mary got up from her bed and walked into Lily's bedroom. Lily was nowhere to be seen.

Mary became concerned that she didn't hear or see her mother and began calling in a loud voice, "Mom, Mom. Are you here?"

Mary could barely hear a muffled voice coming from the bathroom stating "I'm in here, Denise."

Mary walked into the bathroom and saw Lily sitting in the bathtub that was filled to the top with soapy water. She still had on her clothes from the day before. Her head was resting on the back of the bathtub and she appeared in a perfect state of relaxation.

"Mom, what are you doing in the bathtub with your clothes on?" Mary said, beginning to realize the extent of her mother's mental deficiencies.

"I'm not sure what you mean. Can you help me out of here please?" Lily said as she acted confused and slowly rose up from her horizontal position in the bathtub.

Her wet clothes clung tightly around her body like a wetsuit. Mary helped Lily out of the bathtub and began helping her undress. Mary then began to comb through her mother's closet and quickly discovered that her wardrobe was bare compared to California fashion standards.

"Mom, I'm going to take you shopping today. You need some new clothes now that you've lost weight," announced Mary enthusiastically. She helped her mother dress and then led her to the bathroom sink to help her brush her teeth and comb her hair. Lily, seizing the opportunity, quickly picked up her tooth brush and cleverly placed it in a jar of Vaseline instead of toothpaste.

Lily slowly began to move the toothbrush toward her mouth. As the toothbrush got an inch away for her mouth, she realized that Mary had failed to notice her calculated movements. Lily then repeated the prior movements by putting the toothbrush back in the Vaseline jar and picking it up to draw Mary's attention.

Upon seeing what her mother was about to do, Mary shouted "Mom, Mom stop. Your toothbrush is in Vaseline." Mary grabbed the toothbrush from Lily's hand and threw it in the trash can. "We're going to have to buy you another one at the mall. I don't know, Mom. You're really scaring me."

Once Lily's needs were taken care of, Mary and Lily moved through Lily's bedroom. Mary's eyes immediately zeroed in on Lily's jewelry box like an eagle spotting its prey. It was sitting on the small 1950s style dresser that had been in Lily's bedroom since Dwight Eisenhower had been the President of the United States.

"Mom, in California, a rich girl never goes out of the house without putting on her jewelry. Today, we're going to indulge ourselves and wear some of that jewelry that's been sitting in the jewelry box since God knows when," avowed Mary with continued excitement.

"You know your father gave me most of the jewelry. He loved giving me jewelry on our anniversaries and other special occasions. He tried giving me a different gift on our first anniversary, and that didn't work out too well for him, so he always stuck with the jewelry."

"What was the other gift that didn't work out to too well Mom?" questioned Mary.

"That conversation is for another day. I'll follow your lead today. I woke up and I'm still tired. I guess that's what happens when you're eighty-six years old," aired Lily, woefully anticipating the challenge of the day's activities.

Mary slowly opened the jewelry box as she listened to Lily. Much to her surprise, it was loaded with fine jewelry that at first sight, she knew was real gold, silver, and gem stones. She peered at the jewelry as if she had just discovered the Holy Grail.

"Dad treated you well," Mary acknowledged excitedly as she began scouring through the jewelry. "We don't have to go shopping today.

We can shop right here," Mary joked as she continued to pick up and examine each piece.

"What's your favorite piece? You have it neatly arranged. I'm surprised, considering, oh never mind," hesitated Mary, stopping in mid-sentence not wanting to upset her mother about the disorganization of her house and apparent mental state.

Mary quickly organized some of the jewelry pieces into distinct piles.

"This is what I want you to wear," said Mary as she began to place the jewelry on her mother. "I think a pair of nice hoop gold earrings, a silver topaz ring on your left hand, a gold bangle bracelet on your right, and a gold necklace will make you look like a million bucks."

Mary stepped back to assess her choices.

Mary had an eye for fashion and read every fashion magazine and store catalog that she could get her hands on. Unfortunately for her, she lived on a pauper's budget. Reading the magazines was her way to escape her insolvent existence; and it allowed her to make the best use of her limited clothes, makeup, and costume jewelry and still make her feel attractive.

Her mother's hoard of jewelry sat in front of her for the taking. As she stared at the shiny stockpile, it reminded her of the pile of cocaine she would snort in her sister Sharon's room during their summer college breaks in Baltimore. Mary realized she was totally consumed by the thought of having this much fine jewelry right under her nose. She never had the opportunity in her years spent in California to wear such fine jewelry.

"Mom, I'm going to borrow your jewelry today, just like the movie stars make use of jewelry from famous designers for the Academy Awards. It won't hurt to wear it for one day, will it Mom?" she proposed.

Mary began to put on jewelry without waiting for a response from her mother. Lily couldn't stand what she was witnessing and quietly moved out of the bedroom and headed downstairs to make a pot of coffee. Mary was so focused on her appearance in the bedroom mirror she failed to notice her mother leave.

Mary's first selection was a pair of one quarter carat diamond earrings that were sitting in a top compartment of the jewelry box. Mary placed the earring in her ear and began to move her head from side to side to admire her new stylish look. No sooner was the pair attached to her ear than she reached into the jewelry box again, and grabbed another pair of one carat diamond earrings placing them in a second hole that she had in each ear. Although the appearance was a little over the top, even for Mary, the earrings made her feel rich and beautiful, and that was all that truly mattered to her. She then snatched Lily's three biggest gold bangle bracelets from the box and placed them on her left hand followed by the immediate placement of two diamond tennis bracelets on her right hand. She began to view the full effect of her new on-loan acquisitions.

Next, she grabbed three gold rings that were each filled with sapphire, quartz, and topaz stones. They were all much nicer than the small gold wedding band that was on her left finger. However, upon seeing the other rings on her finger, without hesitation she removed her wedding band and replaced it with another large diamond ring that was sitting in Lily's jewelry box.

The final piece of jewelry was a thick, long gold necklace with a large topaz stone affixed to it.

As she looked at this piece, she began to realize that her father loved her mother very much. The gold necklace must have been given to Lily on a very special occasion. She gingerly placed it around her neck and her wardrobe was officially complete.

As she looked in the mirror to admire her new pieces of jewelry, she began to feel like the beautiful models she would see in the fashion magazines and on the street in Beverly Hills and Santa Monica. The fine jewelry that she was wearing was absolutely stunning and she could now quickly move her mind past the dated clothing that she was still wearing from the day before.

She quickly breezed through the house with pep in her step. As she entered the kitchen, the first words out of her mouth were, "How do I look, Mom?"

Lily looked at Mary and was taken aback by her self-absorption.

"Have a cup of coffee, dear," said Lily as she sat at the kitchen table with a cup of coffee that was filled to the brim.

Mary poured herself a cup and added a touch of cream and a spoonful of sugar. She moved the cup toward her mouth and took a sip.

"Yuck, what is this, mother?" snapped Mary as she quickly moved the cup away from her mouth. "It doesn't taste like coffee. It tastes like Coca-Cola. Mother what's in this coffee?" asserted Mary.

"I'm not sure honey," maintained Lily in an innocent tone knowing that her plan worked perfectly. "Why, what is wrong with it? Mine tastes fine."

"Taste it mother," Mary demanded as her tone became unpleasant.

Mary peered at the coffee pot and saw a liter bottle of Coca-Cola sitting next to it. "Mom, you put Coke in the coffee maker instead of water. What were you thinking?" Mary moaned.

"Are we going to the beach again today?" Lily asked trying to add fuel to the fire to test Mary's patience.

"Mom, if you are this crazy, I can't take this for one week." Mary began to clean up the mess around the coffee maker.

"What time is it, dear?" Lily added, further testing her daughter's patience.

Mary quickly turned her head. "Mom your watch is on your wrist. Let's go and enjoy the day shopping." Her tone was pleasant until she reached into Lily's purse and couldn't locate her car keys. "Where are your car keys, Mom?"

"Did I leave them in the bag on the beach?" questioned Lily.

Mary moved to the refrigerator. The keys were nowhere to be seen. She quickly closed the refrigerator door and opened the freezer where she quickly spotted and grabbed the keys.

"You put them in the freezer. My, my, my, Mom." Mary said as she contemplated the state of Lily's mind. "Mom, I'm worried about you. I think you may need some help. Let's think about it while we're shopping," Mary touted as her mind quickly focused back on herself.

Although Mary's true colors were beginning to emerge as Lily had planned, she knew it was going to be a long and tiring day.

CHAPTER 38

Lily remained upset that Mary wouldn't let her drive her car, but knew she would be back in California in a few days.

"How do we get to Columbia Mall?" inquired Mary to test Lily's navigational skills.

"I'm not sure," admitted Lily. "I simply get in and start driving. I usually figure out where I want to go. I've ended up in some bad neighborhoods every now and then. But the young people standing on the corners are very helpful to point me back towards my house." Lily wondered if Mary would take the bait.

"Mom, you've actually stopped your car and talked to people in drug-infested neighborhoods? They're probably drug dealers. You can get yourself killed or raped or have your purse and your car stolen. Mom, you're absolutely and positively one hundred percent crazy," insisted Mary.

"Well, it's always worked. I've gotten along pretty well so far, dear."

Mary reached into her purse and turned on her cell phone navigation application that directed her to Columbia Mall. Throughout the half hour ride, Lily continued looking up and down at her watch and kept asking Mary what time it was. Lily's plan was working better than she hoped. However, she was realizing that her daughter's personality had not changed as she hoped it had. What she had witnessed over the past twenty-four hours gave her a strong indication that she would not want to leave all of her estate to Mary. However, Mary still had six days remaining in her stay, and Lily thought that there was still a slight chance that Mary could turn over a new leaf.

The Columbia Mall, located south of Baltimore, had many large department stores like Macy's, Nordstrom, Lord and Taylor, and Sears to name a few. It was one of the most popular malls in the area, and attracted patrons from Baltimore and Washington D.C.

As they pulled onto the mall parking lot, Mary quickly found a parking spot near the entrance to Nordstrom's department store. Nordstrom's may not have been as high-class as some of the unique boutique shops that populated the Beverly Hills shopping district, but it suited Mary perfectly fine.

Lily remained in her acting state, asking Mary a question before they exited the car.

"Have I been here before? I don't remember ever being here. What time is it?"

"It is time to go shopping Mom," Mary declared in anxious anticipation of the shopping trip. "Mom, we've come here almost every time I've come into town. We were here five years ago, the last time I came."

As soon as she uttered those words, Mary realized how seldom she came to see her mother. However, she thought that considering her mother's state of mind, it didn't matter what she said or did, because her mother would quickly forget. An instant later, Mary's mind changed course to her shopping mission.

Lily was totally unprepared for what Mary had planned once they were inside Nordstrom.

CHAPTER 39

Mary quickly led them into a clothing area that matched her style and flare. Although she was shopping for herself, Mary held up blouses, pants, and dresses in front of her mother, hoping to fictitiously lead her mother to believe the shopping was for her. However, Lily was much smarter than that and knew that Mary's shopping enthusiasm was selfish.

After Mary spent five minutes of perusing numerous clothing racks, an experienced and sharply dressed saleswoman approached her. Upon inspecting her fine jewelry, the salesperson provided additional attention to the two ladies.

Mary quickly picked out a blouse and pants for her mother and directed her to the dressing room. Mary remained with the saleswoman. She described in meticulous detail her taste in fashion, and the saleswoman shared her knowledge of the latest trends and style tips. The two meandered through various areas of designer collections as the saleswoman pulled clothes off of the racks. Mary quickly found the closest full-length mirror to determine if the items matched her style.

Lily came out of the dressing room, outfitted in the suggested clothing, but Mary and the saleswoman were nowhere to be seen. Lily searched the store and once located, they sincerely expressed how beautiful the clothing looked on her.

Upon their approval, Lily peered at the price tag. Together the price of the two items totaled "$275.00." In the past, Lily would have never spent that much money on clothing for herself. She was too practical; however, she had no problem buying the items knowing that the "I TOLD YOU SO" painting hanging on her wall would soon be auctioned for a hefty sum of money.

"I'll take them. They do look good on me," Lily professed. She figured she might as well enjoy her money while she could.

Once she changed and reached the sales register, she handed her charge card to Mary to pay for her items and sought out a comfortable place to rest, as the shopping was already draining her energy.

Lily sat on a comfortable sofa next to a man playing a grand piano. Mary kept an eye on Lily until she was seated, after which she began moving through the clothing racks with the saleswoman in pursuit behind her.

Lily remained seated as an hour passed. Mary came back to check on her. Another hour passed, and Lily was reaching a boiling point.

Lily made a decision to sit outside of the store on a bench in the mall walkway, hoping Mary would think she was lost.

Shortly after Lily's relocation, Mary came lumbering out from the store and down the mall walkway in a panic. She was wearing a new dress, stockings, and a pair of pumps with stiletto heels. In each arm she had four large shopping bags that carried her newly acquired wardrobe.

As she ran around the mall, Mary caught a glimpse of her mother from the corner of her eye and raced in her direction.

"Mother, Mother! Where were you? I was worried sick."

Lily immediately became suspicious of Mary's purchases after seeing the shopping bags dangling under her arms.

"What happened to your other clothes, dear? These aren't the clothes or shoes you had when we came into Nordstrom's."

Mary quickly realized that her mother's memory was quite a bit sharper than she had thought.

"Can I have the receipt for my clothes?" Lily requested with a shrewd tone and an angry look. She knew what had taken place before Mary even passed her the receipt.

Mary reached in one bag, and then the next, searching from bag to bag. As her hand reached into the eighth bag, she pulled out a receipt that was at least two feet long.

"Mom thank you for buying me these beautiful clothes," insisted Mary with a hesitant, fake grin on her face. "I feel like it's Christmas. It was very nice of you to agree to buy me these clothes. This should make up for all of the past Christmas' when you didn't come to California or buy me a gift," said Mary hoping to pass some guilt onto her mother. "Are you sure you don't mind?" Mary appealed.

Lily knew before those lying words came out of Mary's lipstick-covered mouth, that she had used her charge card. Lily suspected that Mary had planned the shopping long before they arrived at the mall.

Lily looked at the receipt and was shocked by what she saw, "$4,712.42." In order to stay in character, Lily's only reaction to the astronomical total was to look up to Mary with a long stare and declare, "Clothes sure are more expensive today than they used to be, aren't they, Mary?"

Mary just smiled with a cowardly grin and quickly changed the subject in hopes that her mother would forget about what had just happened.

"Mother, I need to get you home. You need to rest," acknowledged Mary as she helped Lily to her feet and then they quickly excited the mall for the ride home.

Lily had had enough of the mall and Mary to last a long time. However, it wasn't going to be as easy to escape Mary as it had been at the mall.

CHAPTER 40

Driving slowly, Mary pulled up in front of Lily's rowhome. A parking space was available right in front of her doorstep. As they exited the car, an African American woman was sitting on her front porch steps. Mary was quite taken aback by the person sitting on the step.

Can I help you?" Mary asked in a short unpleasant tone.

"Mary, I know who this person is. She's here to help me now and when you and your sisters leave."

"Mom, I thought you wanted to move to California with me," said Mary.

"I will, if you'll take me," countered Lily, wanting to put Mary back in the right frame of mind.

Mary looked toward the aide, hoping to change the direction of the conversation.

"It is good to see you again Lee," said Lily.

"Hi, Mrs. Lily. It is good to see you again, too." Lee turned her head toward Mary. "I was interviewed by Mr. Jake Snyder and your mother last week and accepted the position." She reached out to shake Mary's hand.

Mary reluctantly shook Lee's hand and then reached back into the car to grab the clothing bags.

"Can I help you with those bags? It looks like to me you both had a good day," stated Lee.

"I think she had a real good day at my expense," conceded Lily in a low muffled voice.

At that statement, Mary turned her head and began wondering how her mother could act brilliant one minute and totally dim-witted the next.

Realizing that she may have tripped herself up, Lily quickly looked to Mary for the keys to the house. Mary handed them to her and she began to fumble with the front door as if she didn't know how to put a key in the keyhole. Lee quickly came over to offer assistance.

"Can I help you, ma'am. I sometimes have a tough time getting my keys into my front door, too. You think they would've made keys and door handle locks better by now, wouldn't you, Mrs. Lily?" expressed Lee in a calm and caring tone.

Lily had seen this same kindness on their first meeting and considered it a good sign.

"I'm sorry we weren't here at the start of your first day," declared Lily. "You know you'll be paid from the time you were supposed to start. I appreciate you staying here until we got home. How long have you been waiting?" questioned Lily as she walked into the house, followed by Mary and Lee.

"I've been waitin about two and half hours Mrs. Lily. But that's okay. I think you're gonna be worth it. I got a good feelin about you the first time we met," admitted Lee, not showing any sign of being bothered by the long wait.

Mary checked Lee up and down, taking notice of their similar age, her taller-than-average height, and her light brown skin.

"You have beautiful green eyes," acknowledged Mary, as her temperament began to change after seeing how caring Lee was to her mother.

"Are you African-American?" Mary rudely questioned.

"I'm not sure what I am," said Lee in a defensive tone. "Do you know what you are?" countered Lee in a fast-paced response to Mary's question.

"Well I'm not sure what I am, but my mother does all of the genealogy research for our family. In your time with her, why don't you ask her about it? She can go on for hours talking about her dead relatives she never knew," joked Mary.

"Well, I sure wish I knew mine, because my mother is dead and she never told me that much about my family. I guess she had her reasons," countered Lee.

Before she could get another word out, the burglar alarm on Lily's car began to go off. Mary quickly looked out the window and saw no one by Lily's car. Both Mary and Lee turned around and saw Lily trying to turn on the television with her car's key fob.

"I can't get this T.V. channel selector to work." Lily kept pressing the panic alarm on her car's key fob.

"Mom stop," yelled Mary in frustration. "You have to stop acting like this," ordered Mary as her face turned as red as a beet.

"You have some nice jewelry there," said Lee calmly trying to reduce the tension in the room. "Mrs. Lily, let's go over the things you and Jake wanted me to do during the time I spend with you," Lee said as she calmly grabbed the car key out of Lily's hand.

Lily and Lee began to review the to-do-list that they had created a few days prior. "Well I think the first thing I need to do is get to the food store and do some shopping for you Mrs. Lily," advised Lee.

The doorbell rang on the T.V. and Lily immediately sprang back into her acting role.

"Mary, will you get the front door, please? Someone's ringing the doorbell. It might be Sharon or Denise. Hurry and answer it."

"Mrs. Lily, that's not your doorbell, that's your T.V. Don't worry. You simply rest your eyes," advised Lee in a comforting voice.

Lily was now also convincing her aide that she had signs of Alzheimer's disease, knowing that she had to fool everyone to successfully implement her plan.

Mary paraded up the steps to the second floor to try on all of her newly acquired clothes and to see if there was any new jewelry she might consider wearing over the next week.

Lee made a food list after looking in the refrigerator and discussing with Lily what she liked to eat.

In reality, Lily needed Lee's help. She was tired and knew she would need assistance from this point forward, at least for part of the day. As the day progressed into the evening, Lily remained in her chair resting, not knowing what tomorrow would bring.

CHAPTER 41

The next morning the doorbell rang at 8:00 a.m. Mary quickly moved down the stairs to the front door where a small statured woman stood at the door.

"Well, who are you?" questioned Mary. "I haven't even been here three days and each day is full of new surprises," noted Mary, confused by the person standing there.

"I'm da home health aide for Lily Clarke. I'm Connie. Connie Smith, hon," said the woman. "You look familiar. Hey hon. That's some nice jewelry you got on. I think I saw some jewelry like dat at da Goodwill store last week. Deys gots some good bargains down dare to find, if ya know how da hunt. Ya know whata mean?" proclaimed Connie with her strong Baltimore accent.

"Whatever," responded Mary not fully understanding or comprehending what Connie said. Connie mentioned her jewelry and the Goodwill store in the same breath, and from Mary's standpoint, Connie was in a different economic class, even though their actual economic class was the same.

"Come on in," Mary conveyed reluctantly. "I'll bring Mom down in a few minutes. Make yourself comfortable."

Mary went upstairs to check on her mother who was already up to her crafty ways again. Prior to Mary coming up the steps, Lily had filled a cup with water at the sink. As she heard Mary coming up the stairs, she carefully knelt down next to the toilet, making it appear that she was drinking water from it. Mary looked in the bedroom and could not find her mother. She quickly walked from the bedroom into the bathroom and saw Lily beginning to drink a cup of water that she had obviously filled from the toilet.

"Mom what are you doing? Stop, Mom, stop!" Mary screamed as she rushed to Lily and removed the cup from her hand.

Lily remained silent with her head down and slight grin on her face that Mary couldn't see.

"Mom, what are you doing? You can't drink water from the toilet," pleaded Mary.

Mary reached down and carefully lifted Lily up from the toilet. "Let's get you dressed," sighed Mary as she walked with her mother into the bedroom.

In the meantime, Connie began to start the same pattern she did at every house where she worked. Knowing Mary was fully engaged with Lily on the second floor, she began going through every drawer in the living area of Lily's rowhome. Every drawer was opened, fingered through, and then closed at lightning speed. After she moved through the living area, finding nothing of significance, she quickly moved into the kitchen. Drawer by drawer, her action was swift and accurate, as if she had performed these searches a thousand times before. As she moved through the drawers, Connie became distracted, concentrating on information contained in the drawer.

Unbeknownst to Connie, Mary came down the steps looking for a bottle of hand soap for the upstairs bathroom and spotted Connie going through the drawers.

"What are you doing?" Mary barked with a sharp tongue as Connie's head popped up.

Connie's face immediately turned blood red. "I'm looking for paper and a pen to take some notes," she explained in a defensive tone.

"The paper and pen are right over there on the counter top," snapped Mary, pointing to a piece of paper and pen located a short distance away from where Connie was searching. "The next time you go into my mother's drawers without a good cause, I think your services here will no longer be needed. This is not a good start. You say your name is Mrs. Smith?"

"Yes it is. I'm sorry. It won't happen again. For sure, hon," confessed Connie. "What can I do to help your mother?"

"Go up and help her with her drawers, and stay out of them, too," Mary commanded as they proceeded through the house and up the steps.

The next few days remained rather routine for both Lily, Mary, and the aides. Mary used her iPad to stay in touch with her friends and family in California. She sent pictures of herself wearing her plundered jewelry to her husband and children. Lily was able to rest comfortably each day, while Mary began to grow restless towards the end of her stay.

CHAPTER 42

On the day before she was scheduled to head back to California, Mary grew nervous about what might happen to her mother when she returned home. Although Lily continued to act somewhat depressed, despondent, and forgetful over the course of her stay, Mary knew she had to settle a few issues before she headed home. While Lily was sleeping, Mary dialed the phone from her bedroom to speak to Jake Snyder. Jake immediately answered.

"Hi Jake. It's Mary." Mary hit the speaker button on the cell phone.

However, Lily was not sleeping as Mary had assumed and had the hearing of an elephant. Upon hearing Mary mention Jake's name, Lily got up and moved directly outside of Mary's bedroom door, worried where the conversation would lead.

Jake still had no idea of the scheme Lily was implementing and Lily grew concerned knowing that whatever Mary may say could totally upset her intended plot.

"Hi Mary. What's up? I'm on a conference call right now. How can I help you?" stated Jake in a hurried voice.

In the background, mumbling could be heard on the speaker phone in Jake's office.

"Jake, I'm concerned about my mother's health. I'm wondering what your thoughts are in regards to her coming to California to stay with me."

"You're crazy, Mary. Why would she want to do that? She doesn't know anyone there, and you have a tough enough time taking care of yourself. I don't think that would be a good idea. Who had that hare-brained idea?" grilled Jake as if he was talking to an opposing client's attorney. "I've known your mother for a long time and the last thing I think she would want to do in her condition would be to move to California."

Upon hearing that, Lily became afraid that one more inquiring question would place her whole plan in jeopardy.

"Well, that is what she said she wanted earlier in the week," countered Mary backpedaling from her previous statement.

"The week must be going better than expected Mary," answered Jake.

"What do you mean by that Jake? What did you expect when I came in?" disputed Mary as she grew disturbed by Jake's response to every raised opinion and point of view she expressed concerning her mother.

"Look, Mary, I gotta go. If you need to talk to me, call me tonight," recommended Jake as the muffled conversation on the speaker phone continued.

"I'm leaving in the morning, Jake."

"Don't plan on taking your mother. Trust me. That would be a huge mistake. I know her better than anyone. She needs to rest and enjoy her remaining days. Bye, Mary," Jake advised as he hung up the phone not letting her get in another word.

Mary quickly opened her bedroom door and saw Lily standing immediately outside the door.

"Mother, I'm leaving tomorrow. I know you wanted me to take you with me back to California. I'd love to do it, but Jake doesn't think it's a good idea. He has your best interests in mind mother."

Mary felt relieved. She would be able to head back home with her new bag of clothes and the jewelry that still clung to her body.

As the evening grew longer, Lily was helped into bed and fell fast asleep.

Early the next morning, Mary soundlessly walked into her mother's bedroom, leaned over and kissed Lily on the forehead. Her next words would be the last words she would ever say to her mother face to face.

"I'll be back again soon. I enjoyed my stay. Dave and the girls will come next time. I wish things could be different." Through the years, the few times Mary came to Baltimore, she had always repeated the same story before she left.

Lily remained motionless and pretended to sleep as she listened to Mary's every word.

As Mary exited the bedroom, Lily laid still hoping to hear Mary say, "I love you, Mom." Nothing else mattered, since her expectations of Mary's character had faded during her stay. Although Mary left Lily with a larger charge card bill than she had ever had in her life, and left with a large stash of her jewelry, none of the material losses meant anything to her.

Lily was nearing the end of her life and she simply hoped that Mary would express her love. Mary's stay had confirmed that she hadn't gotten beyond her own insecurities and materialistic traits, or gained the ability to love her mother. Once Mary left the room, Lily silently sobbed knowing Mary had failed to achieve her minimal expectations, and crazy Sharon would soon be arriving. She began to question the wisdom of her plan.

CHAPTER 43

Sharon arrived next. Lily knew that her week with Sharon would be one of the biggest physical and mental challenges of her life. She was tired from Mary's stay, and could already see small decreases in her energy levels with each passing day. Her joint pain and headaches were beginning to increase, and she was starting to take advantage of the prescribed pain medication.

Lee and Connie were in the routine of preparing meals, washing clothes, cleaning, and taking care of Lily's daily needs. On the day that Sharon was scheduled to arrive, Lee was on duty. Sharon was scheduled to arrive around noon. Lily prepared herself mentally exactly like she had prior to Mary's arrival. However, the arrival of Sharon created additional challenges for her acting role. Her aides had organized and cleaned her house, leaving Lily the inability to shock Sharon with her disheveled appearance and her home's initial disarray.

"What time are you expecting Sharon?" asked Lee.

"It's almost noon, and she should be here any minute," stated Lily. "I'm never sure what to expect from her. While she is here Lee, expect the unexpected. You need to be on guard, in case she still has her problem," confided Lily.

"What problem Mrs. Lily?"

"Some sort of drug problem. I'm not sure what, but she is always on and off whatever it is. I'm hoping that when she is here, she is not on it, so I can see my real daughter. If she is on it at her age, I'd have thought it would have killed her by now. I gave up trying to help her years ago," confessed Lily.

Lily waited with great anticipation of Sharon's arrival. In the past, when she came into town, she usually came in like a tornado and left like a hurricane, devastating everything in her path. As Lily sat, the minutes and then hours began to tick away. Lily grew tired knowing that Sharon's late arrival was an indication that she had things on her mind other than her mother. Lily immediately knew if the flight was not delayed, Sharon would arrive at her house hopped up on drugs.

Lee also had enough instinct and sense to understand what was going on, even though she had never met Sharon. However, she had seen enough addicts over her lifetime to know that Sharon would be a challenge as soon as she arrived at Lily's house.

"Mrs. Lily, I've seen and dealt with my share of drug addicts," disclosed Lee.

"Sharon is the only one I've ever known. It is so troubling seeing my daughter destroy her life and knowing I can't help her."

"They've got to learn to help themselves, Mrs. Lily. You can't do it for her. I'm afraid if she hasn't done it by now, she's never going to. How old is she Mrs. Lily?"

"She's sixty-one years old. I was married almost two years when Mary was born, and feisty Sharon was born a year after her."

"I'm six years older than Mary, Mrs. Lily. My mother spoiled me. Did you spoil her, Mrs. Lily? I thought the first child is always spoiled. I was my momma's first child and always felt special," professed Lee with a big smile.

"I don't know what happened to my girls. I guess we spoiled them by letting them leave town to go to college. That was the biggest mistake of my life based on how they turned out."

"Mrs. Lily, I'll stay as long as you want me to today to make sure you're safe," avowed Lee.

"To be honest with you Lee, I would appreciate that. The later in the day or early evening she arrives, the more I anticipate she'll be acting crazy."

As Lily was speaking to Lee, she began to realize in the short time since Mary had left, she was sounding and acting like a mentally competent person. She had stopped acting as soon as Mary had left and Lee was now witnessing another side of her. Lily looked up at Lee.

Lee looked down at Lily and could see she was not feeling well.

The day flew by, and it was almost 8:00 p.m. with no sign of Sharon. Then, Lily heard a car pull up and stop in front of her house. Inaudible loud voices came through the front window. Lee looked out the window and could see a woman leaning on an open door, screaming at the taxi cab driver.

Lee moved to the front door and opened it, knowing it was Sharon arriving in a whirlwind, exactly as Lily had predicted. As the front door opened, the woman's voice was now audible.

"Go fuck yourself, you rotten turban bastard. You fuckhead are rippin me off. Go ahead and call the cops. If you do, they'll export you back to India with all of your other 10 billion friends. Eat shit, you asshole."

As the yelling continued, Lily pointed to Lee to get her pocketbook. Lily whipped out one hundred dollars and pointed to Lee to go take care of the problem. Within two minutes, the yelling completely stopped, but Lily could overhear Lee repeatedly saying "sorry" and "thank you." Lily heard the taxi cab pull away.

The "tornado Sharon" had arrived.

The first person to walk through the door was Lee, who immediately gave Lily a wink and placed the leftover change from the taxicab fare into Lily's hand.

Banging could be heard coming through the door as Sharon dragged her suitcase up the marble steps into Lily's rowhome. She walked through the door backwards, dragging an older model suitcase. Before turning to Lily and Lee, she straightened her hair with her hands, moved them up and down her blouse to straighten it, and made sure her sleeves were covering her arms. She took a full minute to do this as if no one was behind her, but Lily was watching her every move.

"Hello. Hello, honey," blurted Lily.

Sharon, appearing anorexic, slowly turned to respond to her mother. Her jaw was open wide as she turned around. Her lips and chin appeared to be wet with drool, probably as a result of the candy she always had in her mouth. Her hair was totally gray, and the little bit of makeup that she had on was smeared around her eyes, which were more bloodshot than Lily had ever seen them.

As she approached Lily, she stumbled slightly and wiped the sweat off her face with the palm of her hand, sniffling at will. All in all, she was a wreck. It appeared that she hadn't bathed in days and her body odor was beginning to reach Lily's nose, in deep contrast to Mary's perfume.

"Thanks for helping me out, sister. Hopefully that's okay to say that, sister. I mean, you know, we're cool right?" Sharon said swaying nervously.

"I doubt if you're my sister, judging by the looks of you. If you were my sister, we'd have the same mother. Mrs. Lily, are you my mother? Did you ever gives birth to a black woman from West Baltimore," proclaimed Lee putting Sharon in a defensive mood.

Lee and Sharon both looked at Lily waiting for her to respond.

Lily hesitated a few seconds, got anxious and blurted out, "Well, we both have green eyes."

"What in the hell is that supposed to mean Mom," protested Sharon. "I think you're getting crazier by the year."

Lee kept her eyes focused on Sharon, hoping she wouldn't do anything to harm Lily in her fragile state. If she did, Lee knew she would be her protector.

"That's calling the kettle black," countered Lily as Sharon drew closer. "Where were you dear? We were worried about you."

Sharon got closer to her mother and looked directly at her with her bloodshot eyes twitching slightly, and her head moving back and forth like a flag on a light breezy day. She appeared to be contemplating what excuse she was going to use.

"I got a ride from the airport. When they picked me up they said we hadda make a stop. We stopped at their friend's house, the cops came, and we ran out the back door, and I had no idea where I was. I stayed away for a few hours in some vacant house and then picked up my suitcase from my friend's car once the coast was clear and took a taxi here. You look great, Mom. Got any food in the fridge?" asked Sharon as she got up and went into the kitchen.

Lily and Lee could hear her scurrying through the refrigerator.

"As ragged and skinny as she appeared, I'm glad she's eating. But that's about all I'm glad about," claimed Lily with a rejected look on her face. "Maybe she'll sleep it off and be better in the morning."

"Tomorrow is another day, Mrs. Lily. Once she goes to sleep, I'll make my way out of here. Okay, Mrs. Lily?"

"I appreciate all you do for me, Lee. Have you always been this way?"

"I've always tried to lead a good life. We always went to church for most of the day on Sunday and my mother always told me how lucky she was to have me. I always appreciated what I had and didn't think much or waste time worrying about what I didn't have."

"What didn't you have, Lee?" replied Lily.

"Mrs. Lily, my mother told me I was special from the day I was born. To tell ya the truth, the day I was born my mother said that."

Before Lee could finish her sentence, there was a huge crash on the kitchen floor.

"I hope and pray she didn't overdose, Mrs. Lily," voiced Lee as she quickly moved toward the kitchen.

Lily remained in the recliner, still tired from Mary's visit and the stress of worrying about Sharon's visit.

As Lee walked into the kitchen, she could see Sharon thrashing on the floor. Surrounding Sharon was the fruit from a large fruit salad that Lee had made for Lily to provide her with some healthy food.

Sharon was lying on the floor moving her arms and legs like a snow angel through the watermelon, cantaloupe, honeydew, strawberries, blueberries, and grapes. Looking at the ceiling, she laughed in delight when Lee walked in the room.

"What in the hell are you doin woman?" barked Lee sounding like a stereotypical 1950's Catholic school nun.

Sharon stopped and rolled on the floor to look up at Lee. "I think I had a little accident. But the strawberries taste great," she mumbled as she popped one in her mouth and began to slowly lift up off of the kitchen floor. "It's been one crazy day. But I'm feelin good now," Sharon assured her as the fruit juice dripped down her hair. "I think it's time for me to go to bed."

"You'll be needin a shower before you think about climbin into one of Mrs. Lily's beds," demanded Lee.

Knowing this would be the end of the first day of chaos with Sharon, Lee stared her down as she moved out of the kitchen and up the steps. Lee followed her up the steps until she reached the bathroom on the second floor.

"I'll be waiting for ya out here, Mrs. Sharon," vowed Lee.

Lee remained silent as Sharon turned on the shower.

Sharon took her time in the shower, enjoying the smell of the soap and shampoo that she remembered as a child. She felt comfortable, knowing she was in her childhood home. It wasn't a comfort she had felt in years. Her normal living spaces were usually small apartments; from which she was usually evicted after a short period of time for not paying the rent or because her friends quickly grew tired of her antics. On occasion, she was even homeless and forced to live on the streets with other drug addicts.

During her shower, Sharon opened the shower curtain and peered about the bathroom. The mirror and medicine cabinet hadn't changed since she was in college. Sharon felt a sense of tranquility knowing that for the next week she would be living in a safe and friendly environment.

She didn't want to take her drugs through the airport on her flight to Baltimore, so when she arrived in Baltimore, she needed to find heroin before arriving at her mother's house. That drug deal, including two hits of heroin was enough to last only one day. Three hits would have suited her daily needs much better.

As she continued enjoying the feel of the warm water covering her body, there was a knock at the door.

"Sharon, are you okay in there? You are taking a long time," contended Lee.

Sharon immediately turned off the shower. It had been a long day for her, and as she dried herself with the towel, she began to realize how tired she really was. The combination of heroin and travel were too much for a sixty-one-year-old drug addict.

After a few minutes, Sharon came out of the bathroom and Lee directed her to the bedroom she would occupy for the week.

"Are you stayin' here all night, Lee?" inquired Sharon.

"I'm staying here until you is asleep," declared Lee.

"I forget why I came here. I wasn't in the best shape when Mom asked me to come," Sharon let slip with a dumb look on her face.

"Well, you got all week to figure that out, don't you?" suggested Lee as she headed downstairs to take care of Lily and get her ready for bed.

Lily was sleeping silently on her recliner. Lee gently shook her awake.

"Come on, Mrs. Lily. Let's get you upstairs. You need your rest for tomorrow. Connie is on duty tomorrow and I'm on duty the day after that. However, call me if you need me. I'm only a few minutes away."

"Thank you Lee. I'm sure glad you are here. I don't know what I would have done if I hadn't found you," conceded Lily in a tired voice as she slowly lifted up off the recliner. "For some reason, I think you were meant to be here helping me."

"I'm glad I found you, too, Mrs. Lily. Now let's get you to bed," proposed Lee as they both headed up the stairs.

CHAPTER 44

As Lily lay in bed the next day, she realized that her first day with Sharon had not turned out as she had hoped. Sharon's late arrival coupled with the fruit incident did not give Lily the opportunity to engage her. She was now going to have to plan for her second day with Sharon as if it was their first day together. Lily's goal today was to convince Sharon that she had Alzheimer's disease.

As Lily began to move about, Sharon heard her, and came into Lily's bedroom.

"Good morning, Mom."

"Good morning, nurse. Am I going home today?" questioned Lily.

"It's me, Sharon, your daughter," insisted Sharon, appearing baffled and confused by her mother's state.

"Are you going to take me home, dear?"

"Mom, you are home. You're confused. Are you okay?" probed Sharon as she now became even more befuddled by her mother's responses.

"You're right, Sharon. I guess I am home. This does look like my bedroom come to think of it."

"Mom, why did you want me to come to Baltimore to see you? Did you want me to come because you get confused and forgetful sometimes?"

"I'm glad you came. I think I invited you because I've been forgetting a lot lately," acknowledged Lily, acting as weary and helpless as possible.

"Based on what I've seen so far, I think you need help."

"Do you think I should go and live with Mary, or do you think I should still be living alone? Mary took the keys to my car last week. I think I put them back in my pocketbook. No one is going to tell me I can't drive my car."

"While I'm here, I'll drive," insisted Sharon.

"Do you think I'm forgetful?" repeated Lily wanting to keep Sharon on point.

"I think something is going on with you Mom. Are you taking any drugs, because you sure are acting like it?" questioned Sharon.

Lily intentionally didn't answer Sharon's question and they both began to make their way through the house and into the kitchen. As they reached it, they saw that Connie had already arrived and had breakfast prepared.

"I'll have what she's having. I like my coffee with cream and a lot of sugar, and I'd like a lot of grape jelly on my toast. Don't burn it; I don't like it that way," ordered Sharon expecting Connie to prepare her a breakfast like Lily's.

"I'm not the butler, hon. I'm here to help your mother. If you want some food, yous got the legs the good Lord gave ya," uttered Connie.

Sharon looked disgusted at Connie, shrugged her shoulders, and moved to the refrigerator. She looked into it and then the freezer, and removed a half gallon of ice cream.

"I'll have me some of this stuff. It's the breakfast of champions," burst out Sharon as she began to laugh hysterically. Lily and Connie didn't join in the laugh, thinking it was rather disgusting to eat ice cream in the morning.

Lily cleverly picked up the newspaper and began to stare at it. She would normally read it from cover to cover, but today, after fifteen minutes of staring at it, she was hoping Sharon and Connie would clearly pick up on her mental impairment.

"Mom, you've been reading that newspaper for fifteen minutes and you haven't turned a page yet," said Sharon.

"And you haven't eaten yet either, hon," Connie added.

"What are you reading about, Mom?" Sharon snapped.

"Nothing important. The same old stuff."

"Mom, can you remember what you read?" Sharon contested.

"Remember what?" questioned Lily.

"Never mind, Mom," uttered Sharon as she made a circle around her right ear with her arm, insinuating to Connie that her mother was crazy.

Lily, in an effort to further confuse Sharon, picked up her table knife and began to eat her eggs without much success in getting the food to her mouth. Both Sharon and Connie began to take notice.

"Mom, you're using a knife to eat. Pick up the fork, Mom," said Sharon shaking her head and chuckling with Connie. "Mom, you watch FoxNews all of the time. Who do you think will be our next President?" quizzed Sharon.

"I think Richard Nixon has a lot of talent. I think he can win again. Don't you?"

Both Sharon and Connie began to laugh hysterically, which made Lily furious. Their laughing began to feed upon each other as tears began to roll down their faces.

Connie followed up in an agitating tone stating, "What year is it Lily?"

"1972, isn't it?" countered Lily.

Sharon and Connie immediately began to laugh even more uncontrollably. The laughing continued over a long minute. As each second passed, their laughing grew wilder and Lily grew angrier and angrier by the second. As Lily grew angrier, they laughed even harder.

Lily became frustrated and shocked by their sheer insensibility. She wanted to react to their utterly despicable behaving, but didn't want to give away her secret.

She began to think about what she could do to immediately settle the score. Without fully or clearly thinking, she suddenly pushed her chair away from the table. Lily slowly walked in between the two of them, seated on the opposite side of the table from where Lily had been. She slowly moved her head, looking at them both. Their laugher began to die down. Lily held onto the back of Sharon's chair with her left hand, and Connie's chair with her right hand. She squatted down a little bit, and began to urinate on the floor. Sharon and Connie were in shock at what they were witnessing. After she urinated on the floor, Lily bent down a little more, pulled down her underwear to her knees and pooped on the floor with gusto.

Sharon and Connie didn't move an inch. When she was finished, Lily straightened up her body, gently pulled up her underwear, grabbed the newspaper and marched her way upstairs into the bathroom to clean up.

Not only had she gotten even with both of the ladies, but she also convinced them that she was mentally unstable and in the advanced stages of Alzheimer's disease.

Lily cleaned herself up, went into her bedroom, sat on a chair and began to actually read the paper. Sharon came up an hour later and tried to open the door. It was locked. She didn't knock on the door, but instead went downstairs and headed out the front door.

Connie snuck up the stairs to see what Lily was doing. Behind the closed locked door, Lily continued reading the newspaper and thinking about what had occurred over the past hour. She then decided to pick up the telephone and call Jake.

Connie was still standing outside of Lily's bedroom door.

Jake immediately picked up Lily's telephone call.

Connie could hear Lily talking, but couldn't hear Jake on the other end of the telephone.

"Hi Jake. It's Lily."

"How are you feeling, Lily?" asked Jake. "Not so good today, she said. I'm sorry to say we have to fire Connie. She's been mean to me, and I don't want her coming back. She was laughing at me for, oh, never mind, Jake. She was extremely hateful to me and I don't want her here."

"I'll call the company sometime today and tell them. I'll see you when I can, Lily, and then we can talk more about your will,"

"I've been thinking about it quite a bit Jake, and I don't know what to do."

Upon hearing only Lily's part of the conversation, Connie became confused and scared all at the same time.

"How could this woman who was so incoherent an hour ago, now be sounding like a normal person?" Connie thought to herself.

Connie went downstairs while Lily and Jake finished their conversation. She grabbed her purse and began her quick exit. Before she reached the front door, she saw Lily's purse sitting on the floor next to her recliner. She quickly grabbed a large portion of the twenty dollar bills stuffed in Lily's wallet and bolted out the front door, never to be seen or heard from again.

CHAPTER 45

Sharon's third day at Lily's house began at the crack of dawn. Lily could hear Sharon scuffling around downstairs. Lily felt unsettled, knowing Lee wasn't scheduled to come until mid-afternoon. Not knowing what Sharon was doing, Lily got up and went downstairs. As she approached the kitchen, she saw Sharon nervously pacing.

"Mom, I gotta get out of here and run an errand. I need to run out and pick up a prescription. Don't worry, I won't be gone long. I'm gonna write you a note telling you where I'm going," pledged Sharon as she tapped her hand on the table like a woodpecker on a tree. "I'm taking your car to run the errand. It will be good to put a few miles on it since you never drive it. No sense in letting it sit."

"I want to go with you, Sharon. I haven't been out of this damn house in so long, and you're not going without me," insisted Lily.

Sharon stopped what she was doing and looked up at her mother.

"Okay, you want to go with me, huh. Well why not? Suit yourself, Mom," Sharon grumbled. "If I take you, you won't know where we're going or remember where we went anyway," Sharon mumbled under her breath.

Sharon needed to hurry out of the house to pick up her hits of heroin from the neighborhood drug dealer. She hadn't had a shot of heroin since yesterday and her patience was in short supply.

"Let's go, Mom," Sharon uttered as they headed out of Lily's house and into Lily's red 2005 Toyota Camry.

As they got into the car, Lily felt uneasy, even though Sharon told her they were only making one stop at a local pharmacy. Little did Lily know, Sharon's targeted destination was a curb side pharmacy in a drug infested neighborhood located a short distance from Lily's house.

Pulaski Highway, a four lane road that ran through Baltimore City, was an invisible divide between middle and low income residents. On the south side of Pulaski highway, the neighborhoods were housed with young professionals, college students, Starbucks coffee shops and Panera Breads. On the north side of Pulaski Highway, it looked like a war zone in most places, with low-income residents and abandoned houses. Children, grandmothers, and neighborhood residents involved in the drug trade were often shot; it was an unfortunate part of life for the residents stuck living in this section of Baltimore.

Lily lived on the south side of Pulaski Highway. In less than five minutes, Sharon had driven the car across the invisible divide. She was now driving through neighborhoods that were the entire opposite of the neighborhood they had just left. Lily quickly became worried as they drove further into this deteriorating section of Baltimore.

"Where are we going, Sharon?" probed Lily.

"Mom, we're going where I told you I was going before," said Sharon.

As they came to a full stop at the next corner intersection, the teenagers on the corner looked at them.

"They're staring at us."

"We'll be there soon, Mom. I was here two days ago. I think I know where I'm going," reassured Sharon as she continued to tap nervously on the steering wheel.

"I don't think there are any pharmacies over here honey, only Chinese carry outs and Korean grocery stores. I don't think they have pharmacies," challenged Lily, trying to sway Sharon to change the direction of the car.

Sharon hit the brakes of the car, stopping it in the middle of block and looked at Lily with a deadly stare.

"Good job remembering, Mom."

She then hit the accelerator and made a sharp right hand at an intersection.

Lily became terrified as she came to realize true intent of Sharon's trip. She closed her eyes as the car continued to make right turn after right turn, as it circled the block.

Sharon slowed the car to a stop and lowered the driver's side window. A young black man standing on the corner approached the car in a quick rocking motion, walking like the Stay Puff Marshmallow man in the movie "Ghostbusters", in an effort to keep his pants from falling below his knees.

"What you and great grandma doin' round here?" questioned the young man.

"I'm lookin' for some candy for today and tomorrow," divulged Sharon.

"Well yous come to da right place," verified the young man.

Sharon handed him a small roll of cash, concealing her money the best she could. It was money she had taken from her mother's pocketbook the day before, prior to Connie's heist. Upon grabbing the cash, the young man turned and began to quickly run away.

Sharon began to yell, but before she could get a sound out, the young man turned around with a big smile as he rocked back toward the car.

"Just kiddin' grandma. Here's ya damn Medicare smack," teased the young man.

Sharon looked at the four small bags of heroin the young dealer had placed in her hand. She gave a nod of her head to the dealer and hit the accelerator. Lily still had her eyes covered; she couldn't believe what her daughter had just put her through. She couldn't believe that her daughter would place her in such danger at this point in her life.

As Sharon was speeding away, Lily finally opened her eyes to get a bearing of their location. She was happy to know that Sharon was heading back to their house, but unhappy to see the heroin sitting in the center console of her car.

"I'm glad you won't remember any of this by the time we get back to your house. I'm sorry I brought you here, but I truly didn't have a choice. I'm an addict Mom and have been on and off for thirty years. It wasn't your fault. I can barely deal with the difficulties I've had in my life, and the drugs take away the pain."

Sharon drove Lily's car right through a stop sign within sight of a Baltimore City Police K-9 patrol car that was parked on a perpendicular street corner. As soon as she passed the intersection, a police siren began blaring loudly as the patrol car quickly pulled up directly behind their car. Their car was only four blocks away from crossing Pulaski Highway to the safer section of Baltimore.

CHAPTER 46

As the Baltimore City police car parked behind their car, panic set in.

"Oh shit, motherfuck. If the cop finds these drugs, I'm gonna do some time. Oh God!" Sharon burst out. She kept her body fairly still, but kept her mouth moving one hundred miles an hour in her alarmed state of mind.

Sharon reached down in her panic and grabbed the small bags of heroin that were sitting in the car's center console. In one swift motion Sharon pulled on the front of Lily pants and underwear and shoved the bags of heroin into them.

Sharon looked in the rear view mirror and could see the police officer and his Labrador Retriever. The dog was sitting in the caged section, in the back of the patrol car. Sharon was hoping the police officer wouldn't bring the drug sniffing dog up to their car or else she and her mother would probably get arrested for possession of drugs and the car would be impounded.

"Act retarded if you wanna go home today," advised Sharon as the police officer got out of his patrol car and slowly walked towards the driver's side door.

Sharon wound down the window.

"Know what you did?" questioned the policeman in a serious tone.

He stood more than six feet five inches tall, and appeared more like a National Football League football player than a policeman.

Sharon nervously responded, "Yeah, officer. I'm trying to get my mother to her medical treatment at Johns Hopkins Hospital and I think I took a wrong turn. I'm lost, officer. Are you okay Mom? Don't cry. She has Alzheimer's and is dying of some other disease that I'm not sure of," said Sharon not knowing that half of what she said was actually true. "That's why I'm taking her to Johns Hopkins Hospital. She's dying for sure. Ain't you Mom?"

"Let me see your driver's license and registration." requested the officer, without changing his tough, no nonsense expression.

Stalling for time, Sharon commented to the officer, "That sure is a pretty dog you have. What's the dog's name?" she uttered as she tried to sidetrack the officer.

"His name is Coco, because he can find cocaine and any other drugs with ease. He's the best," the officer boasted as he looked proudly back at his patrol car. Coco could be seen obediently and anxiously waiting for the police officer's return or his next command. "I'll go get him and show him to your mother. That might make her feel better. Dogs do that, ya know?" His demeanor changed; he began to appear more relaxed and a slight smile appeared on his face.

"Have your license and registration ready when I come back," ordered the officer as he moved slowly back to his car to retrieve Coco.

Sharon was in a full-fledged panic.

"Mom, I don't have a driver's license. Repeat Mother, I don't have a driver's license. I think I'm gonna run Mom, I gotta get out of here," Sharon indicated as she began hyperventilating.

Having never been in this or a similar situation, Lily didn't know how to react. Sharon may have run when she was younger, but being sixty-one years of age, she quickly realized that if she ran, she wouldn't get very far.

"Give me your license. That'll work. I look like you. Don't I?" Sharon began to quickly fumble through Lily's wallet.

Lily was stunned, not knowing what to do, and sat perfectly still in the car while the chaos ensued around her.

The police officer reached into his patrol car and tugged Coco out of the patrol car. Coco's tailed wagged as the officer and Coco moved toward the car.

"Oh shit. Here comes the damn dog," blurted Sharon. "We're fucked big time," she vented in a panicked whisper, as her body remained as motionless as possible.

The police officer moved toward Lily's car. As he reached the car, he grabbed the passenger side door knob and slowly opened the passenger side door, where Lily was seated. As soon as the door swung open wide enough for the dog to enter, the dog's head and long nose swiftly plunged between Lily's legs.

The police officer quickly noticed the movement of his prized dog.

Suddenly, loud gun shots could be heard around the corner. Lily, Sharon, and the police officer looked in the direction of the shots to see three young African American men, including the man who had sold Sharon the drugs, run quickly through the intersection and down a perpendicular street. The man who sold the heroin to Sharon struggled running, as he continued pulling up his low hanging pants with each step he took.

Another man appeared in the intersection trailing behind them, with a gun pointed directly at the three men, firing at will.

The police officer looked at Lily and Sharon and snapped, "Gotta go. Look after my dog while I'm gone."

He handed Lily the dog's leash. The police officer took off running after the drug dealers as the dog's snout remained buried in Lily's crotch.

"What should we do now?" questioned Lily as she began to laugh at their situation.

Sharon remained in a panic tapping her hand nervously on the steering wheel. Sirens could be heard in the background heading in their direction.

"I'm gonna put the dog back in the car. I think that's what I'm gonna do," babbled Sharon whose face was blood red.

Sharon quickly got out of the car, moved to the passenger side and grabbed the police dog's leash, yanking Coco away from Lily. She raced Coco back to the police car, looking like a trainer parading a dog in the Westminster Dog Show. She quickly placed the dog in the back seat of the patrol car and closed the police car door.

It was a hot summer morning and was going to be a hot day. Sharon became concerned about the dog's health.

"If I leave Coco in the patrol car unattended, the heat may kill the damn dog," she yelled to her mother.

She smashed the front passenger window of the police car, knowing that the dog couldn't escape the enclosed cage in the back seat of the patrol car.

After her demolition had the intended outcome, Sharon ran back to her mother's car, got in and hit the accelerator, driving the car away as quickly as she could; running through another stop sign at the next intersection. Sharon could hear and see three additional police cars whizzing through another intersection in her rear view mirror, heading in the direction of the shooting.

Sharon continued to speed away, reaching Lily's house in a few short minutes. She pulled the car into a parking spot a few doors away from Lily's front door, turned off the car, and hastily exited the car.

"I'll see ya in the house Mom," declared Sharon as she ran into the house to shoot up the heroin.

Lily remained seated in the car exhausted by the events of the morning. Soon the car door began to open. Much to her surprise, Lee was standing there.

"What are you doing here, Lee? You weren't supposed to be here for another five hours," exclaimed Lily.

"Mrs. Lily, I woke up thinking about you and I had a funny feeling in my stomach. Mrs. Lily, the good Lord told me to come and see you. So here I am. Are you okay, Mrs. Lily? You look worn out and it is only noon."

"It was an interesting morning to say the least. Please help me in and keep an eye on Sharon to make sure she's okay. God bless you, Lee."

Lee helped Lily into the house and got her settled into her recliner. As soon as Lily was comfortable and resting, Lee went into the kitchen and began cleaning up the mess Sharon had created minutes earlier.

Lily now knew beyond a reasonable doubt that her daughter was still a drug addict. She wasn't sure what the next day would bring, but she knew she already had spent an adequate amount of time with Sharon to determine her true character, and Sharon still had four days remaining of her visit. Lily wasn't sure she could physically survive four more days with Sharon. The way she felt, she thought it was possible that the stress Sharon was putting on her fragile body might kill her before the week's end.

The rest of the day passed uneventfully since Sharon had enough heroin to last the next forty-eight hours.

CHAPTER 47

After all the commotion Sharon had caused, she was determined to start behaving better for her mother's sake. However, as the day began, she had a problem; she only had enough heroin to get her through the day. She contemplated how to raise capital for her next heroin fix.

After Sharon and Lily finished breakfast, Lily settled in for a restful day in her recliner. She watched FoxNews as Sharon paced around behind Lily, looking for a solution to her drug habit. Lee was not scheduled to arrive until the afternoon.

"I bet I can find something valuable in the basement. Mom will never miss it," Sharon muttered to herself as she immediately moved toward the basement door that was located in the kitchen. She hadn't been down there in more than twenty-five years.

The unfinished basement felt and looked like a time warp to Sharon. Her father's workbench stood exactly as she remembered it. A dehumidifier hummed off in the corner; her father had always stressed that he didn't like humidity in the basement, though she never knew why. The washer, dryer, and steel laundry tub sat in the back of the basement, just as she remembered. The basement toilet sat all by itself in a back corner, without any walls or doors, exposing an open air view of the entire basement.

"Time has passed me by, and yet some things still remain the same," she thought.

After staring at the room for a few seconds, Sharon quickly got back to the task of trying to pilfer a few items from it. She peered around the room and suddenly focused her attention on her father's hand crafted, half a century old work bench to see what she could find.

Sharon began going through the workbench looking for anything that would provide a means for her to raise quick cash. As she opened a drawer, she could see an old knife from what Sharon assumed was from the Vietnam War or World War II.

Sharon mulled over how easy it would be to sell the knife at a pawn shop. She placed the knife on top of the workbench and began looking through other drawers.

As Sharon bent down to pull out a lower drawer, her arm hit the knife, knocking it to the ground. As she bent down to pick it up, she could see a small open slot in the back of the workbench.

Sharon peered through it for a few seconds trying to determine what was inside. However, she was unable to get a clear view.

Lily began calling her loudly from the top of the stairs.

"Sharon, hurry, I need you," cried Lily.

Sharon laid the still lit flashlight on the workbench, grabbed her knife and moved up the stairs hearing her mother saying loudly, "Sharon, Sharon, help me please."

As Sharon entered the kitchen from the basement steps, her mother was nowhere to be seen. She placed the old knife on the kitchen table and continued searching.

Lily sat resting on her recliner, her shirt soaked from a self-induced iced tea spill. Lily knew that Sharon was wandering through the basement for too long, and she became concerned Sharon might locate the hidden paintings.

"What's wrong with you, Mom?" moaned Sharon.

"I spilled my iced tea and need some paper towels."

"You called me all the way up from the basement just for that?" chided Sharon.

"I'm sorry, dear. My clothes are soaked."

Sharon ran into the kitchen and grabbed paper towels. Lily was satisfied that Sharon was no longer in the basement.

Sharon rushed back to Lily's recliner to help her soak up the spill, but her addict's mind remained on the task of trying to raise cash.

"Mom, I can't believe Daddy never finished the basement. It looks exactly the same as it did when I left for college."

"It's an antique, like every item you see in this house, including me," boasted Lily.

As soon as she said that, Sharon's eyes began to move around the room looking for antiques or items of value.

As she peered around the room, her eyes came across a painting, which had been hanging on the wall for as long as she could remember.

"Where did you get that old painting Mom? Is it an antique? It must be since I'm an antique, too, and it's older than me."

Lily was concerned that Sharon was asking about her million dollar painting hanging on the wall.

"I don't know anything about that painting, dear. I think we bought it at the Five & Dime store for $2.00 back in 1952. I actually don't know dear. -How are you feeling today, Sharon?" asked Lily attempting to get Sharon to change the subject.

Sharon said nothing for a few seconds, as she stared at the painting wondering how much she could get for it at a local pawn shop.

"Oh, Mom, I'm feeling much better now. I think you're helping me more than I'm helping you." Sharon said as she continued to stare at the painting like a cat setting its sight on a mouse.

"In my state, I don't think I can help anyone," complained Lily. "I spilled my drink because of my prescription medicine. It makes me tired sometimes and then I start dropping things."

"Oh, I didn't know you were taking medicine," commented Sharon now realizing that there were prescription drugs in the house.

Lily totally missed that she had tipped off a drug addict. However, even with those words Sharon remained focused on the painting that was hanging right in front of her, not knowing which drugs her mother was taking.

"Mom, you need your rest. I'll turn up the volume on FoxNews and you can get a little rest."

Over the next hour, Lily and Sharon sat watching television. Sharon kept her eye on Lily's awakened state. It was becoming late morning and it was time for Lily's customary nap, which she took every day, even when she was healthy.

Lily slowly dozed off. Sharon watched closely, waiting until she knew that her mother was in a sound asleep.

Sharon slowly raised up from her chair and eased into the kitchen, she grabbed the aged knife she discovered in the basement and grabbed a trash large bag from under the kitchen sink. She stopped in front of the "I TOLD YOU SO" painting and removed it from the wall.

She immediately headed out the front door of Lily's house. Once outside, she set the painting's edge on the sidewalk and placed a garbage bag over it before sitting it on the front seat of her mother's car.

She drove off, and immediately began a search on her cell phone to locate the closest pawn shop.

As she pulled up to the pawn shop that sat on the corner of Pulaski Highway and Rose Street, she could see its name in big red letters, "CITY PAWN."

Just then, her mother was beginning to awaken from her short nap.

CHAPTER 48

"Sharon! Sharon!" Lily pronounced loudly.

Sharon didn't answer.

"Sharon, are you here?" Lily shouted with concern.

As Lily began to stand up from her recliner, she immediately noticed the bare spot on the wall where her prized painting, "I TOLD YOU SO" had been hanging.

Seeing the painting missing from the wall hit Lily like a gunshot to her stomach. She immediately became short of breath and doubled over trying to catch her breath.

"Oh my God. She didn't!" Lily burst out as she absorbed what had taken place.

She searched the first level of the house in a futile attempt to locate the painting. Then she looked out her front window and noticed her car was also missing. She was beside herself and began to cry knowing what had taken place.

"I'm a failure, Frank. I never thought she would have done this, not in a million years. Where did we go wrong, Frank?"

Lily reached for her telephone and called Jake to try to determine what to do.

At the same time, about one mile away, Sharon grabbed her purse and the wrapped painting, exited the car and rang the buzzer of the heavy gated and fortified City Pawn storefront. The door lock buzzed, allowing her to enter. As she moved into the store, Sharon's eyes moved back and forth observing the guns and large construction tools that filled the glass display cases. As she walked up to the counter, she peered at the dozens of knives displayed in the glass counter.

"Hey," stated a large dark skinned African American woman, sitting behind the counter; her head bobbing up and down to the rap music that was playing over the store's sound system. She was sitting on a high top stool, leaning over the counter with a body hugging tube top exposing a significant portion of her large breasts. Tattoos dotted the exposed skin of her chest and arms. Her big gold earrings swung back and forward as she moved her head.

"Whats you got?" probed the woman.

"I gots, I mean got this knife from World War II. I think my father always told me it came off a dead German he killed somewhere over there, way back when," Sharon hesitantly claimed, attempting to get her best deal.

"Can I see it? As you can see, I know my knives," bragged the woman.

After the woman inspected the knife for a quick minute, she disputed Sharon's claim. "This knife came from a Sunny Surplus store back in the 70s. Either you or your Dad are good liars because it wasn't used to kill no German."

Sharon was surprised by the woman's frankness and knowledge of knives.

The woman proposed, "I'll give you $25.00 for it. Someone will want it because it looks like an old knife. We sell a least ten or so knives a week," boasted the woman in a decisive manner.

Sharon's shoulders slumped in disappointment.

"What you got next?" questioned the woman in eager anticipation of what was in the garbage bag.

Sharon removed the painting from the plastic bag and placed it directly on top of the counter. The woman looked at it and immediately began to laugh at the subject matter of the painting and the fact that someone was bringing in what looked like an original painting to pawn in her neighborhood.

"Baby, do you know how many people in this neighborhood will want a painting like this, of a white boy with a lobster stuck on his finger? Baby, most people in this neighborhood ain't never seen a lobster much less want to hang it and a white boy on their damn wall. Yous crazy lady for wanting to bring in this painting," explained the woman humorously. "Ma Man Rashid in the back there might know a little bit about paintings, but he's tied up on some eBay sale right now," pronounced the woman looking at a man sitting behind a glass window, staring at a computer screen.

Sharon sat silently contemplating if she was going to get an offer for the painting. She was hoping for a generous offer of a few hundred dollars.

"I'll tell you what. I'll give you twenty-five dollars for the painting, not knowing anything about it and hoping I can sell it on eBay."

"I was hoping for three hundred dollars," admitted Sharon.

"Baby, yous is one crazy white lady," declared the woman in a hysterical laugh. "I got about as much of a chance of selling that painting, as I do getting into your skinny ass clothes."

Sharon smiled tightly at her comments as she became irritated at the cut-rate offers she was receiving for both items.

"Twenty-five is all I can give you. Sorry baby," maintained the woman in a more business like tone knowing the offer and sale was going nowhere.

Sharon looked at the painting and slowly moved it toward the woman as if accepting the offered price. The woman placed her hand on the one side of the frame and then moved her other hand to the other side of it. Sharon had not yet let go either of her hands, as she was still indecisive. Both women were slowly nodding their heads like the sale was almost a done deal. As the pawn store woman began to pull the painting toward her to acknowledge that the sale was complete, Sharon obnoxiously and abruptly tugged back the painting. The pawn shop woman's hand offered little resistance to Sharon's tug of the painting.

"I can't sell it for twenty-five dollars. I can't. I truthfully can't," objected Sharon as her arms and hands began to nervously tremble.

"If you want to wait around, I can see if Rashid will give you more," advised the woman.

Sharon crankily countered, "I'm done. I'm done. I want to get out of here. Give me my twenty-five dollars for the knife and I'll go," she moaned, nervously swaying from side to side, as she began to feel the guilt from trying to sell her mother's painting. She now began to feel spasmodic, knowing she was still short of cash for her next drug buy.

The woman gave Sharon the cash for the knife and Sharon quickly covered the painting with the garbage bag and headed toward the door. As she got halfway to the door, the man in the back room had completed his sale and was moving toward the display counter.

"Hey, baby?" yelled the woman addressing Sharon in a loud voice. "You wanna come back and I'll have Rashid take a look at that cheap ass painting you got in the garbage bag?"

Sharon turned, looked at Rashid, looked down at the painting covered by the plastic bag.

"No, thank you. I think my mom wants to keep it," said Sharon in a rejected voice with her head down and shoulders slumped over as she headed out the door.

Sharon drove home and rushed into Lily's house with the painting under her arm in hopes she would still be asleep. Unfortunately for her, that was not the case. As she entered Lily's house, she carefully laid the painting on the floor, under the location where it had previously hung. She ran around looking for her mother. She briefly stopped and looked at the workbench to consider searching to see what was behind it. However, in her panic, she rushed up the basement stairs trying to determine her next steps.

She saw a scribbled note on the kitchen table saying "Sharon, out looking for you with Jake, Mom."

Sharon sat for a minute contemplating her next steps. She then sprang into action, going from one kitchen drawer to another, opening it and closing it. She did this over and over, looking for the prescription drugs her mother mentioned earlier in the day.

Sharon looked down at her cell phone that had been on a silent mode and saw that her mother had called her numerous times. She put the phone back in her purse and continued her vigorous search. She ran upstairs and began to ransack her mother's bedroom for prescriptions. Not finding anything in her mother's drawers, she began going through her father's drawers. As Sharon tugged on her father's second drawer, she could hear a different sound than she was accustomed to. Inside the drawer was a treasure trove of her mother's medications.

"Thank you Daddy," she screamed as she ran and got her suitcase and began to stuff the pills into it, looking at each medication before she threw it in her bag. There were pill casings loaded with what appeared to be morphine, hydrocodone, oxycodone, and methadone. Sharon never had this large of a supply of prescription pills in her entire life. She could use them or sell them. Between the drugs and her monthly Medicaid check, she calculated that she had enough disposable assets to cover her needs for the foreseeable future.

Sharon packed her bags, stuffed a few pieces of her mother's jewelry in the bag that she thought she could sell in a pawn shop, and headed to the kitchen.

She took the note that her mother wrote to her, turned it over and scribbled, "I'm sorry Mom. I never got over you letting Mary marry Dave. It ruined my life. Sharon."

Next, she grabbed her bag and headed out the door, back to her home town of Chicago, Illinois. Sharon would never physically see or talk to her mother again.

Two hours later, Lily pulled up to the house with Jake. Lee was sitting on the front step. She could see that Lily was overwhelmed and shaken.

"Are you okay, Mrs. Lily?" inquired Lee.

"Have you seen Sharon?" questioned Lily.

"No mam Mrs. Lily. I've been waitin here for about 90 minutes and haven't seen a soul."

Lily, Lee, and Jake moved into Lily's house. Lily saw immediately that her painting was sitting on the ground right below its position on the wall, with a garbage bag hanging loosely from it.

Lily looked at Jake as they both acknowledged the painting was still safe. However, it was a sober acknowledgement. It was not a happy occasion.

"Take it with you when you leave and do with it what we agreed. We should get a good price for it at the auction."

Jake shook his head in agreement acknowledging Lily's wish.

Jake moved into the kitchen and yelled, "Sharon! Sharon! Are you here?"

There was only silence.

Lily eased back into her recliner and collapsed from the impact of Sharon's stress on her leukemia-ridden body.

Lee saw a note on the table, silently read it, and handed it to Jake for him to consider reading it to Lily.

"Do you think we should let Lily see it?" Jake debated cautiously to Lee.

"In the time that I've been here, Mr. Snyder, I've noticed Mrs. Lily acts real forgetful when her daughters are around, and then other times when they're not here, she's as smart as a switch on my butt. I'm not sure what's goin' on with her, but I think you gotta give it to her. I don't think it's for me or you to decide. I'm real fond of Mrs. Lily and don't know what happened between them girls. But she's the one who has to be at peace. Not us."

Jake reached over and gave Lee a hug.

"I'm sure glad we hired you, Lee. Lily needs someone strong like you now. You know we lost Connie yesterday. She's no longer working here and we are short on staff, and Lily may be short on time the way things are going. I want you to think about moving in with Lily for the next few months. I know you're retired, have Social Security, and don't need the money; but I'll pay you around the clock to be with Lily for the next few months. Let's say four months. If you need to go home, simply keep track of your hours. I trust you, or I should say, Lily trusts you and that's all that truly counts."

Lee appeared surprised by Connie's firing, and she was taken aback by the request to live with Lily for a few months.

"I'll think about it, Mr. Jake. Let's get this note to her before she falls into a deep sleep. I can't take holding it in my hand anymore knowing it's going to make her feel bad."

"Could you give it to her?" Jake said. "I think it will be better coming from a woman. I'm not a softy."

Lee walked into the living room where Lily sat on the recliner with the television blaring. Lee hit the mute button and looked at the exhausted woman resting in front of her.

"Mrs. Lily, Sharon left you a note. In truth, I don't want to give it to you, but I think you need to see it," Lee spsaid calmly.

Lee handed Lily the note. Lily read it and continued to stare at it. She began to sob and weep. Lee bent down and hugged Lily to make her feel better. Lily wouldn't let go. Lee slowly kneeled in front of Lily. They hugged for a long time until Lily stopped sobbing and eventually slowly let go of Lee. They looked each other in the eye and Lee confessed, "You gotta help me up. I'm think I'm stuck."

They both began laughing out loud as they began to ponder how to get Lee out of her predicament at the foot of Lily's recliner.

CHAPTER 49

With the sudden exit of Sharon and Connie, Lily and Lee were left on their own. Lily had three and a half days to gather her thoughts and get her house in order before Denise's arrival.

A few hours after Sharon's quick exit, Lee began to clean up the kitchen. Lily also sat in the kitchen with Lee, sipping on a cup of afternoon tea.

"Mrs. Lily, you're a good supervisor keepin' a watch over me while I clean up this kitchen."

"While you're here Lee, Lo que es mío es tuyo, y lo que es la suya en la mía."

"Say what, Mrs. Lily?" Lee blurted as she began to laugh.

"I said, while you're here, what's mine is yours, and what's yours is mine. You never heard that saying?"

"Not in my neighborhood. I know some Korean from going to the corner store, but not Spanish. The Mexicans are too afraid to come to my neighborhood. The Koreans like our money and they ain't afraid to come and get it. I think I'd be more afraid in their neighborhood than they'd be in mine."

"Why would you be afraid in their neighborhood, Lee?"

"You know they eat dogs in Korea. If I take my daughter's dog through their neighborhood, there's no tellin' what might happen to it," concluded Lee as they both laughed hysterically.

"Mrs. Lily, between Sharon makin' a little mess in the kitchen and a big mess upstairs, do you think she made a mess in the basement? Do you want me to check the basement?"

"Please go down there Lee and see what she may have done."

"Okay Mrs. Lily," answered Lee as she began walking down into the basement and then right back up the basement steps.

"Mrs. Lily, it doesn't look like she did anything other than disturb the workbench down there. It sure is a pretty workbench. I had to bend down the whole time I was down there because I felt like I was going to hit my head. How come you never finished the basement other than that pretty workbench?"

"That's how all of the rowhomes' basements were around here Lee. When they designed them, the only reason people had basements was to store coal for the furnace and to do the laundry. Frank always had to bend over when he was down there, as did almost all of the other men in the neighborhood. We lived simply and never thought about finishing it because the ceiling is so low. We never spent time in the basement years ago like people do today."

"All of the rentals I've lived in are the same way, Mrs. Lily."

"You've never owned your home Lee? Paying rent is a waste of money. You need to own your own home," asserted Lily.

"I think I'm too old to own my own home, Mrs. Lily. If I did, it wouldn't be paid off until I was almost one hundred years old."

"Well Lee, if you ever end up owning one of these rowhomes, I'd recommend you spend some money and have a contractor dig out the basement. The young ones moving into the neighborhoods around here are all digging out the basements, making them deeper and repouring the concrete slab. It gives them almost one third more living space and increases the value if they ever sell it. I think I'm still one of the only basements left around here where the gas and electric meter readers and the washer and dryer repair people hit their heads on the ceiling once or twice before they leave."

"Well Mrs. Lily, if I ever get one of these rowhomes, which I think you have a better chance of turning black like me than I do of owning one of these nice rowhomes down here by the park, I'd definitely have the basement dug deeper, so I didn't feel like I was goin' to hit my head each time I went in it," maintained Lee.

"You're not that dark, Lee. Maybe you're well on your way to owning one of them," kidded Lily.

"Mrs. Lily, I'm goin' to call the police and have them come and file a police report so that you can get your prescriptions refilled. Are you sure you want to file a police report on Sharon?"

"I don't think I have a choice Lee. If I don't, I don't think they'll let me refill my prescriptions and I definitely need them for my headaches and joint pain," indicated Lily as she began to rub her hand across her forehead.

"If you don't mind me askin', what's goin' on with you Mrs. Lily, with your health I mean?"

"Well Lee. I'll tell you more after Denise comes and goes. I want you to know that when she comes, don't ask me any questions about how I'm behaving. I'll fill you in on my crazy antics at some point in the future."

"Okay, Mrs. Lily. I trust you, but what you said sure makes me confused because you sure can act senseless sometimes. It seems to me, just like that painting hanging on your wall, you're doin a good job of painting deception."

"It makes me confused, too, Lee. All I think I am doing is deceiving myself," confessed Lily. "If you think you're confused now, you ain't seen nothing yet. Wait till Denise comes into town. She'll probably make both of our heads spin at the same time. I think she may be the biggest surprise of all."

CHAPTER 50

The next three days Lily and Lee spent together were some of the most relaxing and tranquil days Lily had spent since she had been diagnosed with leukemia. However, Denise's arrival was now at hand, and Lily was beginning to feel anxious.

Lily spent most of her time resting in her recliner, but her mind remained as sharp as a tack. Over the three days before Denise's arrival, Lily and Lee began to delve into deeper conversations about their perspectives on life and love.

"So why does your youngest daughter still live with you Lee," inquired Lily.

"Well, it's hard to find a good man in Baltimore City. They is either dead, dealing drugs, or can't find a job. It's hard. If my momma was still alive, she'd probably tell me I didn't teach my daughters the Rule of Three."

"What's the Rule of Three?" inquired Lily.

"My momma had this rule she taught me and the women in the neighborhood. And she was always right about it. The rule of three goes like this: A woman gots to have two of three things if she wants to attract a man. That's right, two of three to attract him and keep him. First you gotta take care of him," Lee pronounced as she held her index finger in the air.

"Second, you gotta be good looking," she expressed as she held up her middle finger.

"And third you gotta give him good sex," said Lee as she began to laugh and rock her hips back and forth in a sexual movement.

"If you're taking care of him and you're as ugly as a dog, you better be givin' him good sex, or you ain't gonna keep him. If you're taking care of him and you look like Beyonce, you don't have to lay down with him if you don't want to, cause he'll stick around. And if you look like Beyonce and give him good sex, you don't have to take care of him. He'll cook, he'll clean, and he'll act perfectly like a little puppy dog. That's what my momma used to say," uttered Lee as they continued to laugh hysterically.

"I had someone tell me something like that a long time ago too," insisted Lily.

With that, there was a strong, loud knock at the front door that startled both Lily and Lee.

As Lee moved quickly to the door, she turned and asked Lily in a low tone, "Are you goin' to start playin' dumb again Mrs. Lily?"

Lily nodded her head in an embarrassed fashion and shrugged her shoulders showing Lee the discomfort she had being deceitful to her daughters.

As Lee opened the door, a stout person with tight short black hair, a pair of blue jeans and long sleeve white flannel shirt that was tucked in their jeans stood before her.

Lee quickly looked her up and down and admired her new pair of blue corduroy deck shoes.

"Can I help you?" questioned Lee expecting to see Lily's daughter Denise at the door.

"I'm here to see my mom," replied the person in a deep masculine voice.

At this point, Lee became very confused. She was expecting to see a woman at the front door, but the person had the appearance of a man. Lee quickly looked the person up and down again and reluctantly let the person into the house.

"Mrs. Lily, someone's here to see you," Lee announced cautiously.

As the person grabbed their large carry-on bag and moved through the front door, Lily got her first look at her daughter Denise. She squinted her eyes, as if unable to fully see the person in front of her and she put on her glasses.

"Oh, Denise. It is you," Lily answered perplexed by her daughter's appearance, even though she was truly happy to see her again. "Come over and give me a hug," said Lily as she reached out her open arms to her daughter.

Denise quickly and fearlessly responded. "Mom, I want you to know I'm going by a different name now; I'd like you to call me Denny," he said wanting to get his new sexual identity out in the open at the very start of his visit.

"Okay Dear. Okay Denni," stated Lily as she said the word and mulled over in her mind the correct spelling of her daughter's new name. "Is that D E N N I or D E N N Y honey?"

"It's D E N N Y Mom. The way a man spells it," voiced Denny adamantly.

"It makes my heart happy to see that you look content and self-confident," professed Lily.

"I'm happier now Mom than I've ever been. You know I always felt different from everybody else. I always felt that people looked at me not for who I was, but what they wanted me to be. I'm only sorry it took me about sixty years to get here," explained Denny.

"You were always beautiful to me Denny," conceded Lily.

"Mom, you were very understanding, but Daddy never was. I'm not sure if it was because I was the last daughter and wasn't a boy, or because I was a girl and always acted like a boy. Daddy was always insensitive to my dreams and aspirations. We never seemed to be on the same page, and I always felt like I was a big disappointment to him."

"Well, the times have changed, Denny," acknowledged Lily. "If you would have been born today, it would have been different. Daddy and everyone else would have been much more accepting and broad-minded to your desires and needs, whatever they might have been."

"I guess, for some things, but surely not everything," hinted Denny.

"What do you mean dear?"

"Well, I've identified myself as a man now for three years Mom. I've changed everything. I finally feel free. Since then, I've also gotten married," revealed Denny.

Lily's jaw dropped as she absorbed this new information.

"Mrs. Lily, I'm gonna go in the kitchen and get you a drink. Any of you want a drink?" announced Lee wanting to remove herself from the personal family discussion.

"No thanks," noted Denny as sweat began to fill his brow and his face began to turn red.

"Oh, dear. What does that mean? I'm confused by what you just said. Did you marry a man or a woman?" inquired Lily with a puzzled look on her face.

"Well, Mom," expressed Denny hesitantly realizing that the information he provided his mother over the last few minutes appeared to be overwhelming her. "I married a woman since I now identify myself as a man. We love each other like any other couple," confided Denny.

"You should have brought her with you," suggested Lily. "Why didn't you?"

"I thought it would be too much for you, Mom, at this point in your life. If you want, I'll bring her the next time I come," said Denny.

"I would have liked to have met her. If you're married, it's legal and if that's what they're doing today dear, I'm fine with it."

"Mom, I'm almost sixty years old and surely don't care what anybody thinks at this point in my life. I simply want to do what makes me feel fulfilled and live my life the way I want. If someone doesn't like it, they can go to hell as far as I'm concerned. I like women instead of men because I think they are attractive. They always seem to like to take care of me and there are a few other reasons, but I can't talk to you about how they treat me in the bedroom, if you know what I mean," boasted Denny as he began to blush.

"Oh dear, honey. I'm glad you have a happy bedroom, too," acknowledged Lily, not knowing exactly what to say. "We were talking about why men are attracted to women a few minutes before you came."

"Why did you want me to come to town Mom?" inquired Denny.

Lily realized at this point in the conversation that she was in trouble. She had been so surprised by her daughter's appearance, she forgot to act like she had Alzheimer's disease. She knew she immediately needed to make a few adjustments to her personality and the conversation to put Denny's mind in the right place regarding her mental state.

"Well Denise," she said hesitantly switching into her Alzheimer's character and thinking what to say next.

"I'm Denny, Mom," implored Denny.

"I'm sorry honey. I invited you here to get your opinion regarding my mental state."

"What do you mean Mom?"

"While you are here, I want you to let me know if you think my mental condition is so terrible that I need to go into assisted living or a nursing home, God forbid. Your sisters already took away my car keys when they were here. Sometimes I think I'm losing my mind, I'm so forgetful. You'll have to ask your sisters how I'm doing." Lily reached down into her pocketbook and began to shuffle through it.

"What are you looking for, Mom?"

"I forget honey. I think my charge card is in here." Lily began pretending to rummage through her wallet looking for her charge card until she eventually found it.

"I was holding your father's charge card too, because he never uses it. It's somewhere in here, I think," she said continually moving her hands in her pocketbook.

"Mom, Dad has been dead for five years. Are you sure you have his charge card?"

"I'm not actually sure, Denise. Where do you think he could have put it? Frank. Frank," yelled Lily.

"Mom, I think you're acting crazy. You're definitely scaring me."

"Don't get scared. It's hell getting old," grumbled Lily.

"Now you're making some sense Mom. I was wondering now that you understand where my transformation is heading, if you could lend me some money for an operation I need to complete it."

"What are you transforming to Denisey?" asked Lily.

"Mom, it's Denny. I'm transforming to Denny, Mom. I want to fully complete the transition from a woman to a man."

"Well honey. What have you done with the money you made working for the government?"

"Well Mom, I retired a year ago, but I support a lot of charitable causes, and I mean a lot of causes. I got myself involved in too many of them. They're always asking for money and I have a tough time telling them no."

"Like what kind of charitable causes honey?"

"Let's see. I support the LGBT community and all of the legislation that's been recently passed. I support organizations like PETA that support the rights and health of animals. I also try to raise money to make polygamy legal. Polygamists have rights too you know. I support other causes like the Naked Clown Foundation, The Marijuana Policy Project Foundation and I've recently become involved in an organization that arranges services such as erotic massages, if you know what I mean, and much more for the physically disabled. I also raise money for the Blind Association. I needed to do something in retirement, but between my new wife, my sex transformation, and raising money to help underdog causes, I'm tapped out of money if you know what I mean, Mom."

Denny lifted his head after he finished thinking about all of the charities he was involved in. He looked up at his mother, only to find her fast asleep in the recliner.

"I guess I wore her out," concluded Denny as Lee was returning from the kitchen with a drink in her hand. "You make me tired, too, Denny with all of the charities you're involved in."

"What's your plan over the next week while I'm here?" inquired Denny.

"Jake Snyder wants someone here with your mother all of the time. So if you're going out, I'll make sure I'm here. If not, I'll go back home. I don't live far away. What's your plan Denny?"

"I plan on catching up with my mom and spending time on a few Baltimore street corners raising money for my charities. I do it every day. I get enjoyment out of raising money for these charities. I especially like helping the less fortunate and disadvantaged people and animals that are left out in our society. I know how the less fortunate feel and I think I can devote some of my time and money helping them."

Lily was now up from her very short nap and listening to each and every word Denny said.

"If I had a million dollars, I'd give it all away to these charities. What am I going to do with the money, other than complete my transformation? There are a lot of people that need money a whole lot more than me. The least I can do is help them. My wife isn't happy with me for giving so much money away, but it's my money," countered Denny.

"Everyone's gotta do what they gotta do and right now your mom needs to get some rest. Let's work out our schedule over the next few days," stated Lee.

Lily rested in her chair listening to every word. Denny's last comments were shocking to her.

"Mary and Sharon needed money and Denny gives it all away," she thought. "How could this be fair? How could it be that I could have children on such far ends of the spectrum when it comes to their money?"

Although her first two daughter's visits were challenging, Denny's visit was very eye opening in terms of how people could run and ruin their lives. However, exactly like Mary and Sharon, Lily knew there was nothing in the whole world she could do to control the path Denny had gone down. She was at peace with the decisions of Denny's sexuality, but deeply troubled by his free-wheeling use of the money that always seemed to pass quickly through his hands.

CHAPTER 51

As the morning of day two began, Lily wanted to continue to confuse Denny regarding the state of her mental health. She eagerly started her playacting before she got out of bed.

"Frank. Frank. Could you please come in and help me? Frank. Frank," Lily shouted.

Denny opened Lily's bedroom door and could see his mother unscrewing a light bulb out of a lamp that was sitting on an end table.

"Mom, what are you doing yelling for Daddy? He's been dead now for five years."

"I can't get this light turned on and I need your father's help. He's always so good at fixin' things. Did he already leave for work?" Lily responded in a convincing manner.

"Mom, he's dead. Plain dead," insisted Denny as he began to move his right hand back and forth across his throat indicating his father's dead. "Mom, you're plum crazy. I don't know what I'm gonna do with you. Come on. Let me help you get up, get dressed, and get some breakfast. Lee is coming soon and I gotta get out and do some collecting during rush hour."

"Don't they call that panhandling, Denny," countered Lily.

"Not if you're doin' it for a nonprofit organization. If you do it for one of them it's called "fundraising," insisted Denny, convinced that there was a difference between the two types of street corner panhandling. "I don't get you, Mom. Sometimes you are missing your noggin, and sometimes you sound like Albert Einstein. What's going on with you?"

After breakfast, Lee arrived at Lily's house. Denny was dressed in her costume ready for the day.

"Who are you raising money for today?" asked Lee.

"I'm raising money for the blind. I have a walking stick and a sign that I use all the time."

Denny held up the sign for Lily and Lee to see. On the front of the sign it read "PLEASE HELP, BLIND" and on the back of the poster it read "ASSOCIATION."

"Isn't that sign a little misleading? I think you're misrepresenting who you are. I don't think you want to do that again," contested Lily sassily referring to Denny's identity change.

Denny became irritated at his mother's inference and peered at her peevishly.

"Whatever I gotta do to raise money for the cause is worth it," insisted Denny. "People generally only give me the extra change from their cars. But it mounts up, nickel after nickel, dime after dime, and quarter after quarter. I raised almost $200 one day acting like a Naked Clown," recalled Denny as he moved his head up and down in confidence.

"What's a Naked Clown do?" questioned Lee with a befuddled look on her face.

"It's a non-profit organization that raises money for multiple sclerosis. They actually don't go naked. But they have a relaxed dress code. I had a big sign that covered my body and stated in big letters Naked Clown. When people saw the sign in front of my body, it appeared that I was naked. But I actually wasn't. I merely had on skimpy clothes."

"That must have been a dazzling sight," teased Lee as they all began to laugh.

Denny then stated, "If you two were celebrities, I could get a lot of money selling your bras for the Bras/Panties/Underwear for Charity organization. You two must be related because your breasts both look like someone would want to buy one of your bras to determine your actual bra size. I'm glad I got the small ones Mom. I must take after Dad's side of the family," conceded Denny as they all continued to chuckle.

"My favorite charity to raise money for was "The Welfare Group for Disability and Sexuality" organization. To raise money for this group, I took a good-looking woman who was confined in a wheel chair and gave her a leg and back massage on a busy street. The police made me stop after two hours because I caused two traffic accidents and created a huge backup in the main intersection leading into the city. It was backed up for miles. I even made the local news that night."

"You are crazier than your mother," said Lee, unintentionally helping support Lily's aim of convincing Denny she has Alzheimer's disease.

"Unfortunately, I only raised $75.26 that day. But I didn't give up. I've been fundraising for them ever since, whenever I can get a new disabled participant. They usually don't last too long. You need a person dedicated to supporting sexuality for the disabled," noted Denny.

"I gotta go," proclaimed Denny as he put on the thick sunglasses given to patients after eye cataract surgery, which would lead an unknowing person to think that he was totally blind. "Do you like my fundraising costume?" he asked as he exited the front door not waiting to hear Lily's or Lee's response.

Denny parked his car a few blocks from his street corner panhandling location. With his orange bucket and sign in hand, his cataract glasses filling his face and his walking stick thrown over his shoulder, Denny walked to the end of Interstate 83 that dumped itself into one of Baltimore City's main thoroughfares. It was almost 8:00 a.m. in the morning and the traffic was already beginning to pick up as workers travelled to their offices in the heart of the city.

As Denny reached the intersection, he walked like an able bodied person. When he reached his spot at the end of the highway, he looked up at the light to count the timing between the red and green lights. After seeing the light's timing, he knew he had fifty seconds to panhandle the commuters when the light was red. During this time he needed to count to fifty to ensure he did not get stuck in the middle of the traffic when the light turned green.

As Denny got prepared, he held the walking stick and bucket in one hand and the sign draped around his neck in big letters saying "PLEASE HELP BLIND." He had learned over time that it was too ineffective to hold the sign and work the drivers into giving him dollars and excess change. He had to engage the drivers and his free hand helped him to do it. All of the money he collected would go to the charity and he was committed to do his very best.

Denny moved up and down the line of cars walking confidently, moving the stick from side to side every now and then for effect. As the hour went by it seemed that every other changing of the light provided him with the extra change from a caring soul.

All of that changed when a shiny Land Rover pulled up in front of him. Unbeknownst to Denny, the man in the shaded window was watching every move he made. As Denny approached the Land Rover, its driver's side window began moving down. Denny assumed some loose change would soon be heading his way.

"I ought to have you arrested. You're a big fat fucking fraud. You're not blind. I'm going to call the cops on you," the man argued belligerently.

"I'm not a fraud. I'm raising money for the Blind Association," claimed Denny as he turned the sign around for the man to see the word "Association."

Denny's explanation made the man more furious.

"Why do you have the glasses on if you're not blind? And why do you have a walking stick if you're not blind?" interrogated the man.

At this point the fifty seconds had passed and the light at the end of the interstate turned green. Cars began to move in all of the lanes except for the lane where the man in the Land Rover continued to argue with Denny.

"These are my sunglasses, asshole," admitted Denny as the cars behind the Land Rover began to honk their horns. "And this walking stick helps me to keep my balance. I'm sixty years old dumb shit," maintained Denny as both of their voices began to rise.

The man's eyes began to bulge out of his head as he peered at Denny with a menacing look.

"You look like a ninety-year-old woman, fat ass," quarreled the man as he slammed his foot down hard on his Land Rover's accelerator and speedily moved through the traffic light as it turned from yellow to red.

Although the man hadn't genuinely intended to hurt Denny, he had. Calling him a ninety-year-old woman hit Denny like a fatal blow from a sledge hammer. He was mortified and immediately zapped of his energy and enthusiasm for his cause.

Denny grabbed his bucket with its total of twenty-nine dollars and seventy-three cents and sluggishly worked his way back to his mother's car. His plan was to go back to bed and rest for the remainder of the day. His sixty-year-old body now felt its age.

CHAPTER 52

Day three brought new hope for Denny. An optimist, he always assumed that each day would bring new promise and prospects. His first day of raising money on the streets of Baltimore had been a disaster. He knew today would be a better day, but he had to come up with an innovative plan to raise money for his "cause du jour." After gathering his thoughts of the prior day's events, he theorized that his unfamiliarity with the city had thrown his thought processes off, and he had given up too easily. However, today was a new day to support a charity he felt deeply committed to helping.

As Denny made his way down the bedroom steps at 6:30 a.m., Lily was already up and resting on her recliner.

"Mom, I've decided I'm going to raise money for the Alzheimer's Association today. We're going to go where I went yesterday, and we're going to raise a lot of money. If the drivers see two old unassuming women sitting on the side of the road, they'll happily donate money," insisted Denny.

"Who else is going with you dear?" questioned Lily.

"You, Mom. We'll make a good team. It's like old times again, when we used to beat Dad and Sharon at double solitaire," contended Denny in a serious, headstrong manner.

"I surely don't think I'm healthy enough to go into the city and help you panhandle on a busy street corner. I need my rest dear," Lily professed.

"Mom, the fresh air will make you feel better," claimed Denny.

"I don't think the car fumes are exactly fresh air, Denny. I think you're as crazy as I think I am sometimes," admitted Lily.

"Mom, I only need you for two hours during rush hour. We'll get there at 8:00 a.m. and we'll leave by 10:00 a.m. That's it. Okay?" insisted Denny forcibly boxing Lily into a corner.

"Well, it doesn't sound like you're leaving me much of a choice," conceded Lily. "You'd better not leave me. I get lost whenever I leave the house."

"I'll bet. Let's hurry up and get moving. It'll be great working together, Mom."

Denny and Lily arrived at the same spot Denny had attended the day before, at ten minutes before 8:00 a.m. He parked the car one block away and they slowly made their way to the busy intersection.

"Mom, you sit on this chair right here on this concrete median and keep this sign on your lap," directed Denny.

Lily slowly sat on the chair, already exhausted from the morning activity. Her chair straddled the edge of the end of the interstate, where the traffic whizzed by on each side of her at changes in the traffic light. She was doing her absolute best to hide her real illness from Denny.

The sign Denny prepared and sat on Lily's lap read in big blue letters on the first line, "I HAVE ALZHEIMERS." The second line read, "PLEASE HELP." As soon as Lily got situated, Denny was ready to start hawking the cars. His sign said in big letters "MY MOM HAS ALZHEIMERS. PLEASE HELP."

"We're going kill it today, Mom. I know we are," pledged Denny.

"I think the only thing you're going to kill today is me," mumbled Lily under her breath.

A few minutes after 8:00 a.m., Denny began industriously moving through the cars between the red, yellow, and green lights. As each car would see him and then his mother, car windows would quickly open and dollar bills or loose change was thrown into his orange bucket, with no questions asked. After seeing Denny panhandle the cars, Lily immediately closed her eyes, not wanting to think about what she had agreed to do or the activity that was taking place among the drivers as they headed to work. Denny hustled them with great enthusiasm.

As the time got close to 10:00 a.m., the traffic began to ease up and Denny slowed down his pace. Lily knew that he had raised enough money from his panhandling to be satisfied and was ready to call it a day. But before Denny finished his morning duty, a dirty homeless-looking man with dread locks down to his waist approached the intersection.

As he got within ten feet of them, Denny finally noticed him.

"Hey man," mumbled the person with a deranged look on his face, as the traffic continued to pass them by. He was obviously high on drugs. "You're on my corner. I charge people to be here. I've never seen you before. You can stay for fifty dollars," said the wild looking man.

Lily began to become afraid for her youngest child.

"Bug off asshole. We're leaving now, but you'd better leave me the fuck alone if you know what's good for you," urged Denny as he immediately and aggressively began a frontal attack.

The homeless man didn't know what to say. Most people had shied away from him, but this crazy person went on the offense.

"Okay, okay. Give me twenty-five dollars and I'll go away."

"You stay here and I'll bring you back a hot corned beef sandwich from Attman's deli," proposed Denny.

"I don't need any food. I get that for free. I just need some money," slurred the man.

"Well go ahead and start asking drivers. The Lexus drivers give out the most money. I did better tapping hard on their windshields to get their attention," urged Denny trying to get the man's attention diverted onto something other than him.

With that said the man's brain went into action and he began canvassing the cars in front of him with his crunched and worn hand written sign. Denny immediately grabbed his mother and walked back to the car. As they crossed the street, the homeless man turned his head towards them, and saw them cross the intersection. By this time, his intoxicated and unhinged brain had totally forgotten that he had had a conversation with Denny.

As they reached the car, Denny felt relieved that they had averted a confrontation with a homeless drug addict.

"That was a close one Mom. I've had that happen a lot. You simply need to yell back and stun them, and hope for the best. It always seems to work for an old guy like me," Denny explained looking down into his bucket full of loose change and dollar bills.

"I'm exhausted. Please take me home. This was not a good idea," said Lily, who felt like she was on the verge of passing out.

As they arrived home, Denny quickly made his way out of the parked car and into the front door of the house. Lee was waiting inside. She had slept at home the night before knowing that Denny would be taking care of Lily.

"Where were you?" Lee questioned Denny, as Lily slowly made her way into the house.

"We were both collecting money for the Alzheimer's Association at the end of Interstate 83. With Mom there, we almost made a killing until a crazy homeless man interrupted us at our spot," boasted Denny with little concern for his mother.

"Well it damn well looks to me that you almost killed your mother in the process. What in God's name were you thinking?" Lee hollered as she began to lift her index finger and move it from side to side. "While I'm in this house, you will never do something like this again or I'll call the police and Mr. Snyder on you. This is borderline abuse, Denny. Your mother is eighty-six years old. She can't do what you can do," said Lee in an angry manner.

As soon as Lee said this, Lily grabbed onto her as she began to fall over and collapsed towards the floor. Lee quickly grabbed her as she was falling, and clumsily placed Lily on her recliner. Lily was now as pale as a ghost.

"Now see what you've done," scolded Lee.

She ran into the kitchen, grabbed a hand towel, and put cold water onto it. She also filled up a glass with cold water. She rushed back into the room and placed the cold hand towel on Lily's forehead. Within a few seconds, Lily opened her eyes.

"What happened?" Lily murmured as her color began to return to normal.

"You passed out, Mrs. Lily. Now drink this water and relax," Lee calmly responded.

"I'm so sorry Mom," Denny said regretfully. "I should have known better. I simply think of you the way you used to be. I still think I'm young, and you're my strong Mom who could do anything and everything. I'm sorry Mom. We got old. How did we get here, Mom?"

Lee continued to give Denny a look of disdain as Lily's condition improved.

After an hour or so had passed, Denny began to count the money in his bucket, placing it in various piles.

"Yahoo, Mom. We collected two hundred and forty-six dollars and thirty-seven cents in two hours. In all of my years of panhandling, that's a record. You always had a golden horseshoe in the right place Mom," declared Denny with misguided exuberance.

"There will be no more records this week," noted Lee. "You may have collected a lot of money today, but look at the cost. You almost killed your mother," insisted Lee, as she peered at a Lily, who still looked pathetic as she rested in her recliner.

"Well, I'll have to go at it alone the rest of the week. I think tomorrow I'll collect money for the Naked Clowns. I bet no one has ever collected in Baltimore for them before," continued the self-absorbed Denny.

As Lee and Denny looked over at Lily, they realized that she was fast asleep.

During the week, Denny continued the same routine each day, collecting money for his causes, counting it, and placing his daily heist into manila folders to be donated to the appropriate cause. His thoughts were centered on his causes and he seemed completely unconcerned about his mother's mental and physical health.

As the week progressed, Lily became uncharacteristically silent and let Denny do most of the talking, who couldn't get beyond his own needs.

By the time Denny woke up on the seventh day of his stay, he had totally forgotten why he came to Baltimore in the first place. Benjamin Franklin once said that guests begin to stink like dead fish after three days, and Denny was beyond rotten after seven days.

Lily on the other hand, was content knowing that Denny was happy with his life and had found his passion, which included helping others. She also concluded that any inheritance she bequeathed to Denny would more than likely end up in the hands of a charity of his choosing. Now that all three of the children's visits had ended and their trips had the intended result, Lily was left to decide how to will her six million dollar estate, as her health continued to steadily decline.

CHAPTER 53

Early the next morning, shortly after Denny left for the airport, Lily made her way down from the bedroom to her recliner. She sat in it and began to contemplate what had taken place over the past three weeks now that all three children were gone.

"I probably will never see them again. I'm not sure what I should do now. My children are each a mess," she thought.

"I'm not sure if I did the right thing inviting them, but it had the result I was hoping for. I'm just not happy about what was revealed. I hope you and God aren't mad at me for what I did to our children, Frank," Lily reflected.

"I sure stirred the pot during their visits. I feel dirty doing what I did. It's left a putrid aftertaste and there's nothing I can do to make it fade from my senses. They've worn me out mentally and physically. I should have known their personalities wouldn't have changed. I am not even sure if my life has been worthwhile based on how they've turned out. I think I'll be exiting this earth soon, leaving it in worse shape than when I entered it," Lily further contemplated.

Lily heard the front door knob jiggling and opening. Lee quietly walked in, assuming Lily was asleep. As she walked through the door, Lee saw Lily sitting quietly in her recliner.

"Good morning, Mrs. Lily. What you doin' up? You should be in bed," suggested Lee.

"What are you doing here, Lee? You should still be in bed, too."

"I got to worrying about you, Mrs. Lily. I think those children of yours took it out of you over the past few weeks. I couldn't sleep last night thinking about you and figured I might as well come here and make sure you're okay. I figured if you were sleepin', I'd be able to sleep knowing you were restin'," confided Lee.

"Thank you, Lee. I don't know what I'd do without you. You're a godsend," said Lily as she tucked the palm of her hand under her left ear to rest her head.

"Now that they're gone, I hope you start acting normal again. I want to see the real Mrs. Lily. I'm getting tired of the crazy, dumb acting Mrs. Lily," admitted Lee.

"Do you think I deserve an Academy Award Lee?" asked Lily looking for some reassurance.

"I think you deserve the one, but not the Mother's Choice Award. I don't think your children will be too happy when they find out the truth about your act."

"Do you think they'll be upset when they find out I have a terminal case of leukemia and didn't tell them? I only have another two or three months to live Lee. I'm gonna die soon. That's why I invited them to see me."

"Oh, I'm so sorry, Mrs. Lily. I didn't know that."

Lee got up from her chair and gave Lily a big hug. Lily began to sob.

"The only person who knows is Jake. When my daughters were here, I felt so lonely not being able to tell anyone about my illness. Sometimes I felt like I was by myself on a rowboat in the middle of the ocean."

"I'm here for you, Mrs. Lily, but I'm still not sure why you acted crazy while they were here."

"That's a story for another day. What do you think of my three crazy children now that you have seen each one of them Lee?" asked Lily, trying to change the discussion.

"Well Mrs. Lily, I only saw them for a few days. I've seen crazy in my lifetime. What I've learned from seeing my family and friends is that we're all different. You have three children and each one of them has their own unique personality, yet they came from the same mother and father. Mrs. Lily, if you had twenty kids, they'd all have different personalities. Hopefully, not twenty crazy ones," concluded Lee, as they both began to smile.

"What about your mother and father? What was your brother like before he was killed? Did you have any crazy people in your family?" inquired Lily.

"Mrs. Lily, my personality wasn't actually like my daddy or my momma. I know that because I was adopted," revealed Lee.

"You never told me that," proclaimed Lily. What hospital were you…"

Before Lily could get out another word, the telephone rang. Lily slowly moved her hand toward the telephone.

"Good morning Lily," voiced Jake. "Sorry to wake you so early. I wanted to make sure you are okay, now that your daughters have all left town. I want to talk to you about your will. I hope you've put some more thought into it. I want you to know that …"

Lee went into the kitchen and began to make coffee and breakfast. Jake continued on for one hour talking to Lily about what she needed to consider in her will.

After Lily hung up the phone she followed her nose into the kitchen as the smell of fresh cooked bacon and morning coffee awoke her senses. As she reached the kitchen, a plate in front of her usual seat was filled with eggs, bacon, and grits. Steam was still coming from the coffee mug.

"Mrs. Lily, I want you to sit down and I'm gonna tell you some more about me. We got the rest of our lives to be together, and now that your daughters are gone, we need to get to know each other better. We got nothing else better to do and I've got to get in my five thousand words each day, and right now I'm only at about word two hundred."

"You know I haven't been my hungriest lately. I'm not sure if it's from my children upsetting me, or the side effects of my medications. Either way, this is the first time I've been hungry in three weeks," admitted Lily as she began to eat the breakfast Lee prepared for her.

Lee sat down at the table, taking pleasure in watching Lily eat.

"I lost my daddy when I was seven years old Mrs. Lily. Your daughters were lucky they had you and your husband for such a long time. It's a shame they don't appreciate that."

"Oh my. What in god's name happened?" probed Lily.

"He was workin' at the Bethlehem Steel plant. He made good money and they paid him a lot of overtime at the steel mill. He was so proud of supportin' me, my brother, and my momma. He was proud because he grew up poor, dirt poor. But we had a lot of money, or so we thought, when Daddy worked there."

Lily continued listening to Lee's every word and finally felt like she could relax and enjoy some real conversation after her Alzheimer's disease character role.

"My Daddy was a laborer at the plant. I was told by my momma that he did lots of jobs in the furnace area. They'd dump scrap steel into the furnace where he worked. It was real, real hot there and the furnace was made of brick, even the roof of the furnace was made of brick. If anyone wants to walk on top of the furnace, they had to wear wooden shoes and asbestos suits, otherwise, your clothes and shoes would melt or catch on fire. Daddy used to say he felt like he was standing next to the sun, the heat was so hot and powerful.

"On the night when my daddy died, his job was to open the furnace door and see if all of the scrap metal had melted. The scrap metal's impurities would rise to the top of the bowl. They called this stuff slag. It would leave a thick covering over the melted steel. When my Daddy pulled open the door, he fell onto the bowl of crusty slag and melted steel that lay underneath it. Unfortunately, the crusty slag cracked like ice on a river, and my Daddy fell in it. There was nothing left of him. The steel was two thousand degrees and all they brought us was a brick-sized slab of steel from the bowl Daddy fell into. He was gone as soon as he fell in."

"The superintendent from the plant came to tell my momma. We later learned that it happened quite often down the steel plant. Daddy was a good man, he …"

Lee continued to talk, as Lily listened to stories about her father. Hours had passed and Lee began making lunch for the two of them.

"What about your mother? She must have been lost without him because he was such a strong man," mentioned Lily.

"He may have been a strong man, but momma was stronger. She ran the house, did the cooking, the cleaning, and controlled our activities on the calendar. Daddy worked and gave her the money and momma gave him an allowance. That's the way it was and they were fine that way."

"When Daddy died, things got hard for us. She never got over Daddy dying. Momma never dated again. She was too proud of being with Daddy and too busy raising us to have time for a man. Momma took two jobs but had some health issues and we ended up on welfare. She did the best she could, but times were hard for black women back then. It was tough getting a job, and the ones she had didn't pay much. For the most part, we was still living under the remnants of the old Jim Crow system, and that wasn't the easiest way to live.

"Once me and my bother came into momma's life, she prayed every day to the Lord to help her cherish every day with us, and she did, even when we were living in the Layfette Court projects. She'd walk us to school, walk us home, and make us do our homework. She did it all, even though we didn't have much."

"When my brother was a teenager, he got caught selling drugs in the projects. Then it got even harder, cause we got kicked out. That's right. My momma, me, and my brother got kicked out of the projects. People think there are no rules in the projects. Well, let me tell ya, the city government will kick your family out if you get caught selling drugs. That's when things began to get tough. When we got kicked out, we initially moved to …"

As the day passed, Lily moved back to relax on the recliner. She kept asking Lee one question after another. Lee responded by going into detail about her life and family. Between the stories, Lee cleaned the dishes, gave Lily her pain medication, washed clothes, and did other house chores.

As her health continued to deteriorate, Lily became more dependent on Lee. The three weeks she had spent with her daughters had drained her both mentally and physically. The effects of her age coupled with advanced AML leukemia made Lily short of breath simply walking up and down stairs, and her body was bruising very easily.

The next few weeks would bring much more of the same with television, board games, bible reading, and discussions of life lessons thrown into the mix. It became a happy time for Lee, but much more so for Lily. Lee quickly became Lily's trusted companion, who by the grace of God, was giving her a sense of calm and passing of the days which would have otherwise dragged on.

CHAPTER 54

Lily was beginning to realize that her health was rapidly declining, and she was becoming more dependent on Lee.

"Lee, you're here early in the morning and leave late in the evening. I'm getting weaker by the day. Would you please move in with me? We know what is going to happen to me sooner than later. I don't want to go to hospice. I'd always assumed I would die in this house," stated Lily as she stared into Lee's eyes trying to reach her inner soul.

"Mrs. Lily, I've already talked to my daughter about that. I would have brought it up to you, but I didn't want to make you uncomfortable. I'd be happy to stay with you, Mrs. Lily. I'll sleep at my house tonight to get my house in order, and I'll start staying overnight with you starting tomorrow, if that's okay," suggested Lee.

"That's perfect. Just keep track of your hours. I'm lucky to have you Lee. I thank God you were brought to me," vowed Lily. "I don't know what I did to deserve you at this point in my life Lee. You would have thought I could have relied on my daughters. If they had stayed here, I'd already be dead," said Lily as they both began to chuckle.

"Well, I heard you snore, Mrs. Lily. I think they left because of your snoring," joked Lee as their humorous conversation continued.

"Lee you're Catholic. I didn't know there were Catholic churches that were predominantly African American," questioned Lily.

"My church is in the heart of West Baltimore. There ain't a white person living within five miles of my church on Edmonson Avenue. But my St. Bernadine Catholic Church isn't like the white people's Catholic Church. We've got a black Jesus on both sides of the altar," said Lee as she held her two arms up pointing as if she was making a gesture toward the church altars.

"What are you talking about Lee? I've never ever heard or seen that before," acknowledged Lily.

"That's right, Mrs. Lily. Some Catholics, the black ones of course, think that Jesus was black. They pray to the black Jesus at my church, just like the southern NASCAR folks pray to the baby Jesus like they did in that movie "Talledego Nights," declared Lee as she began to cackle out loud between her words.

"Jesus was a Jew, Lee, wasn't he?" disputed Lily.

"If Jesus was a Jew, Mrs. Lily, then why did the German Catholics kill six million Jews in World War II? That never made any damn sense to me that they pray to a Jew and then they kill them all. I don't get that. They must have known Jesus was black, too," insisted Lee.

"You know your history Lee," affirmed Lily. "But let me ask you this question. Do you know how many Russians died in World War II? I'll give you a hint. Five million Germans were killed."

"Eight million," countered Lee, guessing at the answer.

"Twenty-five million," revealed Lily. "Five times more than the Germans. How come no one ever talks about the twenty-five million Russians that were killed because of Hitler? I love history. I love doing research about my ancestors, too," mentioned Lily. "Have you ever done any research about your family?"

"I've never done any because I was adopted. I've never actually thought about making the effort to find out about my birthmother until recently. Now that my daddy, momma, and brother are all gone, I've thought about my birthmother quite a bit wonderin what she was like. I've just never done anything about it."

"Well, if you would like some help, I'm pretty good at researching the various ancestry websites for family information and may be able to help you, if I have the energy."

The doorbell rang. As Lee opened the door, Lily could hear a commotion.

There were a few voices saying, "Surprise. Happy Birthday, Mom. Happy Birthday, Grandma."

After the commotion quieted down, Lee peeked her head around the front door entrance.

"Mrs. Lily, do you mind if my family comes in and we celebrate my birthday for a little bit? I'd like you to meet them too," indicated Lee with a huge smile on her face.

"Please do. I'd love to meet them," insisted Lily enthusiastically.

Lee's daughter walked into the door, followed by her three adult children. Her daughter appeared to be in her forties. Her children were dressed professionally as if they had just come from church.

"Mrs. Lily, I'd like you to meet my daughter, Ella."

"Nice to meet you, Mrs. Lily," expressed Ella. "I've heard a lot of good things about you. I hear you and my mother have a good time together. Truth be told, she enjoys your company immensely. I hope you're feelin better today and we aren't comin at a bad time."

"Of course not, dear. You all have a wonderful mother and grandmother. I don't know what I'd do without her," admitted Lily.

"Let me introduce you to my grandchildren, Mrs. Lily," boasted Lee as she smiled at each one of them and then introduced them like they were receiving a huge award.

"This young man is my grandson Elijah. He is in his residency at Johns Hopkins Hospital. He'll be a full-fledged doctor in one year after what seems like thirty years in medical school.

"And this young lady is my granddaughter Tonya. She is a lawyer in the state's attorney's office in Baltimore City.

"Last but not least is my granddaughter who is going to make me a great grandma in about three months. This is my granddaughter LaToya. Her husband works in the public relations department for the Baltimore Ravens and couldn't be here since it is the start of the football season," concluded Lee with a proud smile on her face.

"They are all beautiful, successful children," acknowledged Lily.

"Let's get some cake, mother," announced Ella as Lee helped Lily up and they all moved into the kitchen.

"Grandma, I'm placing six candles on one side of the cake for each decade of your life and eight candles on the other side for each year of your life," explained granddaughter Tonya as she placed the candles into the cake.

"Before we light the candles, let's say a prayer for the victims of 9/11. We can never forget that day and keep the men and women who lost their lives in New York City in our hearts," urged Lee.

"Is today the 9/11" anniversary?" questioned Lily. "I can't believe I've lost track of the days."

"Yes it is, Mrs. Lily," confirmed Lee. Not only that, it is a blessed and cursed day for me. I was born way back when in 1948 at Lutheran Hospital. Children, your grandmother Ella told me that September 11, 1948, was the worst and best day of her life because it was the day she had another miscarriage, and the day she met the woman who gave me up for adoption. God bless Grandma Ella and that other woman wherever she is," exclaimed Lee with thoughtful exuberance in her voice.

Lily heard each and every word that Lee had said. As the granddaughter began to light the candle, Lily felt as if a thunderbolt had rocketed through her body leaving her in a state of utter shock. She felt totally immobile, as if she couldn't move or think as she tried to process what she had just heard.

Lee's family began to sing Happy Birthday to her. Lee continued to look at her daughter and grandchildren's faces smiling from ear to ear. Her daughter and grandchildren didn't notice Lily's blank look and pale gray face. Since they had never met her before, they merely assumed it was her normal state of being.

"Make a big wish and blow out the candles, grandma, if you can," teased Tonya.

Lee laughed and took three breaths to quickly blow out the candles. Everyone clapped except for Lily. She sat in the chair motionless, as her now-pale face began to bead up with sweat. Lee looked over at Lily and could see that something was wrong.

"Are you okay, Mrs. Lily?" asked Lee. "Elijah, get Mrs. Lily some ice water please."

Everyone sat motionless as Lee tended to Lily. Lily looked up to Lee with the eyes of a puppy dog homesick for its mother.

"I'm sorry this may have been too much for you, Mrs. Lily," professed Lee. "I'm sorry."

"They're fine. It's not them," claimed Lily as she stared at each one of them realizing that they were all her biological grandchildren and great grandchildren. "I need to go to bed right away, Lee. I'm not feeling well. I can make it upstairs myself. You all enjoy your time together," insisted Lily as she got up from her seat and headed up to her bedroom.

"Are you sure, Mrs. Lily?" asked Lee as she watched Lily head out of the kitchen. She watched her walk up the stairs before returning to celebrate with her family.

"Thank you all for coming, my beautiful family," said Lee proudly. I'm not sure what happened to Mrs. Lily. I hope she is okay."

As Lily moved closer to her bed, she began to sob uncontrollably and felt alone again.

CHAPTER 55

As Lily lay in her bed, the information she had learned about Lee over the past few weeks now began to make sense. Lily wondered in her thought, "Could it be true that Lee was the daughter I gave up for adoption in 1948? How could a second baby besides mine be born on September 11, 1948, in Lutheran Hospital in Baltimore and have a mother named Ella? There can't be two babies born into this same exact situation."

"Lee also has green eyes, very light skin, and similar-sized breasts," Lily thought.

"Oh my God," Lily pleaded out loud. "This can't be real. It can't be. Please help me, Lord. Please help me, Frank. What should I do?"

"The rule of three, the rule of three, that's it. The woman Ella told me that in 1948, and Lee mentioned it to me, too," Lily realized as her thoughts continued to race.

"Oh, by the grace of God. Oh my God. Her name is Lee and they are the initials to my maiden name, Lily Elizabeth Ewing. Her mother Ella told me in the hospital that she was going to do something special so that she would not forget me. Was this it, naming Lee after me?" Lily considered.

"Help me Lord. Give me strength," Lily implored out loud as she began to sob, cry, and take stock of what she had just uncovered. Lily felt hopeless without exactly knowing why as she began living what would be the longest night of her life.

Throughout the night, Lily went through a series of emotions.

"I'm ashamed I gave her up for adoption, and that she never knew me."

She began to undergo the despair she experienced immediately after the rape, reliving the memories and misery of the rape that had been stored for over sixty-eight years.

Throughout the night, she felt the humiliation she experienced in the months leading up to the birth of Lee. She could see the look in her father's eyes, which left her feeling guilty and shameful until she met her husband Frank a few years later.

Her charged emotions were also not only about her. Lily had a deep caring heart, and the scars she bore for a lifetime were now opened again. She felt like she deserted Lee and began to question the meaning of her life.

"How would our lives have turned out if I would had raised Lee? Would Frank have married me if I was raising Lee as a single parent in 1951?" she contemplated.

She felt alone and a coward all at the same time. She wondered how Lee would have turned out if she had raised her.

"Would she have turned out like my dysfunctional daughters?" she thought.

Lily's thoughts ran the gamut of emotions as she tried to process the rape, Lee's birth, and how sixty-eight years could have passed without her knowing her first-born daughter. Life and time had gone by fast for Lily, and her time was nearing an end. She knew it and felt it more each day.

She particularly felt it more this night because her mind had continued to be strong, even though her body was failing but now they were both in a state of despair and misery. Sorrow plagued every inch of her body throughout the night. She hoped the next day's sunrise would make her feel better.

Even though she had a tough time processing how she felt, it had crossed Lily's mind during the night that maybe Lee was better for not having been raised by her. Through their discussions and seeing Lee's daughter and grandchildren, it appeared that she had a good life. She was raised in a loving household by her mother Ella, who had kept her promise to Lily to love Lily's biological daughter. Lily could see the results of the promise in Lee and her extended family. However, on this first night, her despair outweighed any positive thoughts about the decisions she made in 1948.

As the night became morning, Lily was still wide awake in bed staring at the ceiling. She felt depressed, despondent, and emotionless as she watched the minutes slowly tick away on her nightstand clock. The only movement she made during the night was going to the bathroom and locking her bedroom door so that her newfound daughter Lee would not come into her bedroom in the morning. Lily was not yet ready to face her. She felt what most would consider post-traumatic stress syndrome in the aftermath of her newly aroused anxiety, emotions, and truths that had lay dormant for over sixty-eight years. The truth was real, and it was right in front of her face and in her house.

At 8:30 a.m. there was tapping on her bedroom door.

"Mrs. Lily, are you okay in there? I'm worried about you," said Lee as she tapped on the door again.

"I'm okay Lee," indicated Lily. "I'm just totally worn out. Could you please make me some toast and tea and leave it by the door? Please leave me the bottle of oxycodone. I didn't sleep well last night. I'm not in the mood to see anyone."

"Okay, Mrs. Lily. I just want to make sure you are okay. I'm not used to you being this way," said Lee sympathetically.

This routine went on for three days as Lily stayed in her room and Lee tended the house and made her small meals, which she placed outside of her bedroom door.

By the fourth day, Lily's depression and despair had subsided, and what now remained were the regret, sorrow, and shame for the years they spent apart, even though she knew that she had made the best decision for both of them.

"If Jesus Christ could rise in three days, I think you can, too, Mrs. Lily," suggested Lee standing directly outside of Lily's bedroom door.

"I feel like the devil, Lee. By heavens, not Jesus, that's for sure," disputed Lily faintly from inside her locked bedroom.

"Mrs. Lily, I think it's about time you let me in so that I can see you and know that you're still alive. You need to get up and take a bath. I bet you smell like a bear that has been in hibernation for five months and you're probably hungry like one, too," insisted Lee.

"Roarrrrr," growled Lily.

"Oh I'm so afraid! Are you a bear or the big bad wolf in sheep's clothing?" prodded Lee.

Realizing the truth in those words, Lily eagerly replied, "I'm definitely the wolf in sheep's clothing, Lee."

"Well, you better come out or I'm going to huff and puff and blow your door in," Lee comically declared.

"I'm thinking you're mixing up your fairy tales," laughed Lily.

After three days in her room and the realization of her current situation, Lily mustered the strength to get out of bed and move to the door to unlock it. However, she wasn't yet ready to tell Lee the secret she had been keeping for sixty-eight years. Her husband Frank never even knew that Lily had borne a child four years before he met her. No one else still alive knew the secret Lily was harboring.

As she walked to the door, she stopped and thought, "I hid the secret of the paintings in the basement from Jake and everyone else; I kept the secret of my illness from my daughters; and now I'm keeping the biggest secret of mine and Lee's life away from her." Lily felt like her whole life was a sham as she walked to unlock her bedroom door. However, she was still not ready to reveal the truth to Lee.

Lily slowly opened the bedroom door.

"Mrs. Lily, now look at you. I think you lost 100 pounds in three days. You definitely ain't lookin too good. Now, I'm here to take care of you and you gotta let me do that. You can't be lockin that bedroom door on me, Mrs. Lily. Is that a deal?" stipulated Lee as she reached her hand out as if to shake Lily's hand.

Lily reached out her hand in response and Lee put both of her arms out and gave Lily a much needed hug.

"Now who's the bear?" said Lee as she hugged Lily tightly.

Lily slowly reached up and hugged her long-lost daughter. Lee eased up slightly after a few seconds, but Lily kept hugging her and wouldn't let her go.

Lee assumed that Lily simply needed a hug after being holed up in her room for three days. Lily knew otherwise. She wasn't going to let this precious moment slip away. She wanted to hold on to Lee forever, but still couldn't muster the courage to tell her the truth.

"Mrs. Lily, I was sincerely worried about you, and now I'm even more worried," consoled Lee as Lily continued to hug her.

Slowly, Lily released her arms.

"Mrs. Lily, you don't look so good. Maybe it's all that time you spent in bed. Let's get you a shower. You need one desperately. You smell like my high school locker room. Can you believe I can still remember that smell? I haven't smelled it in more than fifty years," recalled Lee, after feeling relieved at Lily's exodus from her bedroom.

Lily stood motionless, staring at Lee's eyes, nose, ears, lips, and hair pondering if she was actually her daughter.

"Mrs. Lily, are you okay? What's wrong with you? I knew I shouldn't have given you that bottle of oxycodone," debated Lee as she became concerned about Lily's emotional state.

Lily continued to stare and began to sway slightly from side to side after standing in the same place for what seemed to Lee a long period of time. Lee gently grabbed her arm and began pulling her toward the bathroom. Lily followed her commands as she continued staring at Lee. Lily couldn't believe her eyes; the person who was standing right in front of her was the daughter she had borne decades ago. Lily looked calm, but her mind was racing as she desperately searched every square inch of Lee's face for a resemblance to her or her three daughters.

"Mrs. Lily what have you been doin in that bedroom for three days? Your arms and legs are all bruised up," noted Lee.

"It's my leukemia," indicated Lily. "It's not getting any better."

"I think I'm gonna have to call Mr. Jake and have him come here and take a look at you."

"Let's give it a few days, now that I'm up and movin about."

"Okay," answered Lee. "But only a few days."

"I missed you during these last three days, Mrs. Lily."

"They felt like a lifetime to me," agreed Lily. "I don't know how time has flown by so fast," vowed Lily actually referring to the years her and Lee were apart.

Lee had no idea of the true meaning behind her words.

"I'm glad you're the one with me now. The good Lord works in mysterious ways," said Lily as she finally began to feel a close kinship with her oldest daughter.

CHAPTER 56

Lee helped bathe Lily and get her ready for the day, preparing for the same routine they had established over the prior weeks. However, Lily had other plans in mind. She was on a mission to learn as much about Lee's life as possible and share as much about her own life, as she began to sense that her health was descending into the abyss. She needed to know as much as she could about Lee so she could find a way to be at peace with herself before she died. Right now, her mind, body, and soul were still in turmoil.

Lily was taking more medications to relieve the constant headaches and growing joint pain. The health effects of her leukemia were increasingly taking its toll on Lily's overall physical health.

As Lee finished her bath and Lily settled into her recliner, Lily calmly and secretly went to work on the road of discovery.

"Lee, you must be proud of your family. They looked beautiful inside and out. You told me a lot about what it was like growing up and how you had it tough in the projects. What was your mother like and did she ever tell you anything about your birthmother?" Lily blurted, thinking "Why did I say such a stupid thing?"

"Everyone knew I was adopted. And everyone kind of figured I was probably all white or somehow mixed between white and black. Momma used to like me to get a lot of sun in the summer because I darkened up pretty good and after a while, people stopped asking questions. But they always kind of gave me a glance. The green eyes didn't help either."

"Momma didn't tell me about my birthmother until she was close to her death. She said she named me after her. She wouldn't tell me her name, but my name "L" "E" "E" was the first name, middle initial, and last name of the woman who gave birth to me. My momma said she was young and white, and the birth mother told her the father had dark skin. She said she was a kind woman with a kind heart. You know for a white woman to give a baby up to a black woman would be a scandal back in 1948," said Lee matter of factly.

"My momma was grateful and strong willed. She told me before she died that she never forgot the week she spent in the hospital with my birth mother after having so many miscarriages. She said it was the worst and best week of her life, even though the worst week was probably when my Daddy died at the steel mill."

There was silence in the room as Lee felt the lingering pain and sorrow she had for her mother losing her husband. Lily could sense Lee's compassion and pride in her father, who had been dead for quite a long time.

To break the silence, Lily uttered "I've never told you about my family."

"What do you mean?" Mrs. Lily.

"I think I've told you I've been tracing my family members for years, long before Ancestry.com. But I like Ancestry.com and have been using it for six or so years. I had a six times removed great grandfather fight in the Battle of Fort McHenry in the War of 1812. His name was Benjamin Fales. His father, Ambrose Fales came from Dublin, Ireland, in 1779 and owned a bunch of trading schooners in Fells Point. I think they were pretty rich."

"Well that's pretty neat. I guess they owned slaves if they were rich," explored Lee with some distain in her tone.

"Benjamin Fales owned one," admitted Lily. "I didn't have anything to do with that dear. As bad as it was, and I'm sorry they owned them, but I can't do a thing to change that," appealed Lily not knowing how to handle what Lee had said.

"I also had a relative, Frank Schmittel, who served in the Union Army in the Civil War. He was shot in the hip in the Battle of Antietam, the war's bloodiest battle. He recuperated and was shot again in the side of his torso in the Battle of Winchester, three weeks before Gettysburg. He also lost a finger in one of those battles. I hope that makes you feel better that we had relatives on both sides of the slavery issue."

Lee began to laugh. "What do you mean "we?" My family didn't own slaves."

Realizing her slip of the tongue, Lily began to backpedal.

"I'm sorry dear. I didn't mean to throw our families into the slavery issue. That's my family's history and I thought you would be interested knowing the truth about them," Lily innocently suggested.

"I'm glad you're tellin me the whole truth about you and your family, Mrs. Lily," Lee said.

These words made Lily feel ashamed and cowardly as she again began to wrestle with deciding whether to tell Lee about their relationship. Lee could see the saddened and disappointed look on Lily's face based on her previous response.

"I'm sorry, Mrs. Lily. I didn't mean to make you feel bad. I know you didn't have anything to do with slavery or did you?" implored Lee to break the ice, and they both began to smile. "Let me hear about the rest of your family," she said with a little more enthusiasm in her voice.

With that, Lily began going on about her family and showing Lee the information contained on Ancestry.com.

"My password book is hidden in the small electrical outlet safe behind my recliner," revealed Lily as she pointed to it. I keep extra cash there too. Lily slowly reached back and pulled the top of the outlet toward her. The top of it pulled down to reveal a small outlet box containing cash and the password book. Lily slowly pushed it back, closing it.

"Frank put the hidden outlet there after the girls went to college. You can still buy them if you ever need a good hiding place. You're the only person who knows my hiding spot Lee. Let's keep it our secret. Pull the password book out in case you ever want to do some research about your family in my Ancesrty.com account," proposed Lily.

As the week progressed, Lily and Lee grew closer. They shared information about their families, their lives, and their long faded hopes and dreams. Lily was comfortable enough with their relationship to open up to Lee, but not enough to tell her the secret.

"I think my biggest failure was raising my three children," professed Lily. "They left home for college and never thought about coming back or gave a second thought to the people who raised them."

As they sat watching the television through the next week, Lily began to think about her legacy, or lack of one.

CHAPTER 57

"I think my biggest regret was getting pregnant at a young age and raising my daughters fatherless," said Lee. It was hard, real hard. You did it right. You married a strong man and then had your children. I wish I had done it like you, Mrs. Lily. Maybe things would have turned out better for me. But I had a good life. I would have done some things different, but it's been pretty good."

"I have big regrets besides my children, Lee," Lily admitted as she looked deep into Lee's eyes.

"I can see your pain, Mrs. Lily. You don't have to tell me. It's okay. In the time we have spent together, I think of you like my momma. You would have been a good momma if I was your child, Mrs. Lily," pronounced Lee, innocent to the true meaning of what she said.

Lily didn't know what to say. She felt numb again. She knew that Lee's words were true and that she probably would have been the daughter that kept her family bonded together.

"I would have been proud to have you as my daughter," asserted Lily as she looked up into Lee's soulful green eyes that matched hers. Then she blurted out without thinking, "You can call me Mom if you want to. I won't tell anyone. It would make me real happy to have had a daughter like you," insisted Lily with genuine, sincere warmth.

"You got a deal, Mom," pledged Lee in a tender voice, not knowing how to respond to this old woman's somewhat outlandish, but at the same time heartfelt request.

A tear began to fall down Lily's face and Lee squeezed her hand. Lily reached over and hugged her.

"I love you Lee," Lily confessed. "I truly love you. I'm sorry I missed you for all of these years," said Lily as another tear began to fall down her cheek.

The three words "I love you" had never been voiced in Lily's home. She realized this was the first time she had expressed these three words to a loved one.

"Well, it simply wasn't meant to be," claimed Lee, not exactly knowing how to handle what Lily had said. She had absolutely no idea of the true meaning of Lily's statement. "You're clearly upset from the all of that medicine you've been takin, Mom. It's entirely that crazy medicine," repeated Lee trying to rationalize in her mind what Lily had just said.

"I guess so," purported Lily, knowing how profound the words really were. She had finally stated the truth to Lee, even though Lee didn't know it. She had deceived everyone from Jake to her three children, and even her fourth child, Lee. She was still ashamed of the circumstances that led to the birth of Lee.

"How could I tell her that her father was a rapist?" Lily thought. "It could ruin her family by telling her the truth about her biological father. It could ruin the proud family they have all become."

As the late afternoon arrived, Lily went to her bedroom, locked the bedroom door, and called Jake Snyder.

"Jake, I need you to come to my house tomorrow. I need to make a few changes to my will," divulged Lily. "I need you to come sooner than later. I haven't told Lee, but I've been feeling terrible lately and I've been taking a ton of medication to alleviate the headaches and joint pain. I think the medicine isn't working and I've been fightin a fever and cough the past two days. Please come tomorrow Jake. I truly think I need you to help me with my final arrangements in case my end is near. I want you to change my will while you are in my house tomorrow. What do we need to do to make that happen?" asked Lily as a cold sweat moved across her brow and she began to cough like a person exposed to cigarette smoke for the first time.

"Hmmm," contemplated Jake as he hesitated to give Lily an answer. "Lily I usually don't work this way to modify or finalize a will. We usually do the draft in my law office and it takes a couple of weeks to complete."

"Honestly Jake, I don't think I have a couple of weeks the way I feel today. I feel dead already," maintained Lily.

"Okay, okay Lily. We'll change your will tomorrow. But please be ready when I come to your house. It is going to be a busy day, so you better get some needed rest."

"Oh dear. I'm sorry Jake, but I know I need to change my will. I do. I do. I do," declared Lily.

"Lily you sound as desperate as your daughters did when they came to Baltimore. However, I get the point. I'll see you in the morning Lily," promised Jake.

CHAPTER 58

That night and the next morning, Lily contemplated exactly what she would tell Jake.

"I invited each of my daughters into town and I now know their true character, both good and bad; even though there was not much good to be found. Lee's come into my life and I'm not sure what I need to do to correct my injustices of the past and take into consideration my daughter's imperfections of the present," Lily thought.

At 9:30 there was a knock on the door.

"It's open. Come on in Jake," mumbled Lily mustering a weak yell that Jake could faintly hear.

"Hi hon," Jake said to Lily as he gave her a once over. "Lily, I hate to tell you, but you've lost a lot of weight since I last saw you. You're also pale and what's with the bruises you have all over your arms and legs? Lily I think you need to see your doctor as soon as you can," implored Jake with a concerned look on his face.

"I don't feel good either Jake. In reality, I think the leukemia is taking its toll on me. Feel my head," urged Lily as she slightly coughed. "I'm afraid of what lies ahead for me Jake. I'm not ready to go just yet," insisted Lily as she looked up at him.

"I'm sorry you're feeling rotten, Lily. But I do have some good news for you before we go any further discussing your will. Your 'I TOLD YOU SO' painting sold at Sotheby's two days ago for nine hundred and forty-two thousand dollars. Can you believe that," proclaimed Jake as he let out a big grin. "Not bad for an old painting that's been hanging by your front door for more than sixty years."

"Oh my. My heavens," affirmed Lily. "Frank would be so proud right now. Oh, my, my," repeated Lily, astonished by the true value of the painting.

"Why'd you want me to come to your house, Lily? What do you want to change in your will now that you're a millionaire?" quizzed Jake.

"I want you to know that my aide Lee is not presently here. I sent her home for a few hours knowing you were coming. I didn't want her to hear our discussion. I want to change the will you developed for Frank and me about ten years ago. I don't want you to second guess my decision either. I truly want you to trust what I tell you. I also want to give you instructions that are to take place at the reading of my will. Now let's go over how I want my will to read and the instructions in terms of what is to be said to my children when you read the will to them."

It took Lily over an hour to give Jake the detailed changes she wanted in her will and another hour to give Jake the instructions that were to be said to her children at the reading of her will. Through the course of the revisions, Lily gave Jake no indication that there were three more priceless paintings hidden in her basement or that Lee was her biological daughter. Jake had no idea of these pertinent pieces of information. Lily continued keeping these facts hidden from everyone.

After Lily had fully presented her changes and the pronouncements to be read to her children, Jake was taken back by Lily's decisions. She had always made good decisions in the past and Jake had learned through the years to trust her judgement. This was the first time Jake had a valid reason to question the decisions she had made.

Jake leaned back on the chair he was sitting in.

"Are you sure you want to make these changes to your will? I'm not sure why you're making them. It doesn't make any sense to me. Once I modify your will and you sign it and we have it notarized, your family is stuck with your decision. I'll write it up today and have you sign it tomorrow, but I want you to sincerely think about these changes. It seems what you're doing is crazy to me, but it's your decision. How did it go when your daughters came into town?"

Lily stared back at Jake in silence.

"Oh, I see. I guess I shouldn't have asked," contended Jake.

"Jake, I don't know what I'd do without you. You have always been the one stable influence supporting me. But I need these changes completed as soon as possible. I don't know. I've got a bad feeling Jake."

"Okay. Let me get at it Lily. I hope you're feeling better. I'll see you in the early morning. You know it's gonna be a little costly to do it Lily," conceded Jake as he headed toward Lily's front door.

"I have the money from the sale of 'I TOLD YOU SO' painting don't I, Jake," bragged Lily.

"You sure do, Lily. You have no problem with money, even though all of your children do," added Jake knowing Lily's concern about giving her inheritance to her daughters.

Jake exited out the front door before Lily could get in another word.

The next day as Lily and Lee were finishing up breakfast, there was a knock at the front door.

Lee answered and Lily slowly entered the front room of the rowhome and parked herself in her recliner.

Lily could hear Lee welcoming Jake and a few additional voices.

As Jake entered the room, he was accompanied by a professional older looking gentleman with a beard and glasses. He wore a worn-looking, dark brown corduroy jacket, khaki pants, and a wrinkled blue button down shirt with a bow tie. The outfit hung on him like a football player's uniform. He had a small brown leather satchel draped over his right shoulder.

"Good morning, Lily," Jake said as he walked carrying a cardboard box filled with what appeared to be folders and loose papers.

"Mrs. Lily is not feeling too good today. But seeing you and this other man, I guess I'm gonna get going to run a few errands. Call me on my cell phone when you're finished and I'll be back. How long are you thinking you're gonna be here?"

"Lee, with Lily you never know. But since it's 8:30 a.m., I think I'm gonna need all day. Plan on coming back around 4:00 p.m.," recommended Jake.

"Wow. Okay," answered Lee, surprised by the amount of time Jake would be with Lily. "Mom, call me if you need anything."

Jake had a puzzled look on his face. "Mom? She's calling you Mom, Lily. You never let me call you that," objected Jake with a slight grin on his face.

"She is very, very special," responded Lily seriously. "You know you were always like the son I never had, Jake."

"And sometimes you felt like my mother when you'd lecture me, I mean give me advice," joked Jake, hoping to elicit a smile from Lily.

The conversation ended with everyone in the room feeling a bit awkward. Jake knew it was actually the result of Lily not feeling well. Lee said her goodbyes and quickly exited the rowhouse.

"I can see you are feeling bad," said Jake. "Lily, this is Dr. Bennet. He's a neurologist specializing in elder care. As I told you yesterday, we need to do this neurology test so that no one can contest your will."

"It's nice to meet you, Lily. I'm sorry about your health condition. I'm going to conduct a General Practitioner Assessment of Cognition Screening Test. We call it the GPCOG Examination. Once we conduct this, we'll determine if you have any cognitive impairment. I'll write up the findings and you'll have it for your records. I do these all of the time, for elderly patients like you who want to insure their will isn't contested on the grounds of a cognitive impairment. I'll be quick and painless. Are you ready?" asked Dr. Bennett.

"I guess," answered Lily looking a tired as an old dish towel and not knowing what to expect.

"Okay, here we go. I'm going to give you a total of twenty-five questions. I'll give you a cognitive score depending on how many you get right. Question 1: I'm going to give you a name and address. After I have said it, I want you to repeat it. Remember this name and address because I am going to ask you to tell it to me again in a few minutes: Michael Smith, 92 North Broadway, Fells Point."

"Michael Smith, 92 North Broadway, Fells Point," repeated Lily.

"What is the date," said the doctor asking the question without a pad or paper in his hand indicating that he had performed the test thousands of times.

"November 14, 2016."

"Okay. Can you tell me something that happened in the news recently?"

"Yeah. It looks like we got Trump for four years. I guess I won't be around to see how that turns out. Will I, Jake?" said Lily with an inquisitive look on her face.

"Stick to the test, Lily. Let's not get into politics today. I've had enough of it. One week after the election and the news organizations are already talking about who may be a presidential candidate in three years and three hundred and fifty-eight days," griped Jake.

"This is a circle representing a clock. Please mark in all the numbers around the circle to indicate the hours of a clock and then mark in the hands to show fifteen minutes past ten o'clock," directed Dr. Bennett.

Lily picked up the pen and began drawing the information on the clock with just as the doctor had instructed. When she was finished, the doctor quickly asked Lily her next question.

"Okay Lily. What was the name and address I asked you to remember?"

"That easy. Michael Smith, 92 North Broadway, Fells Point," Lily quickly responded.

"Do you pay your own bills?" asked Dr. Bennett.

"I have since my blessed husband, Frank, died about five years ago."

Dr. Bennett continued going through the questions one by one. Lily continued answering each question with confidence over the next ten minutes.

"We're finished," announced Dr. Bennett. "This is an easy one to add up to reach your score considering you got them all right. That happens about 20 percent of the time with elderly patients your age. Congratulations on your brain power."

"I wish I had the body power, too," Lily grumbled.

"Unfortunately I can't do anything about that," conceded Dr. Bennett. "How quick do you need the write-up Jake?"

"I hate to say it, but how about tomorrow? The sooner the better would be great," requested Jake.

"I'll have a courier bring it to your office tomorrow, Jake. Is that okay?"

"That's perfect Gene, like Lily's score," said Jake

"That's the first test I've had since high school in 1946," claimed Lily.

Dr. Bennett gathered his working papers, gently stuffed them into his satchel, stood up, and headed toward the door.

"It was nice meeting you." Short on conversation, Dr. Bennet exited the house.

Once the door was fully shut Jake explained, "He did me a big favor today, Lily. He cancelled a few appointments to come here. But believe me, he owes me. I've done him a ton of favors through the years. Besides that, he's a great guy and is highly respected in his field. He's one of the best."

"Thank you Jake. I'd like to say that you're a lifesaver, but I don't think there is anyone on this earth who can save me from my not too distant fate," reminded Lily in a low tone as she weakly smiled at Jake.

"Now let's get to the will. It's going to take a while to review it. Let's go into the kitchen. I'm going to need a lot of room to spread out," asserted Jake.

Jake and Lily made their way into the kitchen. Jake began to talk in a more direct and professional tone as he discussed how he had changed the will.

"I want you to know that when we finish this document, it is final. It won't be able to be changed, even after you visit the angels," Jake stated emphatically.

"I know, Jake. I know what I'm doing, believe me. You have to trust my decision," answered Lily. "I'm in my right mind as you witnessed with Dr. Bennett. I have valid reasons for the changes I have to make. If you don't make them, I'll be rolling over in my grave and I may even come back to haunt you," promised Lily expressing the critical importance of her decision.

"Okay. okay. As your lawyer, I'll do whatever you want me to do. After we're finished, I have to advise you that the changes will be filed in the courts tomorrow. Once we're finished, I'm going to email the documents to my staff and they're going to print them out on legal paper and two of my paralegals, who are also notaries, will come back as watch you sign the documents. They will then sign the documents and we'll be finished. That's the easy part. Now let's look at the changes I've made to your will that we discussed yesterday."

Jake opened his laptop on Lily's kitchen table and opened the Word file on it containing her previous will with the "track changes" she had directed the day before. Lily was feeling miserable but did her best to hide it. Lily and Jake reviewed the document changes line by line. Once she got started doing the word-by-word review, Jake began explaining the meaning of the changes and how they would impact those individuals noted in the will. The review went on for a few hours until Jake had finally made additional changes to conform to Lily's wishes and true intent.

Afterwards, Lily went back to her recliner and Jake emailed and called his staff with specific instructions on reviewing and printing the document. As another few hours passed, Jake's staff knocked on the front door and brought in the finalized papers. Lily's and Jake's notaries signed multiple copies of the newly modified will. Once all of the copies were signed and stamped by the notaries, they quickly exited Lily's rowhome.

"You know you may be leaving me with quite a mess on my hands when you visit the angels and your children see the will," acknowledged Jake.

"You can handle them Jake. They've always been afraid of you. They're afraid that you already know all of their little, dirty secrets," declared Lily.

"I'm not afraid of them, that's for sure Lily," reassured Jake. "But that doesn't mean I won't have a mess. Disbursing your assets will be challenging enough. You didn't make that part of it easy for me. However, I wish you'd be able to see the looks on their faces when your will is read."

"Even though they are my children, after the way they treated me, I'd love to see the looks on their faces, too. They may not say anything at all, but their faces may tell a different story. However, once I'm dead, I don't, or won't care," concluded Lily as she shrugged her shoulders.

Jake went back into the kitchen to organize his belongings for his trip back to the office.

"Do you want me to call Lee so that she can come back?" asked Jake.

"Please don't. I need some time to gather my thoughts. I'll call her in a little bit," said Lily as she closed her eyes to rest.

Once Jake's computer, papers, and other miscellaneous items were packed, he kissed Lily on the forehead, stared at her thinking about all of the experiences their families shared in the past, turned, and quickly exited the front door of Lily's rowhouse.

CHAPTER 59

As soon as Jake had walked out of her front door, Lily took a note pad and envelope out of an end table drawer next to her recliner and began writing a letter that began with "Dear Lee ..." As soon as she began to write, tears began to fall onto the paper. As she began to write again, her words began to flow. By the time she had finished, she felt a sense of relief. She had finally put on paper what she had wanted to tell Lee for the past few weeks, but she was still too ashamed to admit to Lee the events that took place in 1948.

After the letter was completed, Lily placed it into a small envelope and set it on the end table and wrote on the envelope "For Lee, From Mom".

Next, she grabbed a second piece of note paper and a second small envelope from the end table drawer. She scribbled a note on the front of the envelope, "To be opened by Lee only upon my death". She then grabbed the note paper, scribbled a few words on it and sealed it in the envelope.

Lily pushed the recliner back and stretched her left arm to the side of the chair and quickly popped open the small electrical outlet safe, as she had done hundreds of times. She placed the second envelope in the outlet safe and pushed it closed.

Then, with a mystifying burst of energy, she immediately rose to her feet, and carefully roamed the house trying to decide where to hide the letter. Eventually, she made her way into the basement. As she moseyed about, she passed the workbench and decided to peek into the small slot at the paintings' frames one more time.

As she slowly bent over and saw the wooden frames, a voice from the top of the basement steps burst out, "What are doin down there in that basement, Mom? You need to get up here now."

Lily was stunned hearing Lee's voice. She had the envelope in her hand, and could hear Lee's feet moving down the steps. Without hesitation and in one swift motion, Lily dropped the envelope into the small slot, where it now rested, with the three Haussner's paintings.

As Lee reached the bottom of the basement steps, Lily was already walking back toward her.

Lee reached the bottom, and saw Lily, and began shaking her head.

"Mom, what in the heck are you doin down here?"

"I was looking for something on the workbench and I couldn't find it."

"Ain't nothing that important down here for you, Mom. Let's get you out of this dirty basement," pleaded Lee.

As Lily began to move up the steps with Lee a few steps ahead of her, she quickly became short of breath and began to cough uncontrollably, wobbling back and forth. Lee rushed to her as she collapsed on a step and continued coughing uncontrollably. Lily coughed so hard she had trouble catching her breath and in an instant passed out.

Lee immediately wrapped her arms around Lily in a tight clutch and somehow mustered the strength to slowly drag her toward the kitchen, step-by-step.

Upon reaching the kitchen, Lee immediately called 911 and an ambulance was dispatched to Lily's house. After the call was made, Lily regained consciousness.

"Take me to my recliner, Lee," insisted Lily.

Lee took Lily to her recliner and ran up the steps to gather some of Lily's belongings. An ambulance could be heard blocks away, becoming louder with each passing second as it approached Lily's rowhouse.

Using all of the energy she could muster, Lily grabbed her note pad again, and began scribbling another note. Within half a minute, she jotted down a few words, and hurriedly opened the fake electrical box on the wall next to her recliner. As she was placing the note in the fake electrical box, the ambulance drivers had reached her house and were knocking at the front door as Lee moved down the steps to open it.

Seconds before anyone could directly see Lily, she stretched down to close the wall safe. In one swift motion she pushed the safe closed, and in doing so, fell onto the floor next to her recliner. Her note was now safe, but she was in a very uncompromising position as the ambulance attendants and Lee reached her. She had precariously but successfully implemented the last steps to seal her legacy, but at an enormous and potentially fatal cost.

CHAPTER 60

After Lily was taken to the emergency room, she was admitted into a hospital room for testing. Her cough persisted along with other symptoms that she tried to conceal from Lee so as not to scare her.

"Mom, I'm gonna stay here with you until we get you home, cause this ain't no place for you to be. My momma always preached to me that hospitals ain't no good for black people. You sure ain't black, but they ain't good for you either. These hospitals will kill you, you know," uttered Lee.

"I'm scared too, Lee," Lily admitted. "I don't know what's goin' on, but I feel awfully weird," Lily mumbled as she coughed. "Don't call my children to let them know I'm here. Promise me that Lee."

"I'm not sure that's right, but I'll do as you wish. I promise," swore Lee.

"I've kept my health issue a secret from them this long; it's no sense that they know now. I need rest and peace, not the dysfunction and craziness they'd bring with them. Don't call, email, or text them," stipulated Lily.

"I'll ask the nurse for some hot tea and that should make you feel better," suggested Lee.

As day became night and night became day, Lee stayed by Lily's side. Lily's cough became worse and the doctors began to run more tests on the second day of her stay.

The doctor arrived late on the second day to deliver the test results.

"Mrs. Clarke, it looks like you have pneumonia," disclosed the doctor. "Our tests also revealed that you have sepsis."

"What's that?" inquired Lily.

The doctor continued. "Mrs. Clarke, you've been pretty fortunate that you haven't been in here more often considering your AML leukemia and your age. Because of your age, your leukemia, and your pneumonia, you have been very vulnerable to getting sepsis. Sepsis develops when the chemicals your body releases into your bloodstream to fight an infection instead cause inflammation throughout the entire body. We can see you have a high grade fever, infection, and low oxygen levels throughout your entire body. We're afraid that since your white blood cell counts are now so low, we're going to have a tough time fighting this. If your breathing gets worse, we may have to take some additional steps and maybe, but hopefully not, put you on a mechanical ventilator."

"When can I go home and be with my family?" asked Lily, not fully comprehending the seriousness of what the doctor had just stated.

"Is she your family?" queried the doctor.

"She's all I have and I want her to be with me right now," contended Lily.

"Well, I would recommend you go home and get a good night's rest tonight," advised the doctor to Lee. "This young lady has a big fight ahead of her. We have to hope that the antibiotics work. If not, we may put you on a mechanical ventilator sometime tomorrow to help you breathe."

"Okay doctor. Lee, I want you to go home and get some sleep tonight," insisted Lily.

"Mom, I'm tired after being here all last night. I think that may be a good idea for me to go home and get some needed rest. It will help you to get some rest, too, Mom," acknowledged Lee.

As the late afternoon turned to early evening, unbeknownst to Lily and Lee, Lily's body was not fighting her life threatening infection. Her breathing was becoming more labored even though it was not evident to Lee. Lily did not want to scare Lee, and wanted her to go home so that she wouldn't have to hide her discomfort, unaware of the gravity of her situation.

"Please go home and get some sleep," directed Lily as she looked deeply into Lee's eyes.

"Okay. I am very tired," admitted Lee not knowing the danger Lily was in.

Upon hearing these words, Lily began to sob.

"I'm sorry my dear child. I'm sorry my baby. I love you Lee," swore Lily as her body began to shake with emotion.

"Don't be sorry. It's gonna be okay. I love you too, Mom," swore Lee not knowing the true intent of Lily's words or what her words meant to Lily. "But I'll be back tomorrow right by your side. I promise," pledged Lee as she leaned over Lily.

Lily grabbed onto Lee's hand, looked into her eyes, and wouldn't let go. She thought that this could be the last opportunity to tell Lee face to face the truth about their relationship. She now knew she had to do it in case anything catastrophic happened to her overnight.

Although she only held onto Lee hands for a few seconds, she felt a sense of godly tranquility move from her toes through her entire body. She felt as if the hand of God was giving her one more opportunity to tell Lee the truth. She felt a sense of grace and amazement at the events of the past month, which had now completely transformed her life.

Precisely as she built the courage to spill out her soul to Lee, a nurse came in through the door in a hurry.

"I got to check your vitals Mrs. Clarke. Could you please step outside?" conveyed the nurse to Lee matter-of-factly.

Lily let go of Lee's hand, Lee blew her a kiss goodbye, and she slowly backed out of the room to go home to get some well- needed rest.

CHAPTER 61

The nurse continually monitored Lily's vital signs, updating the doctor of her status. The doctor also checked on Lily intermittently. The nurse's monitoring continued every hour on the hour until 2:00 a.m. Lily was having more difficulty breathing as her cough increased in intensity.

At 3:00 a.m., Lily was exhausted from the constant arrival of the doctor and nurses checking on her throughout the night. A small group of doctors and nurses assembled in her room.

"Mrs. Clarke, your condition is quickly deteriorating. The medications we're giving you are having a tough time fighting the sepsis. Your leukemia is causing your body to be in an extremely weakened state and your body isn't sufficiently combating the infection. You're having problems breathing because the sepsis infection has inflamed your lungs. We need to immediately place you on a mechanical ventilator to assist in your breathing and to help your body fight the infection. The technical term for your condition is acute respiratory distress syndrome. We'll need about 20 minutes to get you ready and then we're going to take you down to an intensive care room. Once we put you on the mechanical ventilator, you'll be considered an intensive care patient Mrs. Clarke. The respirators are very uncomfortable in your throat, Mrs. Clarke, so we're going to give you a strong sedative to put you to sleep. You'll rest better that way."

"Put me to sleep?" questioned Lily. "Will I be awake when my daughter arrives?" asked Lily as she clearly understood the seriousness of her situation and condition.

"You'll be asleep until your breathing improves," conceded the nurse.

Lily began to breathe even harder as she began to panic at the thought of being put to sleep. She had a plan in place to tell Lee the truth about their relationship when she arrived at the hospital in the morning.

"Nurse, nurse. I need a memo pad and pen to write my daughter a note. Do you have a memo pad, please?" asked Lily desperately. "I need to write my daughter a note before you knock me out."

The nurse handed Lily a memo pad and she began to scribble on it as she lay on the hospital bed.

Dear Lee,

They are putting me to sleep tonight to help me breathe. I wanted to tell you last night but couldn't, and I want you to know that you are my biological daughter. I bore you out of wedlock in Lutheran Hospital on September 11, 1948, and gave you to your mother, Ella. I'm sorry. I love you and will tell you more when I'm awake. I love you and am truly sorry for the biggest mistake I ever made in my life, giving you away. Please forgive me. You are my best daughter. I love you.

Your mother, Lily

As soon as Lily finished writing the note to her daughter, she folded it up and the on-duty nurse was busy preparing for her to be moved to the intensive care unit.

"Please give the note to my daughter Lee in the morning," pleaded Lily showing the nurse the piece of paper that she held tightly in her hand.

"Sure," mumbled the nurse half-listening as she continued working to prepare Lily's bed and belongings for her trip to the intensive care unit.

Lily placed the carefully folded note in her hands and crossed her hands on her chest as the hospital staff transferred her fragile body to a stretcher, and wheeled her down the hall toward the intensive care room.

As soon as she arrived in the intensive care room, the nurses began getting Lily ready for the mechanical ventilator. The medical team knew that her health was quickly deteriorating, and it was her best shot for recovery and a few more weeks or months of life.

"Please give this note to my daughter when she arrives tomorrow," implored Lily to the attending nurse.

"Will do," indicated the nurse as she floated around the room preparing the monitors and medical devices.

The medical team came into the room and gave Lily a sedative before placing the breathing tubes far down her throat. Lily held onto the note in her hands as she lost consciousness. The medical team went about its business securing the medical devices and instruments in the right places to track Lily's vital signs.

As the late night became morning, Lily's health began to deteriorate further. The medical team was now concerned that the sepsis was continuing to run rampant, and Lily's vital organs were beginning to show signs of shutting down. Even as she lay in the bed unconscious, Lily's hand continued to hold onto the note she had prepared for Lee.

At 8:00 a.m., a new shift of medical staff arrived. As the new staff arrived, they were briefed on the condition of the patients, including Lily.

"This new patient is in bad shape," noted the nurse who had been with Lily throughout the night. "She has pneumonia, a lung infection, AML leukemia, and sepsis. She is not producing enough oxygen and her vitals are shaky at best. She probably won't last the next twelve hours, and at this point, she's probably braindead from her lungs not pumping enough oxygen throughout her body and brain. It happened so fast for her, as it often does for leukemia patients, much less elderly ones. She has a "do not resuscitate" directive and a woman who said she is her daughter should be here in the late morning. Keep a good eye on this woman," advised the nurse.

"It looks like it's going to be a rough day. Any other instructions?" quizzed the oncoming nurse.

"I'm tired and I can't think of any others. She's been on the ventilator the whole time I've had her," replied the outgoing nurse.

Lily lay quiet and still as her body began to slowly slide towards the abyss. As the oncoming nurse pulled up the sheet and bedspread to look at Lily's legs, she could see that her toes and legs were beginning to turn blue. In addition, her vital signs began looking increasingly grim. Her blue legs and toes were sure signs that oxygen was not properly flowing through her body and the end of her life was near.

The note to Lee remained in Lily's hands for the next hour as she lay motionless on the bed, and her body inched closer to death.

CHAPTER 62

Lee arrived at the hospital at 9:15 a.m. After receiving a visitor's pass and seeing that Lily's room number had changed, she swiftly maneuvered through the hospital, before finally arriving at the nurse's station in the intensive care unit.

"I'm looking for Lily Clarke," requested Lee.

"Mrs. Clarke told us that her daughter Lee would be here in the morning. Are you her daughter, ma'am?" questioned the attendant at the front desk.

"I have to see her. I just know it deep down. Since her children aren't in town or won't be coming to Baltimore to see her, I'm all she has. She must have been confused when she told them I was her daughter," Lee thought.

Lee slowly nodded her head, acknowledging that she was Lily's daughter, knowing that she was conveying an enormous lie to the attendant.

"Wait here please and I'll get the doctor and the attending nurse," stated the secretary.

In Lily's room, the nurse attending to Lily peeked out of her hospital room and could see someone talking to the secretary at the intensive care unit front desk. She quickly and correctly concluded that it was one of Lily's family members. She did what all nurses would do in a similar situation and immediately ducked back into Lily's hospital room and began straightening it up by removing napkins, straws, and any loose papers that littered the room. As soon as she collected what she thought were all of items that littered the hospital room, she threw them in the trashcan.

She could then hear the doctor walking down the hall talking with a woman who she presumed was a relative. As the conversation and footsteps drew nearer, she took one panoramic last look around the room, as the footsteps moved to directly outside of the intensive care room. Her eyes spotted a piece of paper lying next to Lily's hands. It was the handwritten note Lily had prepared for Lee.

As Lee and the doctor entered the room, the nurse quickly snatched the note from Lily's hand and placed it behind her back, in one last attempt to make the room look orderly and clean. She succeeded making the room look perfect, at Lily's expense. With that snatch, Lily's chance to tell her daughter the truth about their relationship while she was alive, had now literally slipped through her hands. Her critical condition coupled with her sedation left little chance for her to have one final happy memory with her daughter, as she had often envisioned over the past few weeks.

As the doctor talked, the nurse slowly walked over to the trashcan specifically utilized for medical waste, and gently dropped Lily's folded note into it like it was nothing more than a blank piece of paper.

As Lee stepped into the intensive care hospital room, the various devices, monitors, and the loud sound of the mechanical ventilator took her by surprise. Lily lay motionless on the bed except for the up and down movement of her chest responding to the mechanical ventilator. The air bag made a swishing sound similar to a large fireplace hand blower. Lee could also see that Lily's heartbeat was speeding up and slowing down on heart monitor machine.

"What happened to her?" demanded Lee to the doctor.

"Your mother took a turn for the worse during the night. Her body's white blood cells couldn't fight the sepsis and the lung infection. These two things were bad enough, but coupled with pneumonia, her lungs couldn't pump enough oxygenated blood throughout her body including her brain. She now has very limited activity in her brain and is essentially brain dead. I'm so sorry. It's only a matter of time before she dies."

The doctor pulled down the sheet covering Lily's body to expose her legs and feet.

"As you can see, her feet and legs are beginning to turn blue which is a sure sign that her end is near. We often see leukemia patients develop lung infections and sepsis. It can sometimes happen this quick. I'm sorry. I'd call your other family members and tell them to hurry to the hospital. Her condition is deteriorating faster than we expected," conceded the doctor.

Lee was silent. She looked down at Lily and began to sob. As she leaned over Lily's body, a tear fell from her eye and landed on Lily's hands, followed by a second and third tear. She had grown so fond of Lily during their time together, and a real bond had developed.

"I only wish I had the opportunity to say a final goodbye," Lee said to the doctor.

The doctor consoled Lee and put his head down as he exited the room, leaving Lee alone with Lily.

"I'm sorry, Mom. I'm sorry we didn't know each other until the end. You would have been a good mother to me," affirmed Lee not knowing how profound her words truly were.

Lee sat down on a chair in despair. Not knowing what to do next and since she wasn't an immediate family member, she reached in her purse and grabbed her cell phone and called her daughter Ella for advice. Her hands were shaking as she struggled to dial her daughter's number.

"Hello, momma. What's up? Don't mind me, momma. I'm drivin' the car as I'm speaking to you. I'm out about running a few errands," said Ella. "I'm meeting all of the children at Panera Bread in a bit to have a morning breakfast and talk about the Thanksgiving and Christmas holidays, and who's doin' what."

"I'm sorry to bother you, dear," exclaimed Lee as her hands continued to lightly shake as she stared at Lily lying unconscious in the bed. "I'm calling you about Mrs. Lily. She took a turn for the worse and she's only got a few hours. None of her family is here and I don't know their numbers, and I truly feel bad for Mrs. Lily. She's such a good soul. What should I do?" probed Lee as she nervously explained the situation to her daughter Ella.

"Do you have her lawyer friend's number?" Ella asked continuing to drive her car.

"I do honey. I'm gonna call him right now. I'm sorry to bother you. I haven't been in this situation before."

Before she could get another word out, Ella interrupted her.

"I know Mom. You don't have to explain. I remember how you felt when grandma died," recalled Ella.

"I feel the same way now. I don't know why. Lily was someone I was merely taking care of. Maybe I need to stop caring for the elderly. But this is the first woman I've gotten emotionally involved with. I've truly grown fond of her. I felt like we had a bond and connection. Damn it. I gotta go Ella. I'm sorry," insisted Lee as she began to cry. She quickly hung up the cell phone so her daughter wouldn't hear.

Lee continued sobbing and slowly regained her composure, she then called Jake's cell phone. The phone rang and rang until the voicemail kicked in and Lee left him a desperate message.

Lee continued to feel distraught as she tried Jake's cell phone three more times over the next hour, while a nurse moved in and out of the room tending to Lily's needs and monitoring the medical instruments dangling around her. The nurse peered under the bedsheets every ten minutes or so to monitor Lily's legs and feet.

"What are you lookin' for?" inquired Lee. "How is she?"

"I'm lookin' for the signs, you know, based on what the doctor reported," explained the nurse not being sure how direct to be with Lee. "Do you have any other family coming? If you do, sooner would be better than later," conceded the nurse as she continued to tend to Lily.

"I'm tryin'. But I don't know. I'm simply prayin' that the good Lord knows what he's doin'. That's all I can ask for right now," vowed Lee as she put her eyes down and began to pray out loud.

"Merciful God please let my Mom go in peace. I'm truly glad I got to know her. Take her in your arms, Lord. I know she has sinned. We all do. Forgive her Lord, whatever they were Lord. Please have mercy on her soul, Lord," said Lee as she rocked back and forth with her hands folded and continued praying and repeating out loud in a low voice, "Have mercy on my Mom, Lord. Have mercy on her."

As another hour passed, Lee continued rocking back and forth repeating her message to God while she stared at Lily.

Lee felt a hand land on each of her shoulders. She lifted her head and slowly turned around. Behind her, grabbing each of shoulders stood her two daughters, Ella and Janet. Behind them stood Ella's three children, Elijah, Tonya, and Latoya coming to support their grandmother. In addition, in the back of the room, stood Tonya's husband and Janet's son and daughter.

"Mom, we were meeting to discuss the holidays, and we all knew we had to be here with you and Mrs. Lily," pronounced Ella.

Lee began to cry knowing that her family had come to support her in this difficult time.

"It won't be long now. Mom's goin' quick," proclaimed Lee as she got up and received big hugs from each of her children and grandchildren who were all dressed in a professional appearance.

At long last, Lily now had Lee's extended family, her extended biological family all together with her. Being with her extended next-of-kin under these circumstances, was not what Lily would have intended. It was either good luck or bad karma.

Lee's family remained silent and one by one walked up to Lily's bed to say a prayer. Afterward, they all held hands and prayed. Their deep faith and strong family bond would have made Lily proud, knowing that she had made the right decision back in 1948. They remained silent standing over Lily as the nurse moved quickly back and forth and in and out of the hospital room lifting the sheets to check on Lily's legs and feet.

As another half an hour passed, Jake entered Lily's hospital room. He looked surprised to see all of Lee's family in the room and looked from person to person until he spotted Lee. He made his way through the family until he reached Lee. She stood to give Jake an extended hug.

"What happened?" inquired Jake.

"She took a turn for the worse during the night, Jake. I wasn't here. I went home to catch up on some sleep and when I got back this morning, they said she was braindead. Her lungs and whole body are infected with all kinds of stuff."

Jake looked at the people standing behind Lee.

"These are all of my children and grandchildren, Jake. They wanted to come and support me," whispered Lee. "The nurse keeps comin' in and pullin' down the sheets. Her feet and legs keep turnin' more and more blue."

Jake remained silent and shook his head knowing what that meant. He looked back among Lee's family and nodded his head in support of them coming to the hospital.

"It was nice of all of you to come to support your mother. Lily would have certainly appreciated it, too. Your mother and grandmother meant a lot to Lily in her final days. She told me recently that knowing you Lee made her life complete. You were very, very special to her, Lee," acknowledged Jake.

"You all should be especially proud of your mother," said Jake as he looked at Ella and Janet. "She is a special lady. Thank you for everything you've done for Lily, Lee. I'm especially glad we found you to help Lily in her final days."

"I truly loved her. I know it's crazy to say, but I truly did," confessed Lee as a tear began to fall from her cheek.

No sooner had she said this, then the heart monitor began to beep. It raced up to one hundred and fifty beats per minute before the nurse quickly came back into Lily's hospital room. As the nurse looked at the machine, Lily's heart rate continued racing up and down erratically. The lung machine continued doing its job, moving Lily's lungs up and down, even though it could not stop her demise.

"This is what we see at the very end. It shouldn't be long now," warned the attending nurse.

"I'm glad I made it here. Thank you, Lee," said Jake.

There was silence in the room. Some of the children and grandchildren kept their eyes closed, remained quiet and prayed over Lily. Others slowly swayed back and forth after standing in place for a long period of time. The room remained silent as the hospital instruments did their job monitoring Lily's deathward spiral.

Forty-three beats, one hundred and thirty-nine beats, two hundred and twenty beats, thirty beats, one hundred and eighty-two beats, the hospital heart monitoring registered over a thirty second period of time. Everyone in the room remained silent. Jake and Lee held hands knowing this was the end.

The nurse stood over Lily and nodded to Lee and Jake expressing that Lily's life was near its end.

The heart monitor continued bouncing like a bingo board, eighty-three, twenty-three, one hundred and thirty, thirty-two, until the heart monitor showed a flat line; Lily's heart stopped beating. Her life was over. Everyone in the room began staring at Lily knowing it was over.

Lee continued staring at Lily, as she experienced Lily's spirit abandoning her body as her face began to turn a pale gray. Jake looked at the ground. Everyone else in the room sat in silence for another few minutes.

Jake eventually stood up. "I'll call her children, Lee. I also have all of her instructions for the funeral. I'll call you when I know the details. She wanted a graveside funeral. She wanted it short and quick. Almost all of her friends are dead, and you know about her family. It's a shame."

Realizing where his discussion was going this shortly after Lily had died, Jake ended the conversation.

"She was a great woman. Her children don't know what they missed," professed Jake as he left the room to talk to the hospital staff about the next steps.

"Children, why don't you all go down the hall and leave me alone with her a minute," requested Lee.

Lee's family nodded silently and left the room.

Lee leaned over to Lily's body as the color of her face continued its change to total lifelessness. She reached down and kissed her on the forehead and grabbed her hand. Lee's daughter Ella was standing just outside the hospital door.

"Momma, stay there one second. Let me take a picture of your hand and Mrs. Lily's hand. They look beautiful together," said Ella.

Lee's hand began to shake as she tried to hold it still. Ella focused the camera on their two hands together and right before she snapped the photo on her cell phone, a tear from Lee's cheek dropped onto Lily's hand. Ella snapped the photo as the tear moved down Lily's hand. Ella looked at the photo and left the room.

Lee remained holding Lily's hand, not wanting to let go. She shook her head from side to side in disbelief at Lily's fast demise.

The nurse began moving the various hospital monitors and the mechanical ventilator away from Lily's bed.

Lee lifted her body up from Lily's bedside and began to walk out of the room, turning around for one more look at Lily, who was now totally lifeless. She then slowly exited the hospital room.

Lily's deception was complete and her secrets remained waiting to be exposed. It may have been the end of her life, but not yet the end of her carefully arranged plan.

CHAPTER 63

Each of the people Jake Snyder had requested to attend the reading of Lily's her last will and testament remained anxious and fearful the day after the funeral. The sudden death of Lily, coupled with her children's incomprehension of her net worth or what might be stated at the reading of the will, made them uneasy. Lee on the other hand, had no idea why she was asked to attend. It was just another day for Lee.

Throughout the previous night, all of Lily's children had common thoughts: I should have been nicer and seen her more when she was alive; I had known she was going to die, I would have talked to her about getting her things in order; why was a fourth person called for the reading of the will; did Mom leave anything for me; I hope she's fair, but I don't deserve anything; she better not give more to my sisters than me, because they both have their issues; did my other sisters steal her money, too?

As they each arrived at Jake Snyder's office, located on South Bond Street in Fells Point, a light south breeze blew off of the harbor. Lee was the first daughter to arrive.

Mary was the second daughter to arrive walking into the office, gave her name to the receptionist, turned her head and immediately saw Lee sitting on a comfortable leather chair in the waiting area.

Mary had on the same jewelry that she had the day of the funeral and the clothes she bought using her mother's charge card.

"Hi, Lee. I'm surprised to see you. What are you doing here? Were you the Ms. Jackson who Mr. Snyder called out yesterday?" quizzed Mary curtly.

"I am Ms. Jackson. You and your sisters never asked me any questions when all of you were in town. That's why none of you knew my last name. I'm not sure why I'm here either. When my name was called at the end of your mother's funeral, I was thinkin' that I may have left somethin' in her house. I think that's what Mr. Snyder wants to give me," said Lee. "I stayed with your mom night and day right up until the end. I could have easily left somethin' in her house. Last night I was thinking about what I was missing, and the only thing I could come up with was your mother's companionship. Even though she was fightin' headaches and joint pain, she always talked about the good times she had with her husband, and how much she enjoyed raising you girls. She said her only regret was sending you all away to college because none of you ever came back."

"Well, I'm not sure why you're here either, but we'll find out in a few minutes, that's if Sharon shows up on time or even shows up at all," asserted Mary.

Denny opened the door exactly at 10:00 a.m., strutting her shoulders from side to side like a rooster as she headed to the front desk.

"I'm here for the 10:00 a.m. meeting," she stated in a deep voice.

"You can go sit with the others. We're waiting for one more," replied the receptionist.

"I know which one is late," concluded Denny as she turned her head and saw Mary and Lee sitting in the waiting area. "I knew it would be Sharon. I hope she is not too late. I have a 2:00 p.m. flight out of here. You know when I turned around, I thought Lee was your long-lost sister Mary."

"What are you talking about," objected Mary.

"I don't know. I had to do a double take because you two look kind of alike. Mary, if you had a real good tan and black curly hair, you two could be sisters."

Lee sat quietly, not wanting to get in the middle of the uncomfortable discussion.

"How would you like it if I told you who I think you look like, whatever name I'm supposed to call you today?" retorted Mary in a condescending tone.

"Uncle, uncle. That was a low blow Mary. Lee is absolutely as pretty as you are, even though she doesn't have the flashy gold you're wearing."

Before the argument could go any further, the office door opened. All of their heads turned as Sharon walked in, looking as soiled and unkempt as she had the day before.

"Well, well. Look what came up from the well. Welcome and better late than never," said Denny nastily.

"Are you this mean because you're taking testosterone or have you always been this mean?" moaned Sharon.

Denny snapped, "I don't know. How did you like taking it? I think you've had every kind of pill or mind and body altering drug ever produced."

Sharon turned her head to the receptionist so that Lee, Mary, or Denny couldn't see her, and made an ugly face insinuating her displeasure with what Denny had said.

"She'sssss act actually a wo wo woman," stuttered Sharon.

"That's okay," conceded the receptionist. "I used to be a man and look at me now," she stated as she pushed her breasts up to show Sharon. "I used to be a man and now I have more cleavage than you," boasted the woman. "You can take a seat over there. Mr. Snyder will be with you shortly," the receptionist said as she showed her annoyance at Sharon by turning her head and going back to her other work.

Sharon sat down on the opposite side of the room from the other three attendees.

"What is she doing here?" broadcast Sharon as she pointed at Lee.

"Why don't you ask her yourself?" said Denny. "She's sitting right there and she does have two ears on her head."

"Never mind," responded Sharon as she sat down, crossed her left leg over her right leg and began to bounce her left leg up and down in a nervous movement.

All three siblings and Lee sat in the room looking at each other. Lily's children had been apart from each other for so long that nothing was going to make their relationship any better. Even Lily's burial the day before was not going to change their estrangement.

After ten or so minutes of them staring at each other, Jake opened the door and invited the four into a conference room.

The conference room was upscale, with a long mahogany table, sixteen black leather chairs and a pitcher of ice water and five glasses on a side table. Pictures of the Baltimore skyline hung on one wall and a huge panoramic window view of the Baltimore harbor served as the other.

Jake sat down at the head of the table, followed by Denny and Mary who sat directly next to Jake on the opposite sides. Lee sat in the chair adjacent to Mary and Sharon in the chair adjacent to Denny. Sharon and Mary were sitting as far apart from each other as possible.

"Would any of you like a glass of water before we start? This may take a while," indicated Jake.

They all sat in silence, each shaking their heads back and forth in anticipation of what would take place next.

"You all know I've known your mother for a long, long time. I think over fifty years actually. She knew me when I was a child and she always had pleasant and positive things to say about me, even when I was a little scrawny and sometimes a bratty kid. After your father died, for some reason I always felt an obligation to lend a hand to your mother. I never had to take care of her. She had enough resources to do that, and that's what we're here to talk about today, your mother's resources. Your mother wanted me to tell you today a few things that won't be in the will."

Jake hesitated a minute as he peered at Lily's children.

"Your blessed mother didn't die suddenly from Alzheimer's disease as you may have thought," disclosed Jake.

All of Lily's children except Lee let out a big gasp and slumped back on their chairs.

"What are you talking about, Jake? That can't be. I saw how bad her memory was when I was at her house," challenged Denny.

"Me too," agreed Mary. "She couldn't even remember our names and was always looking at her watch, and placing her purse and car keys in crazy places like the refrigerator. Once she even placed them in the downstairs washing machine. It took me hours to find them."

All three of the siblings in the room were shocked by the news except for Lee wishing Lily could now see their faces.

"She even peed and crapped right in front of me and that other aide, whatever her name was," insisted Sharon.

"It was all an act," professed Jake. "That's right, it was all an act. I didn't even know what she was doing until she had me work up her final will. We had a good laugh together, even though your mother was deathly sick. It was one of the few times I saw her laugh in the last few months, except when she was talking to Ms. Jackson. They were always laughing together."

"You may or may not have officially heard at the funeral, but your mother died of leukemia. She had a bad case of what is called AML leukemia. I can't tell you what the AML stands for, but between it and two bad chromosomes the doctor said she had after a lot of testing, she didn't have a chance. She knew it too. Her doctor was real direct with her, and she was real strong. She was happy with her life and her faith was strong, so she was mentally ready for the day when she would meet your father and the Lord. She truly believed it. In reality, it helped get her through her illness."

"She had some very strong drugs and pain killers," recalled Jake, as he paused and looked at Sharon, who then cast her eyes to the ground. "They helped her get through the pain and headaches when they weren't being stolen."

Mary, Denise, and Lee looked at Sharon and shook their heads in disgust.

"But that's not what we're here for. We're here for the reading of your mother's will. It's officially called The Last Will and Testament of Lily Elizabeth Clarke. Before I read it, I want you to know, prior to me redoing your mom's will, I had a doctor declare her mentally competent. He's a neurologist who specializes in evaluating the competency of elderly patients like your mom. I've used this physician dozens of times and have never lost a case when a family contested his findings. In addition, I've included a provision in her will stating that if any of you contest her will in any way, shape, or form, you'll receive nothing from her estate and you will be considered as having predeceased the others noted in the will. This was done in accordance with your mother's request."

Jake handed each of them a copy of the will.

"You each have a copy that you can take with you. I'm going to go over with you what it says in plain English. You can read it all later and call me over the next few days if you have any questions."

"I have a question. Why is she here?" Mary inquired, pointing to Lee.

"I'll get to that soon enough, Mary. Let's cut to the chase," insisted Jake.

Jake then unknowingly directed his conversation toward the three children Lily raised.

"Your mother didn't know how much she was worth until after she found out the news about her imminent death. As you all know, with the exception of you Lee of course, your father kept meticulous records and thank God for that. Your mom was able to quickly organize her accumulated assets in an orderly manner, thanks to your Dad. By the way Sharon, honestly, what did you do with that painting 'I TOLD YOU SO,' the day you took it out of your mom's house?"

"I took it to a pawn shop to sell it. It had been on Mom's wall for so long, I figured I could sell it and get her a nice gift," claimed Sharon.

"How much did the pawn shop want to give you for the painting," asked Jake.

Sharon hesitated and admitted, "Twenty-five dollars."

"It's a damn good thing you didn't let them take it," concluded Jake. "Guess how much that painting sold for last month at a big auction house in New York City? Well don't guess. You'll never guess. It sold for nine hundred and thirty-five thousand dollars; a little shy of one million dollars."

The three siblings immediately began to cry, spontaneously rose up from their chairs, joined arm and arm in a circle at the end of the conference table and began wildly jumping up and down. Tears of joy flowed down each of their cheeks as they all screamed in excitement.

Lee sat quietly as the jumping and screaming went on for what seemed like a long stretch of time.

Eventually, all three of Lily's children tired out. Denny's pants had fallen down to her knees, exposing a butt tattoo, Mary's jewelry was out of place and an earring had dropped on the floor, and the red candy Sharon had been sucking on was dripping down her chin and neck.

Mary and Sharon looked at each other when they finally realized they had their arms around each other, quietly gathered themselves back together, and sat back down in their chairs.

"That's the good news," confirmed Jake. "Between the sale of the painting and your mother's other small set of investments, including a few stocks and mutual funds, her overall net worth in cash and investments, excluding the value of her rowhome, is worth slightly over one point two million dollars," Jake disclosed without any obvious fanfare.

"That's unbelievably great," shouted Mary as she and her sisters appeared as excited as children on Christmas morning. "Now, what's the bad news?" she prodded with a bit of skepticism.

"Well there is no real bad news. The cash and investments will be divided up three ways; individual trusts will be set up in each of your names; and you will be able to draw down on the money at a rate of no more than $2,000 per month. Your mother hoped the money would last you all well into your eighties, so that's the way she set it up. You should be real pleased with her decision. Based on your last trip to see her, she was afraid if she gave it all to the three of you right away, you'd have a contest to see who could spend it quicker."

"Your mother thought that Mary would be the first to spend it all on jewelry or clothing. However, after she thought about it a little, she gave me strict instructions to make sure I tell you Mary that you may be the slowest spender of the three because you already got a start on the jewelry purchases by plundering it from her house, when you thought she wouldn't miss it due to her Alzheimer's disease. Boy did she fool you. Trust me, she had accounted for every piece of jewelry she had and knew exactly what you took, and I bet it's the beautiful jewelry you have on today. She even fully accounted for the forty-nine hundred dollars you spent using her charge card at Nordstrom's."

Mary put her head down in shame as Jake turned his head to Sharon.

"Sharon, you hit a triple play when you stayed at your mother's house for a few days."

Sharon began peering out the window as Jake began talking about her.

"You took her on a drug purchase, stuffed heroin down her pants after a cop pulled you over, tried to sell her painting that's worth a million dollars for twenty-five dollars, and worst of all, you heisted all of her leukemia pain medicine before you buzzed out of her house without saying goodbye. I'm not even sure why she gave you any money, because you certainly don't deserve it. I'm saying that as your mother's friend, not her lawyer. I still can't believe you took all of your mother's leukemia medicine. That was heartless and despicable."

She couldn't look Jake in the eye and put her head down in shame when Jake blurted out the word "despicable."

Next Jake turned his head focusing on Denny.

"Denny, your mother had the most sympathy for you. She was fine with your transition to a man and was even fine with you having a new wife. She would have liked to have met her. She simply wanted you to be happy. She was almost ready to give you all of her inheritance as a consequence of your sisters' visits, until you showed her how dedicated you were to your causes. She was incensed that you regularly give almost all of your money away to causes that are most likely giving most of their money to run the organizations and support the senior executive's lifestyle when you should be taking care of yourself. She hopes in the future you use your money to support your family instead of someone else's family. Your mother loved you the way you are and she was happy you're finally at peace with yourself."

"I'll have each of your trusts set up in thirty days to start distributing her inheritance to you. Do any of you have any questions?" concluded Jake as he moved his head, focusing his eyes on each of Lily's three children.

Hesitantly, Sharon inquired, "I have two questions. Why is she here? And what about Mom's house? It didn't sound to me like you included Mom's house in the estate."

"That's a great question Sharon. Your mother's house isn't included in the total I've mentioned so far. Remember, your mother gave me strict instructions to not let anyone into her house. No one has been in the house but me. She had a reason for doing this and was very insistent upon it. She wouldn't tell me why. If you go to page five of her will, you can see your mother is leaving her house and all of its contents to Lee Jackson," disclosed Jake.

All three siblings looked at each other for affirmation, as they shook their heads in disbelief.

"Why would she do that? That's crazy," protested Mary.

All three of the siblings turned their heads and focused their attention on Lee. There was silence in the room as the siblings waited for a response. Lee remained calm and expressionless, shrugging her shoulders three times, signaling her unease at Lily's final decision.

"I'm not sure why she did it. I truly don't have any idea. After spending the few months with your mother, in truth, I learned to love her," Lee confessed as her voice began to slow down and she began to speak very fondly of Lily.

"And I think she learned to love me too, like she did, or does each of you. Your mother had me call her mom in her last month. Since I lost my mother a long time ago, for some reason, I felt real special calling her mom and for some reason she liked hearing it. I can't tell you all sitting here what it was, but we had something genuinely special."

As Lee stated this, tears began to flow down her eyes. The siblings were not sympathetic to what she said, but now began to understand why her mother had placed Lee in the will.

"I guess maybe she felt that way because I never owned my own home, and she wanted me to have one free and clear, all paid up. I can't believe she did that. I feel bad for you guys that she gave it to me. I'll never forget your mom. She became my second mom. I only wish I could have helped her and known her longer. She was surely sufferin' in the end with the sepsis infections and pneumonia," Lee stated as she began to sob again recollecting their time together.

"I'm sorry. I can't help it. I truthfully miss talkin' to her. I know more about your relatives and ancestors from the last three centuries than you'll ever know. For some reason, your mother talked to me about them every day in the last month that we were together. She went quickly once she got to the hospital. The infections killed her so fast. She wanted me to be with her in the end and I was holding her hand when she died. I'm so sorry," professed Lee as she continued to sob.

Jake reached across the table and tapped Lee on the arm to comfort her.

"She always talked highly of you, Ms. Jackson. I wasn't sure either why she did what she did, but all I can tell you is this is what she wanted and insisted on over and over as I tried to make sure she wouldn't have any regrets. I can honestly tell you all sitting at the table that these were her final wishes. This is what she wanted," asserted Jake as the four attendees realized that the meeting was soon coming to an end.

"Oh Lee, in addition, for you to officially receive the title, free and clear, there is a stipulation that you must agree to physically live in it one year before you would agree to sell it" contended Jake.

"I understand Mr. Snyder. I ain't planning on going nowhere," murmured Lee.

"I have a box for each of you containing personal items your mother wanted each of you to have. She divided them up so there would be no bickering. Oh, I also forgot to mention to you Ms. Jackson, that if you look on page seven, you'll see that Mrs. Clarke also left thirty thousand dollars to you to hire a contractor to dig the basement deeper, so that you don't hit your head on the rafters or have to bend over every time you do laundry in the basement. For some reason, she was adamant that I hire a contractor for you to do that. I'll have a contractor ready to go soon. But first, and in accordance with her instructions, you'll have to move in and clean out the basement before the contractors can come in and do their work. For some reason, Mrs. Clarke also insisted you do that before the work on the basement is started. Anyway, that's what all of the new families are doing to these rowhomes. It'll give you a whole floor of new living space."

"Well, thank you all for coming in today. I'll be contacting each of you separately to set up the trusts so that you can each have your monthly allowance in the near future. Ms. Jackson, I'll be processing the paperwork for the house in the next week or so. I'll need you to come in and sign some papers at the settlement for the house. You three children were lucky to have your mother. Her legacy should help sustain each of you for the rest of your lives. I'll be talking to you all real soon and call me if you have any questions."

With that the meeting ended and Jake walked out of the conference room for his next appointment.

The reading of Lily's last will and testament was complete and Lily's two final deceptions remained to be exposed.

CHAPTER 64

Much to Jake and Lee's surprise, it took much longer than expected for Jake to get the title of the house transferred into Lee's name. It was now sixty days after the reading of the will and the house had only been settled on the day before. Lee immediately called her landlord and gave him her thirty day notice.

The day after, Lee drove alone by herself to her new rowhome on Ellwood Avenue, to behold what she never possessed in her sixty-eight years: a house of her own, paid in full. As she parked her car across the street from her house, she looked up at the rowhome that was now hers.

A light south wind moved across the park hitting her back. Lee felt Lily's presence as she stared at her new home. She sensed the wind was actually Lily's spirit pushing her toward the front door of the rowhome.

"I know you're here. I can feel you already, Mom," vowed Lee as godly chills began to form in her neck to back to fill her torso and then her arms and legs.

As she crossed the street and reached the marble steps, she nervously searched for the keys in her pocketbook as her hands shook. As she fumbled to pull them out, she dropped them on the ground. The light breeze now picked up again.

Lee felt Lily's presence again continuing to push her into the house.

"Okay, okay Mom. I'm goin', I'm goin'. I'm as anxious as you are," she verbalized as she turned her head, looking back to the sky.

Lee placed the key into the lock, turned the handle, and slowly pushed the door open. This time it felt different walking into a house she now owned. She quickly noticed a difference in the paint color on the wall where the "I TOLD YOU SO" painting once hung.

Her hands shook and her knees trembled as she moved slowly to Lily's recliner chair. She sat on it and began to sob. She wasn't sure if the tears were tears of joy or tears of sorrow missing her close friend. She looked around the house and pushed the recliner back and lay back in the same position Lily would have. A smile came upon her face.

After a few minutes of contemplation, she slowly got up from the chair and moved to the upstairs, looking in the rooms and noticing slight disturbances in the house from when Jake removed the personal items he gave to Lily's children. The jewelry box drawer was empty of its jewelry and all of the family photographs that hung on the walls were no longer there. It felt empty.

Lee went back down the steps and moved into the kitchen.

"Oh my," she thought. "The refrigerator and freezer must be a moldy mess."

As she opened the refrigerator, the smell of rotten food took her breath way. She quickly grabbed a garbage bag and began cleaning. Moldy milk, moldy cheese, followed by moldy fruit were the first things to go. After seeing these items, Lee began tossing everything in it until the refrigerator was totally empty.

The freezer was next. Even though some of these items may have still been good to eat, the fact that they were in the same unit as the moldy items, left Lee with no choice but to pitch them all. After all of the items were in the garbage can, the only item remaining was the ice which was now solid and packed together. Lee picked up the ice and dumped it into the sink.

After finishing, Lee headed back to Lily's recliner for a quick break. As she pushed back the recliner, her head peered to the left noticing Lily's secret electrical outlet safe with its hidden compartment. Only Lily and Lee knew its existence. Lily slowly reached down and pulled it open, exposing its contents.

Lee could see what appeared to be an envelope stuffed inside it. She slowly pulled it out and could see Lily's shaky handwriting on it.

It read "To be opened by Lee only upon my death." As she opened the envelope, she saw a piece of paper with Lily's handwriting.

"Lee, when you read this note, I request you immediately dismantle my husband's workbench, so that you can get started making the basement deeper. Do it alone. Trust me, Love, Mom."

Lee didn't comprehend the intent or meaning of the note. However, she decided to honor Lily's wishes and take a better look at the workbench and see how the basement would look once the floor was dug two feet
deeper.

As she walked down the stairs, they creaked and the basement smelled a little like mildew. She quickly realized that the dehumidifier was no longer running, as it had been when she was taking care of Lily. Lee focused her eyes on the workbench.

"It sure must have been pretty a long time ago. It's ashame it has to be torn down," she thought.

The workbench appeared as if it hadn't been used in years. Lee moved toward the desk and slowly began to remove the items from it, placing them on the concrete floor. A surge of energy began to take hold of her. She felt Lily's spirit telling her to move faster. Once all of the items on the desk were removed, Lee quickly and efficiently removed the ones that hung on the shelves above the workbench and placed them on the basement floor. As the basement floor pile grew, Lee felt great anticipation and impatience, without knowing why.

She sat down on the wooden workbench chair that Frank had used and looked slowly up and down at the workbench as she tried to determine the meaning of Lily's note. She pulled the top right drawer and it, like the workbench tabletop and shelves, was filled with Frank's tools. Lee began to remove the items from the three drawers on the right of the workbench and the three drawers on the left side of it. Some of the them she threw carefully across the pile of items that began to accumulate in a circular pattern around her on the basement floor.

Once the drawers were empty, she sat still looking at the workbench again. "What is it, Mom?" she said out loud. "Come on, Mom. What is it that you are trying to tell me?" she said as she peered at the workbench searching for the sign or clue Lily may have left her.

She reached down and haphazardly pulled out each drawer hoping to find an answer. After each drawer was slung across the piles of items on the floor, she looked at the workbench confounded by what it was trying to tell her.

After a few minutes of sitting and staring, Lee began to tiptoe over the pile of rubbish she had created and decided to head back upstairs as Lily's hand-written puzzle was still eluding her. As she began to walk to the stairs, she turned around to look at the empty workbench one more time.

A beam of light was shining in from the front basement window hitting the right side of the workbench. The beam of light enabled Lee to see a small slot in the side of the workbench. She immediately stopped and began to move back toward the workbench. As Lee approached it, the sunlight on the side of the workbench grew brighter as the clouds and trees outside moved with the wind. Lee leaned down to peer at the workbench slot and could see there was something inside of it. She noticed there was a significant gap separating the workbench from the concrete wall. In between, a long piece of wooden trim filled the gap.

Lee scurried through the tools on the floor, figuring she might as well bust up the work bench, since this was Lily's request. She grabbed a hammer and futilely hit the side of the wood trim. It did not budge an inch. She tried hitting it again, but her sixty-eight-year old body wasn't strong enough to break apart what Frank had created in 1952.

"What are you putting me through, Mom. I think you may be the crazy one. I ain't never used a hammer before in my life."

After scratching her head and staring at the workbench, Lee placed the claw end of the hammer into the slot hole, grabbed the handle and began to pull it with all of her weight and might. As she leaned back and pulled the handle the wood trim, and the nails began to slightly crack and move. With one more considerable tug on the wood trim, it gave way, causing Lee to land hard on the concrete basement floor and a few of the tools that were scattered about it.

Lee laid motionless on the concrete floor, waiting to feel any pain or bleeding on her body. Other than a little numbness on her left elbow, she had come out unscathed from the tumble.

As she slowly lifted her head to see the damage she had caused to the workbench, she could see the wood trim from the right hand side of the desk lying on the basement floor by her feet. A large cavity loomed behind the workbench.

The sides of two wooden crates stacked on top of each other behind the desk could now be seen, along with a white envelope, sitting on the exposed concrete floor. As she stood up, she pulled the top crate out and saw a third one on the far side of the workbench.

Lee reached down to pick up the envelope. As she turned it over, she could see Lily's shaky handwriting again on an envelope saying, FOR LEE, FROM MOM.

As Lee opened the envelope, for a reason unknown to her, her hands began to shake again. She began to carefully open the letter and took a deep breath. At that moment, she felt a sense of calm.

Silently, she began to read.

Dear Lee,

As you are reading this letter, you know that I am in a better place and free of my pain and suffering. I led a good life, but always had emptiness in my heart until you came along.

The three crates enclosed behind Frank's workbench contain artwork that Frank and I purchased from Haussner's Restaurant in 1952. They have been sitting hidden behind this workbench since 1952. How we came upon the paintings is a long story in itself. I willed you the contents of my house so the paintings would become yours. I estimate the value of the three paintings to be about $5,000,000. When the dust settles from my estate, take them to Sotheby's auction house in New York and auction them. Even Jake doesn't know they exist, only you!

I felt compelled to give you the house and the contents of it for a few reasons. First, you made this old woman's life complete and a blessing. I hope by the time you are finished reading this letter, I have done the same for you.

I didn't mind dying after seeing the strong and proud woman you've become. As you can see, my three children didn't turn out so good. I don't think I was the best mother based on the way they turned out. Your mother did a great job raising you. As you can see from my children's lives, I couldn't have been as good of a mother as Ella was to you.

While I was living, I didn't have the guts to tell you a secret that I learned during your stay with me. I was too ashamed and too embarrassed by what you would think of me. I am so, so, so sorry that it was my decision not to tell you, but I thought it would be easier for you and me, and would keep my children away from you for a long time into the future, if you want it to be so. You can make that decision yourself.

Back in 1948, when I was eighteen, I unfortunately had a baby out of wedlock. That baby was you. Although I don't think it's prudent to go into the details about how I became pregnant, I did not know your birth father. I met your mother Ella in the hospital and decided to give you to her through adoption. She had had five miscarriages and could never bear children. She so desperately wanted children and I knew you would be loved. I was young and unmarried, and couldn't raise a child alone in that era, much less a darker-skinned baby.

You have my green eyes. Your birthday was on the same day that I gave birth to a baby I gave up for adoption to a woman named Ella. I truly never forgot your mother. When I learned at your birthday celebration when you were born, the hospital, and your mother's name, my world stood still for a long time. I can still picture your mother's face as I write this letter. She even taught me the "Rule of Three," exactly like she did for you.

In the short time we were together, I learned to love you, my first daughter, with all of my heart. I'm sorry for leaving you twice, at your birth and my death, without being able to tell you I love you in person. I genuinely and truthfully couldn't. I was too ashamed and thought I would lose you again, forever.

I now have you forever in my heart and I hope you can forgive me for what I did. I hope I am always in your heart, too.

I love you forever and hope I will see you again in heaven. You were chosen by God to enrich those less fortunate than yourself. Thank you for making my life enriched, fulfilled, and complete.
Your mother, Lily

After Lee finished reading the letter, a burst of light came through the basement window onto her face. Lee looked at the window and smiled and the light splashed upon her face with delight as it danced through the clouds and trees in Patterson Park. Lee felt Lily's warmth fill every ounce of her body. She closed her eyes and nodded her head, letting Lily know that she now knew the truth and understood what

Lily was saying to her. After a minute, a cloud slowly moved across the sky, blocking the light as Lee felt Lily's presence abate.

Lily's final earthly deceptions were fully exposed, and she was now free to be on her journey into heaven.

Lee began to sob uncontrollably thinking of the joy she had experienced meeting her birthmother and the sorrow of losing her before she could express to Lily her feelings of true forgiveness and pure love.

Lily's legacy was now fully complete and the last vestiges of her existence were passed on to her one truly worthy daughter.

Made in the USA
Columbia, SC
22 November 2018